To

JEAN

ROBIN FORSYTHE
THE SPIRIT MURDER MYSTERY

Robin Forsythe was born Robert Forsythe in 1879. His place of birth was Sialkot, in modern day Pakistan. His mother died when a younger brother was born two years later, and 'Robin' was brought up by an ayah until he was six, when he returned to the United Kingdom, and went to school in Glasgow and Northern Ireland. In his teens he had short stories and poetry published and went to London wanting to be a writer.

He married in 1909 and had a son the following year, later working as a clerk at Somerset House in London when he was arrested for theft and fraud in 1928. Sentenced to fifteen months, he began to write his first detective novel in prison.

On his release in 1929 Robin Forsythe published his debut, *Missing or Murdered*. It introduced Anthony 'Algernon' Vereker, an eccentric artist with an extraordinary flair for detective work. It was followed by four more detective novels in the Vereker series, ending with *The Spirit Murder Mystery* in 1936. All the novels are characterized by the sharp plotting and witty dialogue which epitomize the more effervescent side of golden age crime fiction.

Robin Forsythe died in 1937.

Also by Robin Forsythe

Missing or Murdered
The Polo Ground Mystery
The Pleasure Cruise Mystery
The Ginger Cat Mystery

ROBIN FORSYTHE

THE SPIRIT MURDER MYSTERY

With an introduction
by Curtis Evans

DEAN STREET PRESS

Published by Dean Street Press 2016

Introduction copyright © 2016 Curtis Evans

All Rights Reserved

Cover by DSP

First published in 1936 by The Bodley Head

ISBN 978 1 911095 18 7

www.deanstreetpress.co.uk

Robin Forsythe (1879-1937)
Crime in Fact and Fiction

Ingenious criminal schemes were the stock in trade of those ever-so-bright men and women who devised the baffling puzzles found in between-the-wars detective fiction. Yet although scores of Golden Age mystery writers strove mightily to commit brilliant crimes on paper, presumably few of them ever attempted to commit them in fact. One author of classic crime fiction who actually carried out a crafty real-life crime was Robin Forsythe. Before commencing in 1929 his successful series of Algernon Vereker detective novels, now reprinted in attractive new editions by the enterprising Dean Street Press, Forsythe served in the 1920s as the mastermind behind England's Somerset House stamp trafficking scandal.

Robin Forsythe was born Robert Forsythe—he later found it prudent to slightly alter his Christian name—in Sialkot, Punjab (then part of British India, today part of Pakistan) on 10 May 1879, the eldest son of distinguished British cavalryman John "Jock" Forsythe and his wife Caroline. Born in 1838 to modestly circumstanced parents in the Scottish village of Carmunnock, outside Glasgow, John Forsythe in 1858 enlisted as a private in the Ninth Queen's Royal Lancers and was sent to India, then in the final throes of a bloody rebellion. Like the fictional Dr. John H. Watson of Sherlock Holmes fame, Forsythe saw major martial action in Afghanistan two decades later during the Second Anglo-Afghan War (1878-1880), in his case at the December 1879 siege of the Sherpur Cantonment, just outside Kabul, and the Battle of Kandahar on 1 September 1880, for which service he received the War Medal with two Clasps and the Bronze England and Ireland until his retirement from the British army in 1893, four years after having been made an Honorary Captain. The old solider was later warmly commended, in a 1904 history of the Ninth Lancers, for his "unbroken record of faithful, unfailing and devoted service."

His son Robin's departure from government service a quarter-century later would be rather less harmonious.

A year after John Forsythe's return to India from Afghanistan in 1880, his wife Caroline died in Ambala after having given birth to Robin's younger brother, Gilbert ("Gill"), and the two little boys were raised by an Indian ayah, or nanny. The family returned to England in 1885, when Robin was six years old, crossing over to Ireland five years later, when the Ninth Lancers were stationed at the Curragh Army Camp. On Captain Forsythe's retirement from the Lancers in 1893, he and his two sons settled in Scotland at his old home village, Carmunnock. Originally intended for the legal profession, Robin instead entered the civil service, although like E.R. Punshon, another clerk turned classic mystery writer recently reprinted by Dean Street Press, he dreamt of earning his bread through his pen by another, more imaginative, means: creative writing. As a young man Robin published poetry and short stories in newspapers and periodicals, yet not until after his release from prison in 1929 at the age of fifty would he finally realize his youthful hope of making his living as a fiction writer.

For the next several years Robin worked in Glasgow as an Inland Revenue Assistant of Excise. In 1909 he married Kate Margaret Havord, daughter of a guide roller in a Glasgow iron and steel mill, and by 1911 the couple resided, along with their one-year-old son John, in Godstone, Surrey, twenty miles from London, where Robin was employed as a Third Class Clerk in the Principal Probate Registry at Somerset House. Young John remained the Robin and Kate's only child when the couple separated a decade later. What problems led to the irretrievable breakdown of the marriage is not known, but Kate's daughter-in-law later characterized Kate as "very greedy" and speculated that her exactions upon her husband might have made "life difficult for Robin and given him a reason for his illegal acts."

Six years after his separation from Kate, Robin conceived and carried out, with the help of three additional Somerset

House clerks, a fraudulent enterprise resembling something out of the imaginative crime fiction of Arthur Conan Doyle, Golden Age thriller writer Edgar Wallace and post Golden Age lawyer-turned-author Michael Gilbert. Over a year-and-a-half period, the Somerset House conspirators removed high value judicature stamps from documents deposited with the Board of Inland Revenue, using acids to obliterate cancellation marks, and sold the stamps at half-cost to three solicitor's clerks, the latter of whom pocketed the difference in prices. Robin and his co-conspirators at Somerset House divided among themselves the proceeds from the illicit sales of the stamps, which totaled over 50,000 pounds (or roughly $75,000 US dollars) in modern value. Unhappily for the seven schemers, however, a government auditor became suspicious of nefarious activity at Somerset House, resulting in a 1927 undercover Scotland Yard investigation that, coupled with an intensive police laboratory examination of hundreds of suspect documents, fully exposed both the crime and its culprits.

Robin Forsythe and his co-conspirators were promptly arrested and at London's Old Bailey on 7 February 1928, the Common Serjeant--elderly Sir Henry Dickens, K.C., last surviving child of the great Victorian author Charles Dickens--passed sentence on the seven men, all of whom had plead guilty and thrown themselves on the mercy of the court. Sir Henry sentenced Robin to a term of fifteen months imprisonment, castigating him as a calculating rogue, according to the Glasgow Herald, the newspaper in which Robin had published his poetry as a young man, back when the world had seemed full of promise:

> It is an astounding position to find in an office like that of Somerset House that the Canker of dishonesty had bitten deep....You are the prime mover of this, and obviously you started it. For a year and a half you have continued it, and you have undoubtedly raised an atmosphere and influenced other people in that office.

Likely one of the "astounding" aspects of this case in the eyes of eminent pillars of society like Dickens was that Robin Forsythe and his criminal cohort to a man had appeared to be, before the fraud was exposed, quite upright individuals. With one exception Robin's co-conspirators were a generation younger than their ringleader and had done their duty, as the saying goes, in the Great War. One man had been a decorated lance corporal in the late affray, while another had served as a gunner in the Royal Field Artillery and a third had piloted biplanes as a 2nd lieutenant in the Royal Flying Corps. The affair disturbingly demonstrated to all and sundry that, just like in Golden Age crime fiction, people who seemed above suspicion could fall surprisingly hard for the glittering lure of ill-gotten gain.

Crime fiction offered the imaginative Robin Forsythe not only a means of livelihood after he was released in from prison in 1929, unemployed and seemingly unemployable, but also, one might surmise, a source of emotional solace and escape. Dorothy L. Sayers once explained that from the character of her privileged aristocratic amateur detective, Lord Peter Wimsey, she had devised and derived, at difficult times in her life, considerable vicarious satisfaction:

> When I was dissatisfied with my single unfurnished room, I tool a luxurious flat for him in Piccadilly. When my cheap rug got a hole in it, I ordered an Aubusson carpet. When I had no money to pay my bus fare, I presented him with a Daimler double-six, upholstered in a style of sober magnificence, and when I felt dull I let him drive it.

Between 1929 and 1937 Robin published eight successful crime novels, five of which were part of the Algernon Vereker mystery series for which the author was best known: *Missing or Murdered* (1929), *The Polo Ground Mystery* (1932), *The Pleasure Cruise Mystery* (1933), *The Ginger Cat Mystery* (1935) and *The Spirit Murder Mystery* (1936). The three remaining novels—*The Hounds of Justice* (1930), *The Poison Duel* (1934, under the pseudonym Peter Dingwall) and *Murder on Paradise Island* (1937)—were non-series works.

Like the other Robin Forsythe detective novels detailing the criminal investigations of Algernon Vereker, gentleman artist and amateur sleuth, *Missing or Murdered* was issued in England by The Bodley Head, publisher in the Twenties of mysteries by Agatha Christie and Annie Haynes, the latter another able writer revived by Dean Street Press. Christie had left The Bodley Head in 1926 and Annie Haynes had passed away early in 1929, leaving the publisher in need of promising new authors. Additionally, the American company Appleton-Century published two of the Algernon Vereker novels, *The Pleasure Cruise Mystery* and *The Ginger Cat Mystery*, in the United States (the latter book under the title *Murder at Marston Manor*) as part of its short-lived but memorably titled Tired Business Man's Library of adventure, detective and mystery novels, which were designed "to afford relaxation and entertainment" to industrious American escape fiction addicts during their off hours. Forsythe's fiction also enjoyed some success in France, where his first three detective novels were published, under the titles *La Disparition de Lord Bygrave* (The Disappearance of Lord Bygrave), *La Passion de Sadie Maberley* (The Passion of Sadie Maberley) and *Coups de feu a l'aube* (Gunshots at Dawn).

The Robin Forsythe mystery fiction drew favorable comment for their vivacity and ingenuity from such luminaries as Dorothy L. Sayers, Charles Williams and J.B. Priestley, the latter acutely observing that "Mr. Forsythe belongs to the new school of detective story writers which might be called the brilliant flippant school." Sayers pronounced of Forsythe's *The Ginger Cat Mystery* that "[t]he story is lively and the plot interesting," while Charles Williams, author and editor of Oxford University Press, heaped praise upon *The Polo Ground Mystery* as "a good story of one bullet, two wounds, two shots, and one dead man and three pistols before the end....It is really a maze, and the characters are not merely automata."

This second act in the career of Robin Forsythe proved sadly short-lived, however, for in 1937 the author passed away from kidney disease, still estranged from his wife and son, at the age of 57. In his later years he resided--along with his Irish Setter Terry, the "dear pal" to whom he dedicated *The Ginger Cat Mystery*--at a cottage in the village of Hartest, near Bury St. Edmunds, Suffolk. In addition to writing, Robin enjoyed gardening and dabbling in art, having become an able chalk sketch artist and water colorist. He also toured on ocean liners (under the name "Robin Forsythe"), thereby gaining experience that would serve him well in his novel *The Pleasure Cruise Mystery*. This book Robin dedicated to "Beatrice," while *Missing or Murdered* was dedicated to "Elizabeth" and *The Spirit Murder Mystery* to "Jean." Did Robin find solace as well in human companionship during his later years? Currently we can only speculate, but classic British crime fans who peruse the mysteries of Robin Forsythe should derive pleasure from spending time in the clever company of Algernon Vereker as he hunts down fictional malefactors—thus proving that, while crime may not pay, it most definitely can entertain.

Curtis Evans

Chapter One

The stifling summer day was drawing to a close.

Towards sunset, heavy sharp-edged clouds gathered in the sky, and every now and then a cool breeze rose suddenly, blew fitfully for a while and as suddenly died away. It looked as if the long spell of dry, sultry weather was about to break with a violent storm, but when night fell the clouds had dispersed, the cool breezes subsided, and all was again clear and still, except for the restless and occasional flicker of summer lightning.

John Thurlow sat at a table in his low-ceilinged study at Old Hall Farm, smoking his pipe, his closely cropped hair gleaming in the light of an electric reading lamp in front of him. On the table were several books dealing with the subject of spiritualism. One of these lay open before him, and from the expression on his face and the way in which he kept relighting his pipe, it was evident that he was reading it with great concentration and eagerness.

A few feet from the table, with her back to it so that the light from the reading lamp could fall on her own book, his niece, Eileen Thurlow, reclined in an easy chair. She was a tall, slim woman in her early twenties with a pale face and shining, raven-black hair. Her features were delicately moulded, and the pallor of her face was relieved by a pair of large, luminous brown eyes, eyes with that peculiar aspect of depth which is generally associated with the character of a dreamer. Her mouth was small and well-formed and her chin, firm. If any judgment of character can be based on physiognomy, one might conclude that, whatever propensity for dreaming Eileen Thurlow possessed, she was also endowed with considerable resolution and a capacity for action. Men found her attractive at first, but were soon repelled by a mental aloofness and frigidity which seemed to imply that they did not greatly interest her. Her uncle, relatives, and friends declared that at times she was difficult to understand, and it was generally accepted among them that Eileen was "a bit mysterious." This reputation had been fostered among them by Eileen's confirmed belief and sustained interest in what is called spiritualism. She belonged to a spiritualistic circle, attended séances, felt that she, herself, had certain mediumistic powers, and, though never eager to proselytize, was always ready to discuss the subject with anyone who approached it seriously. On the obstinate sceptic, she would waste no time, and with those who attempted to be facetious, she could be bitingly sarcastic.

Her uncle, John Thurlow, had at first viewed this manifestation of interest in the psychic on Eileen's part with some concern. Not that he doubted the existence of occult phenomena, for he had spent a large part of his business career in India, but he was afraid that such things might have a morbid effect on her mind and be deleterious to her physical health. During the years of what he always called his "exile in the East," he had passed through a phase in which the cult of Yoga had deeply interested him, and he had never quite shaken off the spell of wonder it had exercised over his mind. That sense of wonder was inextricably mixed up with some vague idea that at the core of Yogism lay some secret power which, once attained, could secure material success in mundane affairs. His business, however, had slowly but surely relegated his preoccupation with Yoga to the background of his mind, and it was now, in his years of retirement, transmuted by his niece's activities into a sudden interest in spiritualism.

At first it was a tentative interest of which he was rather ashamed, for he was acutely sensitive to ridicule. During this period, the jocular remark by one of his friends, "Well, John, seen any spooks lately?" was enough to make him utter a flat denial that he was at all interested in the subject. But gradually he outgrew this tentative phase and began to acquire the courage of conviction under the influence of his niece's faith and his own delving into the subject.

The book which lay on the desk in front of him and which he was reading so eagerly was Sir William Crookes's, "Researches in the Phenomena of Spiritualism," for the general bias of John Thurlow's mind was sceptical and he was, he felt, approaching his subject from a sound, scientific point of view. He achieved considerable satisfaction from this reflection; the scientific approach was a subtle screen against ridicule. Not that he knew much about any science except that of making money, but the very word science seemed to have an almost hypnotic effect on his powers of reasoning. For the opinions of famous scientists in any branch of learning he had a deferential awe, and any statement of theirs, no matter how guarded or theoretical, he would swallow with unquestioning credulity.

All at once he rose from his chair, paced up and down the room to stretch his limbs, and as abruptly sat down again.

"Well, Eileen, I'm at last convinced that there is something in spiritualism!" he exclaimed, turning his chair round to his niece as if eager to discuss the subject.

Eileen closed her own book with an air of satisfaction and looked at her uncle with a smile playing about the corners of her lips.

"Belief must be largely a matter of temperament, Uncle. I never required conversion. I must have been born in the faith, so to speak. You've only reached conviction after quite a lot of persuasion and study."

"Well, Eileen, you see, I want scientific proof. I'm naturally sceptical and cautious. But to be half converted, one has only got to think for a moment of the famous scientists who've been confirmed believers in spiritualism. There's Sir William Crookes, whose book I'm reading. There's Sir Oliver Lodge and Camille Flammarion and the rest of them. I'm absolutely convinced at last. You might humbug the ordinary man in the street, but you can't humbug trained observers and exact thinkers."

"I suppose not," replied Eileen somewhat listlessly and, after a pause, added, "but now you're fairly certain that there is such a thing as spirit manifestation, you've only got to keep your mind open and you'll get some actual proof, visual or aural. This old house, in which people have lived continuously for hundreds of years is particularly favourable for such. You're almost certain to hear the faint strains of music which I've repeatedly heard for some time now. I should say a former occupant of this house was a keen musician."

"You're quite sure that this spirit music isn't just fancy? I often have all sorts of tunes running through my head, but I can't say I actually hear them. They're quite different."

"No, no, it's not imagination on my part. I distinctly hear music; it's very faint, but quite audible."

"Can you distinguish the instrument?" asked John Thurlow, after a moment's reflection.

"What a strange question to ask!" exclaimed Eileen with genuine surprise. "Now that point never struck me. I was so excited by the manifestation that I didn't worry about the instrument. When I come to think of it, I must say the music sounded like the faint notes of a church organ."

"The church is a mile away, and even when the wind is in this direction, it's impossible to hear the church organ. Can't be that, for I've checked it up since you first told me of the phenomenon. When did you hear it last?"

"On Tuesday night and it was particularly clear. I was sitting in this room when it occurred. You were out having a chat with Doctor Cornard."

"Yes, I remember. Strangely enough, our talk turned on the subject of spiritualism. I had a hot argument with him. He flatly says he thinks it's all rot. I mentioned this book of Sir William Crookes's to him, and he declared that a famous scientist was usually a specialist in one subject and therefore more easily gulled than the average, level-headed person."

"He puts himself in the latter category with complacent conceit, I suppose. Did you tell him of this music that I've distinctly heard on several occasions?"

"Well, yes, I did. I hope you don't mind."

"Not at all. What did he say?"

"Hinted that the church organist was practising at the time and that some condition of the atmosphere, or the wind, carried the sound as far as Old Hall Farm. He sought a material explanation and wouldn't hear of any other."

"The church organist wasn't practising on Tuesday night. I took the trouble to ask him," replied Eileen quietly.

"Oh, indeed! That's a splendid point. I wish I'd known it. I could have flattened Cornard out beautifully," remarked John Thurlow eagerly.

"It's no use arguing with Doctor Cornard, Uncle. He's one of those men who make up their minds on such a subject without any inquiry. Perhaps it would be fairer to say his education and training have unconsciously made up his mind for him. I think doctors on the whole are a very cynical lot."

For some moments John Thurlow sat in thoughtful silence and then remarked: "I wish I could hear this spirit music you talk about. I wonder when it'll occur again."

"I think we might hear it at any time, if we could only get ourselves into the proper mood. You must be *en rapport*, as they say, or you'll never hear it. These occult phenomena must be diligently sought for, or they remain beyond your physical senses. It's a case of seek and ye shall find. I was speaking to Dawn Garford the other day and she made a shrewd remark on the subject. She said that the average man, who figuratively sticks to the tarred highway, certainly won't find mushrooms. You've got to get off the beaten track and hunt for them."

"A good illustration. I've a great respect for her opinion. She's always bright and sensible," said John Thurlow, and asked: "But how am I to get *en rapport*, as you put it?"

"Well, you must experiment. Let's try it out to-night. Put out the light and we'll sit and listen, firmly believing we'll get in touch with this discarnate musician. I feel certain that I have the gift of mediumship. When I first heard the music, I was in a very peculiar frame of mind. I wouldn't call it a trance, but something like the periods of ecstatic reverie which occur to people with psychic gifts."

"Do you think it wise, Eileen?" asked John Thurlow, looking at his niece with an air of half-scared hesitancy.

"If you're really curious about the matter, there's nothing like making an experiment, Uncle. No harm can possibly come of it. I'm willing to try it out. All the well-known cases of genuine mediumship began with a home circle, and I should like to convince myself I've got the power. Relatives don't stoop to humbugging one another, even if it were possible."

"By jove, I think we ought to try!" exclaimed John Thurlow with sudden eagerness. "I feel a bit nervous, though I don't just see what there is to be scared about."

"If we find that our experiments prove unpleasant or dangerous, we can certainly chuck them up," remarked Eileen.

"Of course, of course," replied John Thurlow and for some moments sat lost in thought. His eyes wandered round the quaint old room with its dark oak beams and wainscoting. Through his mind was passing the thought that for hundreds of years all sorts of people had lived and moved and talked and wept and laughed and loved and quarrelled in that very room. The whole house was impregnated with the spirit of the bygone and bore the indelible imprint of the activities and designs of people long since dead and forgotten. He glanced through the open window at the dark blue sky, now spangled with stars. A vague sense of mystery and wonder stole into his musing. From the particular, his thoughts broadened out to the general. The universe was altogether inexplicable, even to science. How and why did it begin? Whither was it progressing? Where and how would it all end? What relation did this earth and its teeming millions of lives bear to that star-scattered space? Was that vast ethereal sweep peopled by the spirits of all past time? Futile questionings! He turned to his niece and asked: "Shall I put out the light?"

"Certainly, Uncle. For some unknown reason, darkness seems to favour any kind of manifestation. All spiritualists agree on that score. I daresay there's some natural law behind it. When you've done so, sit perfectly still and listen. I'm going to try and get in touch with what is called a spirit guide. I ought to have a spirit guide; all mediums have."

John Thurlow rose from his chair, pressed up the switch on the wall at his left hand, and sat down again. When his eyes grew accustomed to the darkness, he could vaguely discern the various pieces of furniture about the room, and, glancing at his niece, he saw her form clearly outlined by the white organdie muslin dress she was wearing. That dress seemed almost luminous as it caught the faint light filtering in through the windows. Her pale face was a grey smudge above the dress.

"Are you all right, Eileen?" he asked.

"Yes. Let's begin. Try and keep your mind quite free from any distracting train of thought. You'll find it difficult. Now please don't talk any more."

John Thurlow settled himself in his chair and tried to keep his mind quite free from distracting trains of thought. Yes, it was more difficult than he had surmised. His right hand, in his jacket pocket, was fondling the smooth bowl of his briar pipe, and a strong desire to smoke assailed him. Under the urge, he was on the point of asking Eileen whether smoking would militate against favourable conditions, when his attention was suddenly arrested by his niece's heavy, stertorous breathing. He was on the point of asking her if she were all right, but remembered her strict injunctions against speaking and desisted. He sat and listened to that laboured inhalation and exhalation for some moments and wondered if she had gone into the trance state usual with mediums. He was beginning to feel decidedly nervous. Everything was so still and eerie, and he was slowly being overcome by a strong conviction that at any moment some uncanny manifestation might occur, some horror materialize before his eyes. He resolved to keep a firm control over himself and all his faculties alert. He would confront any such wonder in a true scientific spirit of observation. He must not allow himself to be disturbed or thwarted by such an infantile thing as fear. What was there to be afraid of, in any case? Eileen was certainly complete mistress of herself. No trace of fear in her behaviour! But perhaps she was now quite unconscious, in that cataleptic state which is the usual trance of the medium.

He listened again to her breathing. It was painfully heavy, but now quite rhythmic. Had she fallen asleep? He couldn't resist the impulse to ask her.

"You awake, Eileen?" he queried in a whisper.

"Yes, wide awake. Listen attentively!" came the reply in a strained voice, quite unlike Eileen's.

John Thurlow experienced a sudden and sharp insurgence of fear. He felt his skin creep and was quite certain that his hair was standing on end. With a supreme effort, he controlled himself and obeyed the summons to listen attentively. Some minutes passed without anything happening. A clock in another room chimed sweetly and faintly in the almost oppressive silence. Then, all at once, very faint strains of music seemed to hover and quiver in the darkened room. They were full of haunting melody and seemed to have that strange sweetness of music that is heard across a sweep of water. Eileen's breath was now coming in sharp, rasping gasps. John Thurlow sat petrified with amazement. Had he lost touch with reality? Surely his ears, in conjunction with his mental expectancy, had played him some fantastic trick, produced some aural hallucination? He listened again with almost painful concentration. Once more the silence was broken by the ghostly music; at times so faint as to be almost inaudible, and then at intervals so distinct as to render the atmosphere in the darkened room perceptibly vibrant.

As he sat motionless and attentive, his first sensation of terror gave place to a feeling of entranced awe. He now felt certain that he recognized here and there a familiar musical phrase, but could not place it; for, though fond of music, he never could assign to any particular work or composer an aria or passage which he chanced to hear or transiently remember. At that crucial moment, he wished that in the past he had paid more attention to such detail, instead of pleasurably gulping the stuff without noting its title or the name of its creator. Suddenly the unseen musician stopped and repeated more perfectly a passage, as if dissatisfied with his first execution. This unexpected occurrence seemed so characteristically human, that it at once charged John Thurlow's attitude with sceptical alertness. Surely there must be some ordinary and natural explanation of this musical phenomenon? Without rising from his chair, he stretched out his hand and quietly switched on the electric light. He glanced at Eileen. Her eyes were closed and her head had sunk forward on her breast. She seemed fast asleep. In a few moments her loud breathing returned to normal, she quietly opened her eyes, and looked across almost vacantly at her uncle. Noticing that he was about to speak, she raised her hand as if to enjoin silence. They both sat and listened. Once more the faint music seemed to surge gently into the room and roll up and recede with alternate strength and diminution. To Eileen it seemed supernal, ineffably beautiful.

"It's an organ!" exclaimed John Thurlow, unable to restrain himself any longer and, rising from his chair, he opened a door leading from his study into the garden and stepped out into the night.

A little later, he re-entered the room by the same door with a look of amazement on his face.

"It's certainly not the church organ, Eileen!" he said emphatically. "Outside there's not a sound to be heard. This is most mysterious."

"The music has stopped," replied Eileen with an air of annoyance. "Immediately you begin to fiddle about for natural explanations of a spirit manifestation, you simply ruin the conditions. You become a hostile influence, Uncle. You must remember that we're trying to get in touch with a spirit; we're not in a laboratory or a law court. It's well known that in an atmosphere of suspicion, with people whose minds are alert for detecting fraud, or intent on material explanations of supernatural phenomena, nothing will ever occur."

"I'm sorry, Eileen," replied her uncle apologetically, "I'll bear that in mind in future. To-night's experience has been an eye-opener to me. Positively stupendous!"

"And it's only the beginning," added Eileen enthusiastically. "If we conduct our experiments in the right frame of mind, we'll get further manifestations, perhaps some kind of materialization."

"You mean a ghost?" asked John Thurlow with alarm.

"Let's call it a spirit form. I like it better than ghost. The word ghost seems to imply fear, just as the word spook implies fear masquerading as courage. I'm feeling terribly tired. The experience has exhausted me and I'm going to bed. Good-night."

Eileen rose languidly from her chair and noiselessly left the study. Hurrying upstairs to her room, she slipped on a light overcoat, descended again stealthily so as not to disturb her uncle, and wandered out into the garden. There was a strange vagueness about her thoughts which she ascribed to the after effects of her trance state.

On her departure, John Thurlow glanced nervously round his study and then coughed as if to assure himself that he was not altogether scared. Drawing his pipe from his pocket, he lit it, and after a few vigorous puffs, swung round his chair to the table and resumed his reading of Sir William Crookes's book. He had only read a few pages, when to his unbounded astonishment, he heard again the faint sound of an organ being played. With nervous fingers he closed his book, shut his eyes, and listened attentively. Yes he recognized the air, and as he strove hard to recollect it the name all at once flashed into his mind. It was Handel's Dead March from "Saul." He was very familiar with this march, and by some psychological trick his recognition of it at once dissociated the music in his mind from the region of the supernatural. He rose from his chair and, kneeling down, placed his ear to the ground. Surely he could now hear the sounds more clearly! Or was it mere fancy? He could not be certain. Rising to his feet again, he passed once more out into the garden. There, all was silence except for the plaintive hooting of an owl in a fringe of woodland bordering the adjoining paddock. More perplexed than ever, he returned to his study, where the very faint strains of an organ—he was certain the instrument was an organ—were still clearly audible.

"Most amazing!" he exclaimed and added with a note of rising exasperation. "But I'll get to the bottom of this thing, or my name's not John Thurlow!"

All trace of fear had now seemingly left him, and his face had assumed a look of sullen determination. He had reverted to the John Thurlow, successful merchant and financier, intent on getting the best of a deal, and in such a mood he was a man of unshakable resolution. His first thought was to summon Eileen, but remembering her air of complete exhaustion on retiring, he changed his mind and decided to investigate alone. For some moments he stood hesitant and then, thrusting his pipe in his pocket, crossed to his writing desk. Extracting a heavy army-pattern revolver from a drawer, he began silently to search the whole ground floor of the house.

Chapter Two

When Fanny Raymer, one of the maids at Old Hall Farm, entered Eileen Thurlow's bedroom next morning with her mistress' morning tea, her ingenuous face was pale and her round blue eyes were starting from her head. Eileen, who was wide awake, knew on glancing at Fanny that something unusual had happened. At first she was not much perturbed, for a very minor catastrophe, such as the breaking of a tea-cup, was sufficient to produce unduly alarming effects on Fanny Raymer's face.

"You look startled, Fanny. What has happened now?" asked Eileen in a matter-of-fact tone so as to reassure the girl.

"I just took master's tea into his room, miss, and he ain't there," replied the maid.

"Isn't there? What do you mean?" asked Eileen with a puzzled look.

"He ain't in his bed, miss, and he's nowhere about the house."

"Then he's probably somewhere about the garden or grounds," remarked Eileen and calmly poured herself out a cup of tea.

"What I mean, miss, is that he hasn't slept in his bed, and when I went to dust his study this morning, the electric light was burning on his desk and the window was wide open."

Eileen, who had raised her cup of tea to her lips and was about to drink, suddenly returned the cup to its saucer and hastily put both down on a small table beside her bed.

"But he must be somewhere about the house!" she exclaimed with growing amazement. "Have you looked in all the rooms?"

"Yes, miss, even in the wine cellar," replied Fanny with finality.

"Then he'll have gone out with his gun into the paddock after rabbits. Runnacles has been complaining of late about the damage they're doing in the vegetable garden."

"I thought of that, miss, but master's gun is in the spare room where he usually keeps it. I went out and saw Runnacles. He was busy in the potting-shed, and when I asked him if he'd seen master about anywhere, he said: 'No, my darling,' so I ticked him off for bein' so forward."

For some moments Eileen was lost in thought. She had left her uncle immersed in his book at about ten o'clock the previous night. She had a vague recollection of then having gone out into the garden and returned. Her mind, evidently thoroughly exhausted by her attempt at mediumship, had almost been a complete blank for over an hour. She clearly remembered, however, that she had fallen asleep without hearing him come upstairs to his bedroom. It was evident he had not gone to bed at half-past eleven according to his invariable custom. But what had become of him? He couldn't have vanished into thin air. The power to dematerialize was emphatically not within the scope of her uncle, John Thurlow's abilities. The affair must have some simple explanation, however preternatural it might appear. The more she thought of it, the more confused and bewildered she became.

"Was the study door leading into the garden shut, Fanny?" she asked at length.

"Yes, miss, and locked. So were all the other doors leading out of the house."

"Then he must have gone out by the window," remarked Eileen, but she felt there was something quite irrational about the inference. Why should her uncle leave the house by the window? There was clearly no valid reason. The idea was ludicrous. She rose hastily from her bed with an air of resolution, and Fanny, leaving the room, went about her usual household duties.

Eileen breakfasted alone, and her first feeling of amazement at the sudden and unaccountable disappearance of her uncle was giving place slowly to a decided sensation of fear. She argued with herself that as yet there was no cause for alarm, but it failed to stem the slowly ebbing tide of her courage. Before lunch, with the aid of the three maidservants, she had made a thorough search of Old Hall Farm from the attics to the cellars; and Runnacles the gardener, with his assistant, had been through all the stables, outbuildings, and lofts. John Thurlow was not to be found. He had seemingly vanished without leaving a trace.

Just before lunch, Arthur Orton of Church Farm, their nearest neighbour, called about some repairs that were necessary to one of his barns, for Orton rented his farm from John Thurlow. He was shown into the drawing-room and there interviewed by Eileen.

He was a tall* wiry man with a lean, bronzed face and dark, flashing eyes beneath rather abundant and unruly eyebrows. The deep lines from the nose to the corners of his mouth, and the thin upper lip, slightly depressed where it met the lines from the nose, gave him a shrewd, cynical air, but whenever a smile lit up his face, it would alter its whole ascetic cast.

On Eileen's entry, his glance swept over the graceful lines of her tall, well-proportioned figure and glowed warmly. His silent appreciation was not lost on Eileen, for she had experienced it before and found it agreeable. In spite of herself, a faint flush tinted her cheeks, and her unmistakable satisfaction was reflected in her countenance. For Eileen thought Arthur Orton an attractive man, and though there was something about his slightly saturnine air that disagreeably disturbed her, she had for some time been secretly fascinated by him. He was, moreover, a bachelor, a good farmer, ostensibly well-off, and reputed never to have been worsted in a business deal. In the parish of Yarham, he was not popular. He was reserved and inclined to be sarcastic, which was construed as equivalent to giving himself airs, but his worst fault, in combination with these, was that he was a stranger. Though he had now been at Church Farm for many years, he was a stranger for the simple reason that he had not been born in the parish of Yarham. Worse still, he was not a Suffolk man.

His arrival at Old Hall Farm at this critical moment was too much for Eileen Thurlow's command of her troubled feelings. On his sympathetic remark that she looked as if she were upset about something, she frankly unburdened herself and told him the whole story of her uncle's inexplicable disappearance. Overwrought by her morning's excitement and worry, she ended her tale on the verge of tears. Arthur Orton was solidly comforting. He deftly brought bright common sense to bear on the subject, and contrived that a light-hearted breeze should blow away the portentous atmosphere of tragedy from Eileen's outlook.

"When did you go to bed, Miss Thurlow?" he asked.

"I left my uncle in his study about ten o'clock."

"Well, I and my man, Joe Battrum, saw Mr. Thurlow step into a car at about eleven o'clock, just as you enter Yarham village. We naturally thought it was his own car and paid no more heed to the matter. You say his car was never out of the garage yesterday. Then it must have been a friend's car, and they've had a breakdown at some outlandish spot. In fact, the whole of Suffolk's outlandish, so that's easy. You mustn't start worrying about nothing, Miss Thurlow. Your uncle'll turn up when he's downright hungry, or he'll ring you up and let you know where he is and what's happened. I wanted to see him about some repairs to my barn, but it's not urgent and I'll look in to-morrow. In the meantime, if there's anything I can do, you've just to let me know. 'Phone me and I'll be on your doorstep in no time. Don't hesitate."

"That's awfully kind of you, Mr. Orton," said Eileen sincerely. "I hope I haven't worried you by telling you all my troubles."

"My dear girl, there's nothing like getting your worries off your chest. I'm very glad you've told me. I want you to think of me as a friend you can turn to when in trouble."

Arthur Orton's eyes met Eileen's and his glance was suddenly charged with significance. He meant the word friend to be taken at an enhanced emotional value, and Eileen was unconsciously eager to accept it. Her lowered eyelids were an admission to him that she understood perfectly. Orton rose to go, but for some moments stood hesitant as if debating a course of action that was hovering uncertainly in his mind.

"You've searched everywhere, Miss Thurlow?" he asked suddenly. From the tone of his voice his thoughts were apparently not in his words.

"We've ransacked the whole place," replied Eileen emphatically.

"The attics and lofts?" asked Orton, rubbing his chin thoughtfully.

"Yes."

The cellar as well? You have a wine cellar, I believe?"

"Yes, we've searched everywhere," replied Eileen with finality. She was rather disappointed at these matter-of-fact questions. His hesitation had seemed to hint at the possibility of a more intimate expansion on the subject of friendship. That expansion had evidently been checked by caution or nervousness. His rather obvious questions came as a depressing anti-climax to her expectancy.

"Now you're not to worry, Miss Thurlow," he adjured finally. "Your uncle will turn up. Take my word for it."

"But suppose he doesn't return by to-morrow morning. Would you advise me to report the matter to the police, Mr. Orton?" asked Eileen.

Arthur Orton was apparently flattered by the question. It implied that she valued his advice. He saw himself once more as the friend in need. He at once assumed a gravely judicial air.

"Well, yes, I suppose it's about the only thing you can do. Still, I shouldn't be in too great a hurry, Miss Thurlow. Give the matter plenty of time. You mustn't act hastily. Once the affair's in the hands of the police, it becomes public property. It may even be broadcast, much to your uncle's annoyance. He's the sort of man who'd hate anything like that. Now this is Tuesday. If you don't get word by Wednesday night, then I think it would be wise to go to the police. In the meantime, just try and keep control of your feelings, and should you want help, just ring me up."

Eileen again thanked him, and as he was on the point of departure, held out her hand. He took it between both his strong hands, held it and patted it affectionately. In Eileen's rather distracted state of mind it was a very comforting gesture; its intimacy diffused a subtle air of protection. She felt she needed protection. For the moment she was thrilled, but as soon as Arthur Orton had gone, her mind at once reverted to the strange disappearance of her uncle, and, in spite of Orton's matter-of-fact encouragement, her fears returned with doubled force. Surely something dreadful had happened to Uncle John? She sat helplessly pondering over the matter after her lunch, a meal which she had eaten without the slightest zest. Surely their little séance of the previous night could have no possible bearing on this baffling affair? She wondered. It was certain there were evil as well as beneficent spirits. It would be impossible to say what power the former might not be able to exert, if once in touch with the living. One assigned no limits to a spirit s potentialities. Eileen found it inconceivable that anyone could commit murder or suicide, unless driven by something in the nature of a dynamically evil spirit. In everyday language people spoke of the insane as "possessed." In Scripture, they were "possessed of a devil." It seemed feasible that at any time anybody, even an innocent and quite worthy being, might suddenly be seized upon as a temporary habitation by some unclean demon. The thought opened up a vista of horrible possibilities, conjured up disagreeable verbal associations, such as ghosts, furies, banshees, wraiths, ogres, genii, even succubi and succubae! She felt she must banish these morbid thoughts, and, rising from her chair, decided she would walk into the village and call on Dawn Garford. It would do her good to get a breath of fresh air and talk matters over with a friend.

Dawn Garford was twenty-six years old and a widow. Her husband, an aviator, had been killed in a flying accident a year after their marriage. Her real name was Mrs. Button, but she was still known to the villagers as Miss Dawn Garford. Her husband had left her a competence, and she had come to live with her aunt in Yarham. She liked a country life, and in the country her modest income went very much further than in town.

Eileen Thurlow soon made her acquaintance and they had become friends, not because they were strongly attracted to one another, but simply because, in a village like Yarham, the scope for friendships was extremely limited. In temperament they were diametrically opposed. Dawn Garford was an assured, material woman with superabundant energy, a cheerful disposition, and an insatiable desire to exercise her charms on men. Her bold, forceful character and reckless bearing won Eileen's admiration, for the simple reason that she, herself, was shy, modest and cautious.

On arriving at the Garfords' house, a modern villa and incongruous in the general setting of Yarham, Eileen found Miss Julia Garford, Dawn's aunt, in a mental and nervous state bordering on collapse. The arrival of a visitor seemingly revived her instantly, and she hurriedly led Eileen into the drawing-room.

"I've heard all about it," she remarked eagerly. "The whole village knows about it, my dear. Now sit down and tell me all there's to tell. I've been expecting you all afternoon. I've got my own troubles and something very important to tell you afterwards."

Eileen briefly described the incidents surrounding the disappearance of her uncle. Omitting the story of the little séance and the spirit music, which she felt might be met with incredulity, perhaps even ridicule, there was very little to tell. Miss Garford asked innumerable questions, made rather fatuous suggestions, and finally asked:

"Do you think your uncle's disappearance, Eileen, can have any connection with Clarry Martin's?"

"But I didn't know Clarry Martin had disappeared," said Eileen with lively astonishment.

"Well, he has; he's been missing since Friday last. His father and mother have kept the thing very dark. They naturally thought he'd turn up some time or another, but now they've had to let the secret out. I believe they've informed the police."

"Doesn't anybody know what's happened to him?" asked Eileen, a look of bewilderment in her eyes.

"No. He was last seen talking to George Mobbs, the baker, just outside 'The Walnut Tree' Inn. They were old friends and had evidently been making merry all evening."

"Dawn'll be rather upset about it," remarked Eileen, for Clarry Martin was one of Dawn Garford's most persistent suitors.

"I don't think it'll worry Dawn much," said her aunt with a mysterious smile. "Now, when she hears about your uncle, she'll be greatly distressed, for she's really very fond of him. I think he has a soft spot for her, too. People in the village are saying that it looks as if they're going to make a match of it."

"Oh, hardly that, Miss Julia. I don't think their relations with one another have got as far as that," said Eileen guardedly. "My uncle's rather infatuated with Dawn, but I think Dawn treats the matter as a joke."

"Well, the gossip was sufficient to make Clarry absurdly jealous. He quarrelled with Dawn a week ago, and since then they haven't spoken to one another. Dawn confided in me that she thought Clarry Martin was going off his head. She is scared out of her wits about him. This morning she left Yarham, and has gone to stay with some friends down at Midhurst in Sussex until Clarry recovers his senses."

Eileen Thurlow was very much perturbed at this information. She was astonished that the mild and middle-aged attitude of gallantry, adopted by her uncle with the incorrigibly flirtatious Dawn, had been marked enough to rouse village comment and waken Clarry Martin's jealousy. She was about to make some direct reference to it, but desisted.

"Clarry Martin drinks too much," she said casually in reply. "I think Dawn's wise in steering clear of him."

The conversation returned once more to the simultaneous disappearance of John Thurlow and Clarry Martin, but further discussion failed to shed any light on the mystery. After tea, Eileen, having promised to keep Miss Garford informed of any developments, took her leave and returned to Old Hall Farm.

On her arrival she learned that, during her absence, there had been no telephone calls, and no further news of her uncle had come to hand. She was grievously disappointed. All the time she had been talking to Miss Garford, she had been thinking that good news would greet her as she entered Old Hall Farm. A telephone message explaining what had happened and saying that everything was all right; that was what she had anticipated. She had even envisaged herself being annoyed for having been so easily distressed, so ready to read disaster into the unknown, when there was absolutely nothing to warrant such a gloomy outlook. For a while she was roused to a sense of anger against her uncle; he ought to have more thought for her feelings than to leave her in this painful uncertainty. He must know that his absence would cause anxiety, not only to her, but to everyone in the house. But this spasm of indignant exasperation disappeared when she remembered how exceedingly thoughtful her Uncle John always was in everything concerning her comfort and peace of mind. No, something really serious must have happened to him, or he would have managed to communicate with her by some means or other.

She ate her dinner in a mood of growing despondency, and began to wonder how she was going to pass the evening. She suddenly remembered that her uncle had, a day or so before, brought back from London a batch of books on spiritualism, and that they were lying on his desk in the study. She decided to bury herself in an easy chair in that comfortable room and spend the time reading. She felt she must detach herself from the present, get absorbed in her subject, and time would fly.

For a while she read with a lively interest Sir Edward Marshall Hall's *Evidences of Survival from Experiences with Automatic Writing*, but the worries and preoccupations of the day had tired her mind, and she soon found that she was reading without concentration. She finally closed her book, and her thoughts reverted to Miss Julia Garford's remarks about John Thurlow and Dawn Garford.

Now that she began to consider the matter, Eileen became aware that there was a large part of her uncle's character and mental life that was hidden from her. It was not that he was unduly secretive, but that she herself had never been sufficiently curious about him. After all, there might be more in village gossip than she had surmised. For all she knew, her uncle might have proposed to Dawn Garford and been accepted. Unlikelier things had happened. He was fifty-five years of age and Dawn, twenty-six, but her uncle was younger physically and mentally than his years. The fact that he had a considerable fortune was one that Dawn, avid for the good things of life and not too romantic in her outlook, would certainly appreciate. No sooner had this thought flashed across Eileen's mind, than she remembered that she, herself, was the sole beneficiary under her uncle's will. If her uncle married, he would certainly alter the provisions of that will. She had not considered this point before.

Her thoughts then fastened on the subject of Clarry Martin's disappearance. It was very strange that Clarry should have disappeared almost simultaneously with her uncle. They were, so village gossip said, rivals for the hand of Dawn Garford. Could this fact have any bearing on the coincidence? From these musings there suddenly sprang to her mind the thought of murder. Clarry Martin was, according to Julia Garford's story insanely jealous of her uncle's attentions to Dawn, but no, she could not think of Clarry Martin in the role of an assassin. Had her uncle any other enemies? The question brought to her memory a remarkable discussion that had taken place between her father and mother about some youthful indiscretion of John Thurlow's in India. She, herself, was then in her teens, and on the occasion was not thought to be listening too attentively to her parents' conversation. What that indiscretion was, she had never been able to ascertain definitely, but she realized when she grew older that it savoured strongly of popular sensational fiction. There was something about a Hindu temple, a goddess called Kali, and she had a vague recollection that a beautiful native dancer flitted lightly on an atmosphere of veiled sexual hints across the stage of her parents' discussion. That dancer's husband, if she remembered rightly, had been murdered. Eileen had taken the trouble later to probe into the matter of the goddess Kali. Strangely enough, this divinity, at the time, interested her far more than the nature of her uncle's indiscretion, or the part played by the beautiful native dancer. Kali, she discovered, was a goddess of destruction and death. She was black, had four arms, and the palms of her hands were red. Her face and breast were smeared with blood, and blood dripped from her tongue which protruded from her revolting, fang-like teeth. Formerly, human sacrifice was a part of her ritual. The sacrificial victim was imprisoned in her temple at sunset, and in the morning he was dead. Kali had sucked his blood during the night. Ghastly as this description was to Eileen in those impressionable years, it acquired some grander horror from the vague association with her Uncle John. Whatever had happened between Kali and her uncle, he had at least survived the ordeal triumphantly and bore no traces of the encounter.

This reversion of her thoughts to that early story of her uncle's indiscretion, and the sudden recollection of the horror of Kali, began to fill Eileen with a vague and increasing terror. All sorts of tales of Eastern deities, of curses and mummies and rifled tombs, sacrilege and the unescapable vengeance of strange gods flitted incoherently through her mind. She decided that the best thing to do was to go to bed, try to sleep, and see what the morning would bring.

The morning brought Runnacles, the gardener, at seven o'clock to Old Hall Farm. It was an hour earlier than his specified time for commencing work. He demanded to see his mistress at once, and Fanny Raymer ran upstairs, wakened Eileen, and told her of Runnacles' unusual request. Eileen, immediately aware that the gardener was the bearer of important news, slipped on her dressing-gown and came down to hear what he had to say.

Runnacles' information was brief and momentous. The dead bodies of Mr. John Thurlow and Mr. Clarry Martin had been found lying within a few feet of one another on the piece of waste land called "Cobbler's Corner," about half a mile to the north of Yarham village. They had been discovered by Ephraim Noy, who lived in the new bungalow, not a hundred yards from Cobbler's Corner. He had informed the village constable, and the village constable's wife had immediately informed Runnacles' wife. That was all. Runnacles could furnish no further details beyond the fact that the village constable had at once cycled out to Cobbler's Corner. Before leaving, he had said he would call at Old Hall Farm as soon as practicable and give Miss Thurlow full particulars of the tragedy.

On learning this terrible news, Eileen Thurlow did not faint, as one might have expected of a woman of her sensitive and delicate stamp. She quietly dismissed Runnacles and went back to her bedroom to dress. Her mind, by some strange process, seemed to her to have become suddenly detached from her body and to be floating, calmly and quite alert, in some region not actually mundane. As she dressed, she happened to glance out of her bedroom window into the garden below. The sky was cloudless, and the garden was all bright and sparkling in the cool morning sunshine. Her uncle was dead. Clarry Martin was dead. In the language of spiritualism, they had passed over. Nature didn't seem to heed. Nature seemed frigidly remote and indescribably beautiful. A great mystery!

Chapter Three

Anthony Vereker, known as Algernon unabbreviated to his friends, looked critically at the numerous landscape sketches both in oil and watercolour that he had completed since his arrival in Yarham, and then carefully packed them all away with his painting gear in a leather trunk in his bedroom. This operation of putting away his work was performed with some of the solemnity of a funeral rite. For several days he had not handled a brush or opened a sketch book. His inspiration seemed to have burned itself out temporarily, and he knew that it was futile to continue painting in this mood. It was merely exercising a craftsman's skill; its only result could be competently executed but uninspired work. That dying fire of inspiration had been finally quenched by the lighting up of his old passion for detection, for in the very village of Yarham certain startling events had occurred. Those events constituted a mystery the solution of which promised to tax the powers of

Anthony Vereker, amateur detective, to their limit. It was the first occasion, too, in his experience, on which he happened to be near the scene of a baffling crime at the time of its commission.

Vereker had had his first introduction to the beauties of the Constable country during his investigations with Inspector Heather into the mysterious murder at Marston Manor. At the time, he had made up his mind to explore all this southern half of Suffolk in search of landscape subjects, and his lengthy stay at Yarham was the result of that decision. He had just fixed a date for his return to London, and had written to his friend Manuel Ricardo to meet him at Liverpool Street Station. That letter had suggested a mild celebration of his return to civilization after such a prolonged sojourn in the wilds of East Anglia.

Fate had, however, decreed otherwise.

The morning after he had posted that letter to Ricardo, Vereker was mildly interested at hearing of the strange disappearance from Yarham of two of its inhabitants, Mr. John Thurlow and Mr. Clarry Martin. He heard the news from Benjamin Easy, landlord of "The Walnut Tree" Inn, where he was staying. Always interested in village gossip, he had managed to elicit from Ben Easy, by very diplomatic questioning, the fact that the two men were reputedly rivals for the hand of the sprightly and charming Dawn Garford. Ben had imparted this information with such an air of profound secrecy, that Vereker was obliged to assume that he had been favoured with vastly important confidences. He tried hard to appear as if he felt highly honoured. Ben and he discussed the affair with the furtiveness of two conspirators, and as a result, Vereker gradually learned that Ben was convinced that Mr. Thurlow had eloped with Miss Garford, and that Clarry had gone back to London, where he lived and worked, a broken-hearted man!

Early on Wednesday morning, however, the startling news of the discovery of the dead bodies of John Thurlow and Clarry Martin on the waste land at Cobbler's Corner went round the village like wildfire. The attendant circumstances were so extraordinary, that it was not clear to anyone how the two men had really met their deaths. At a first and casual glance, it looked as if they had killed one another in a brief but deadly combat. John Thurlow's skull had been smashed by a peculiar iron bar, called a fold-drift in this portion of the county of Suffolk. This bar lay near the outstretched hand of Clarry Martin, but not actually in his grasp. In John Thurlow's right hand was a .45 army pattern Webley revolver, with one cartridge of the complement of six, discharged. The bullet had passed through Martin's trapezius muscle, above the clavicle bone of the right shoulder. Even to a layman it was apparent that such a bullet wound could hardly have proved fatal. Other features about the bodies of the two men, not at first apparent to a casual eye, came to light subsequently on a closer examination by Doctor Cornard, and rendered the whole business more baffling than ever.

The news of this amazing tragedy, apart from its overwhelming effect on the village of Yarham, seemed to galvanize the jaded Vereker into a feverish burst of activity. Rising from the breakfast table, at which he had just seated himself, he hurried round to the post office telephone box, and at once rang up his friend, Manuel Ricardo, who was as usual occupying Vereker's flat in Fenton Street, London, W.

That you, Ricky?" he asked on hearing a feeble and somewhat sleepy, "Hello!"

Yeah!" came the reply in an exaggerated American intonation. Ricardo was annoyed at having been wakened at such an hour, and knew that this buffooning would act as a mild irritant on his friend.

"For heaven's sake be serious, Ricky, and speak English. I mean the authorized version."

"I sure will, chief, but I'm rather crazy about the revised version since I visited lil ole New York. Now what have yer gotta say, boy? Make it snappy for I'm dangling on this end of the line in my pyjamas and bare feet."

"I want you to cancel our little engagement. I shan't return to town next week, Ricky. Sorry and all that, but I'm right on the scene of a most amazing double murder, or rather, that's what it looks like at the moment…"

"Don't go into details, Algernon," came the immediate interruption; "I can't stand a double murder on an empty stomach. I'm sorry you've decided to postpone our beano for the sake of mere detection. This criminal investigation's getting a complete mastery over you. You're becoming an addict. We'll have to lock you up at Hendon."

"Are you very busy just now?"

"No, I'm at a loose end. I've just completed my new serial for the *Daily Report*, and am making a desultory study of popular Victorian fiction. I've just read a beauty: *The Morals of May Fair*, by the author of *Ought We to Visit Her?* We can't compete with that nowadays, Algernon. There's no May Fair to speak of, and if there is, it hasn't any morals. Modern frankness has knocked all the delightful shudder out of allusive wickedness…"

"You'd better come to Yarham. You're just idling. It's a dangerous thing for a man of your temperament. I'll expect you down to-morrow night. There's a good fast train…"

"Impossible, Algernon. I'm taking Gertie Wentworth to the Broughtons to-morrow night. They're flinging a beer and sausage party."

"Who on earth's Gertie Wentworth? It's the first time you've mentioned her name."

"It won't be the last; it's worth repeating. Algernon, a new star has swum into my ken! She's of the first magnitude."

"Ricky, you're hopeless!"

"On the contrary, I'm afraid I'm over sanguine. She's fabulously rich."

"Then you won't come to-morrow?"

"No, definitely. By the way, Gertie has a most fascinating cast in her left eye…"

"Yes, yes," interrupted Vereker petulantly. "I believe it's a bewitching defect in a wealthy woman. Can't you get out of this infantile beer and sausage business?"

"It would be difficult. Nothing short of a death in the family would work as an excuse. Hilda Veasey threw me over because my favourite aunt died twice within six months. No more fictional obituaries for the present. My memory's only a selling plater and not good enough for classic lying. Too risky!"

"When will you be free?"

"When Gertie finds me out. But seriously, what do you want me to do?"

"I want you to come down here and help. It's going to be an interesting and difficult case. From the look of things, I foresee considerable danger."

"Then I shall be with you the day after to-morrow. My latest craze is to live dangerously. I've started by discarding the use of safety matches."

"I'll expect you by the fast train leaving London at two. You might bring the case containing my investigator's equipment. It's in the wardrobe in my dressing- room. Inside the lid of the case is pasted a list of the equipment. Just check it up and see that nothing's missing. Two or three items you'll have to renew. Wax candles is one. Get an extra electric torch and several batteries. And I feel there's no gum arabic."

"A necessary article, Algernon. You really can't ask anyone to stick 'em up without a pinch of gum arabic."

"That reminds me. Bring my two Colt automatics and a box of ammunition."

"What about a gas gun, to be thoroughly up-to- date?"

"You'll be an excellent substitute, Ricky!"

"One minute, Algernon. I'll jot that down for my article on the difference between wit and impudence. Anything else?"

"Not that I can think of at the moment."

"May I remind you that I'm short of money? Can you see your way clear..."

"Good lord, Ricky, haven't you got your fare down here? I suppose you've squandered your last bob on observing this star of the first magnitude."

"I'm glad you said 'squandered,' Algernon. A cynic would call it a highly speculative investment."

"A cynic wouldn't be such a fool as to credit you with any worldly cunning. Is my man, Albert, in?"

"I smell him cooking the breakfast. Haddocks this morning, I think."

"Ask him to advance you five pounds on my account. That'll have to cover your beer and sausage evening with your latest discovery and get you down here."

"What about the wax candles, electric torch, batteries and so forth?"

"You must allow for those and keep a strict note of the amount."

"Really, Algernon, your financial methods are Procrustean. A measly fiver won't stretch from Gertie Wentworth to gum arabic. Something—something'll snap!"

"You must make it do. I can't waste any more time just now. Ring up Geordie Stewart of the *Daily Report* and tell him I'm their special correspondent at Yarham. Au revoir!"

Vereker banged up the receiver and hurried out of the post office. Borrowing Benjamin Easy's bicycle, he made his way quickly to Cobbler's Corner, the waste land on which the bodies of John Thurlow and Clarry Martin had been discovered by Ephraim Noy.

Arriving on the scene, he found Godbold, the village constable, in command with Ephraim Noy as sole attendant. No one else was present, for though bad news travels fast in other parts of the world, neither it nor anything else travels fast in Suffolk. Speed is an irrelevance in Eden.

Godbold, pocket-book and pencil in hand, was, in spite of an air of importance engendered by the high occasion, looking distinctly worried. Murder, within the area of his authority, was an unprecedented experience for him. Just before Vereker's arrival, he had surreptitiously glanced through his "Police Code" and refreshed his memory, now vague, on the instructions detailed under the heading "Murder." During this perusal, he had turned his back guiltily on Ephraim Noy. He was thinking it was a bit difficult to remember everything connected with a constable's duties. He knew all about the Diseases of Cattle Act, of Cattle Straying under the Highway Act; he was intimately conversant with the Prevention of Poaching Act, and the orders applicable to the County under the Wild Birds Protection Act. But murder? It wasn't quite reasonable to expect...

"Good morning, Godbold," said Vereker, as he came up with the harassed official.

"Good morning, sir. You're the very gentleman I want."

"Anything I can do to help?" asked Vereker genially, for Godbold and he were good friends.

"I want you to take charge here, sir, till I run down to the village and 'phone the sergeant and Doctor Cornard. It'll be some time before the sergeant can turn up, but I'll be back as soon as I can. I'd have asked Mr. Noy, but I don't know the gent very well, and he don't seem too bright in any case. You know what's happened, I suppose?"

"I do, and I'm acting as the special correspondent of the *Daily Report* in the case."

"Very good, sir. Now I want you to prevent any unauthorized person from..."

"I know all the rules and regulations, Godbold. Don't trouble to repeat them. I'll see to things till you return. Do you think it's murder?"

"Mighty like it, sir!"

"Any footprints?"

"None, sir; the ground's as hard as iron after the long drought, and the grass like chaff. Worn't any dag (dew) last night either. But I must be going."

"Right," replied Vereker, and the constable, mounting his bicycle, disappeared at his usual, comfortable, patrolling pace towards Yarham village.

Vereker, on his departure, crossed the few yards of sun-scorched grass that separated the bodies from the winding lane that made a hairpin bend round the small stretch of waste land, called Cobbler's Corner. Meticulously observing all the rules so necessary on such an occasion, he nevertheless made a hurried but searching scrutiny of the two bodies and the *mise-en-scène*. Having jotted down all the details that struck him as vital, he took up his position on the road and awaited the return of Constable Godbold.

A few villagers with time on their hands for adventure soon appeared, but were sternly ordered not to leave the highway. With the habitual regard for authority characteristic of countrymen, they gathered together in a group and tried to elicit some information from Mr. Ephraim Noy, who, calmly smoking his pipe, had taken up his position on a five-barred gate leading into a meadow opposite Cobbler's Corner.

Mr. Ephraim Noy, they discovered, was a man of few words. He told them briefly that he had found the two bodies, lying in their present positions, as he crossed the Corner on his way into Yarham, an hour or so previously. He refused to discuss the matter further. It wasn't his business, and he plainly hinted that it was theirs in a much less degree. Leaving him perched on the gate, calmly observant but uncommunicative, they fell to discussing the tragedy among themselves. In this occupation, somewhat arid at the moment owing to meagreness of detail, they were quietly engaged, when Constable Godbold returned in company with Doctor Cornard.

Godbold at once relieved Vereker of his command and thanked him, adding that the sergeant and inspector would arrive later, accompanied by an official with his photographic equipment. Feeling that the proceedings were now in order, and that the weight of responsibility was slowly but smoothly moving from his own broad but diffident shoulders to those of his superiors, Godbold's face had resumed its habitual expression of official dignity and smug competence.

Vereker, having chatted for a few minutes with Doctor Cornard, whose acquaintance he had made shortly after his arrival in Yarham, decided to return to the village inn for breakfast. He was hungry. Besides, he was well aware that, not being acquainted with Sergeant Pawsey or Inspector Winter, he would have little chance of acquiring any further information about the tragedy than his own sharp eyes had already given him.

"Good morning, Doctor," he said as he picked up his bicycle, which was lying on the grass at the roadside.

"You're not going, Vereker?" asked the doctor, who had just glanced at the bodies and satisfied himself that life was extinct. "I thought you said you were interested in detective work."

"So I am, but not as a mere onlooker. I've seen all I want to see at present, but I'd like to have a chat with you later, strictly *sub rosa* of course."

"Come in any evening. I have a meal at seven o'clock sharp; I can't call it dinner. You'll be welcome. The padre was telling me about your fame as an amateur sleuth, and I'd like to hear your views."

Thanking him for his proffered hospitality, Vereker mounted his machine and left the strange little group of people that had gathered and stood curious and expectant at Cobbler's Corner.

On his way back to the inn, his thoughts were actively engaged on the subject of Miss Eileen Thurlow, John Thurlow's niece. She was the first person he would like to see and question, but he was conscious of the difficulties attendant on such a delicate task. She would certainly be interrogated later by the police, an unpleasant enough experience for a young woman, possibly prostrate with grief, without the preliminary intervention of one whom she might consider a meddlesome stranger, or a hustling newspaper correspondent. Chance, however, was to smooth his oath in an unexpected manner, for as he ran into the outskirts of the village, whom should he encounter but the Rev. William Sturgeon.

James Sturgeon, son of the rector, had been a college friend of Vereker's, and his father on hearing of Vereker's arrival in Yarham had soon made himself known. On now recognizing Vereker, he at once hailed him and asked him where he had been sketching during the morning.

"I haven't been sketching, Padre," replied Vereker. "I've just been to Cobbler's Corner on a much more exciting business."

"So you've heard all about it. When I received the news this morning, my thoughts immediately turned to you. If there's anything mysterious about this affair, I said to myself, young Vereker will soon be up to his neck in the game of detection, instead of getting on with his work. Tell me, what do you think of it?"

"I can tell you nothing yet beyond the fact that I think it's a murder, perhaps a double murder. I've merely glanced at the bodies and the scene of the crime."

"Terrible, very terrible! I'm now on my way to Old Hall Farm to see Miss Thurlow about the whole affair and offer what consolation I can. Why not accompany me? She's a very charming young lady. I'm sure you'll like her, and perhaps you'll learn something to help you in your work of investigation, if such is going to be necessary in the case."

"I should like to see and speak to Miss Thurlow very much, Rector, and was just wondering how I could get round to her diplomatically."

"Then I'm the very man you want. Can you come along now?"

"Certainly. I hope Miss Thurlow will be able to see us. She may be too upset."

"She's a young woman of great force of character, Vereker. She'll not take this blow lying down. If my judgment of her is correct, she'll be very much on the spot and eager to help clear up the terrible affair. Let's waste no more time."

With these words, the Rev. William Sturgeon looked at the bicycle on which Vereker was leaning as he stood talking.

"D'you think you could give me a lift, if I stand on the mounting step?" he asked. "I was only a light weight when I was at college, and no one could put on weight in a living like Yarham."

"It's a borrowed bicycle," remarked Vereker dubiously.

"Then you needn't hesitate!" exclaimed the rector with the prodigious laugh that he always reserved for his own jokes.

A few minutes later, Benjamin Easy's disreputable bicycle was coasting down the hill towards Old Hall Farm, Vereker grimly steadying it, and the Rev. William Sturgeon standing on the step of the back axle, with an almost seraphic smile on his face and his coat tails fluttering gaily in the morning breeze.

Chapter Four

On arriving at Old Hall Farm, the Rev. William Sturgeon and Vereker found Eileen Thurlow about to set out for Cobbler's Corner in her uncle's car. Though ostensibly suffering from the shock which the recent news had inflicted on her, she was completely in command of herself, and there was an air of resolution about her whole bearing. That fortitude was shaken considerably by the rector's words of sympathy and condolence, and tears rose to her eyes in spite of her determined effort to suppress them. She soon recovered her composure, however, and, treating the rector as a trusted friend, she briefly narrated everything that had occurred at Old Hall Farm, pertinent to the disaster which had overtaken her relative.

Vereker had been introduced to her as the well-known artist and amateur detective, and during her narration, she

almost unconsciously addressed herself to him, as if desirous
of helping him in every way in his task of investigating the case.
On mentioning the subject of the spirit manifestation which she
believed to have occurred on the night previous to her uncle's
disappearance, she was particularly pleased at Vereker's very
patient hearing and sympathetic questions about the details of
that singular experiment; the more so, because the Rev. Sturgeon
clearly showed his strong disapproval.

"I warned you, Eileen, to have nothing to do with this cult of
spiritualism. It's a very dangerous cult in my opinion," he had
interrupted.

A little later, she departed for Cobbler's Corner, escorted by
the Rev. Sturgeon, after giving Vereker a very cordial invitation to
call on her at Old Hall Farm at any time, should he wish to consult
her about any-thing connected with the mysterious tragedy.
Thanking her sincerely, and congratulating himself on his ability
to attain access to Old Hall Farm and probe further into Miss
Thurlow's strange story of the spirit manifestation, Vereker took
his departure and returned to his rooms at "The Walnut Tree."

To say that he was beginning to be interested in the new case
that had so unexpectedly thrust itself upon him, would be to
understate the effect that it had on his restlessly inquisitive mind.
He was filled with an excitement which manifested itself in the
rapid and preoccupied manner in which he paced up and down
his sitting-room in the inn, when alone and surveying the various
details already known to him.

His thoughts reverted to Miss Eileen Thurlow. Susceptible,
as an artist, to feminine beauty, he admitted to himself that she
was a very attractive young woman. Apart from her physical
charms, there was something very engaging in the distinction
and frankness of her mind. From fear of the general ridicule
which any reference to the supernatural arouses in matter-of-
fact, ordinary people, she might have been excused if she had
omitted to mention the subject of the experiment in spiritualism

which had prefaced the unaccountable disappearance of her uncle. She had described it very clearly and courageously in her determination to be explicit and comprehensive. On this controversial topic Vereker was very much in sympathy with her. He had always been interested in occult phenomena, and had gradually passed from a state of obstinate scepticism thereof to an admission of agnosticism. Lack of conversion, his spiritualistic friends had often assured him, was due to his habit of weighing evidence from a purely material point of view and to his almost hostile inquisitiveness. These characteristics had rendered him an unfavourable participant in any séance, and had led him eventually to drop his investigations into the phenomena altogether. The sudden resurgence of the subject of spirit manifestation in connection with a case of murder at once revived all his interest, and he felt that he was on the fringe of one of the most exciting experiences of his career.

He recalled to his mind the appearance of many of the mediums whose stances he had attended, and at once recognized the peculiar mystical aspect of Eileen Thurlow's eyes. They were to him a distinctive feature of the genuine psychic. However ordinary the general appearance and deportment of the mediums he had encountered, they had invariably possessed that strange, detached look in the eyes, a look suggestive of seeing through outward forms to some hidden reality beyond. Then he suddenly realized that he was anticipating matters. Perhaps this strange experience of Eileen Thurlow's on the night of the disappearance of her uncle had nothing whatever to do with the tragedy that had followed. The violent deaths of John Thurlow and Clarry Martin might resolve themselves into one of the complicated murder mysteries which had engaged his detective powers on so many previous occasions. He must be patient and await developments without forming theories on insufficient data.

The next two days he spent in a state of restless impatience, listening to the various and contradictory stories of the case as retailed to him by his acquaintances in the village. On the morning of the third day, his friend Manuel Ricardo wrote to him, saying that his visit to Yarham must be postponed, owing to unforeseen circumstances and that Gertie Wentworth certainly came under that category. He added that Vereker's investigator's outfit had been forwarded by L.N.E.R., and had been replenished with an extra electric torch, three batteries, and twopence worth of gum arabic. These had been purchased out of his own money, as Albert had refused to advance more than one pound without a confirmatory note from his employer. He affirmed that he would do his utmost to put in an appearance at Yarham before the murder quest reached the stage of a pitched battle with sub-machine guns. The letter, one of Ricardo's habitually flippant effusions, concluded with the important news that the services of Scotland Yard had been called in to deal with the Yarham murder mystery, and that Inspector Heather, who had been detailed to take charge of investigations on their behalf, had rung up the flat and was on his way to the village.

This final piece of information at once mollified Vereker's annoyance with Ricardo's irrelevancies, and removed his sense of exasperation at his own forced inactivity. He felt that he would now be able to take an active part in this new battle against the forces of crime, and renew the old and exciting rivalry that accompanied his former investigations in conjunction with his friend Heather of the Yard.

During this waiting for developments, Vereker had refrained from taking advantage of the invitation he had received from Miss Thurlow, but he had called on Doctor Cornard and discussed the case very thoroughly with him. He had also been kept in touch with the local police movements by his friend, Constable Godbold, under a promise of the strictest secrecy.

Vereker had just thrust Ricardo's letter in his pocket, when a railway van arrived with the case containing his investigator's equipment. As he was about to take possession of this case, a police car suddenly ran into the cobbled square in front of "The Walnut Tree" Inn, and Inspector Heather stepped out. After an appreciative glance at the quaint architecture and beautiful setting of the old tavern, the inspector advanced towards Vereker with an expression of mock gravity on his round good-natured face.

"This is not playing the game, Mr. Vereker. You've got a long start of me this time."

"I need it. Since our last duel, they've added the Hendon College to help you out of your little difficulties."

"You mean 'The Brain Box'? Well, we'll say we start equal then. What's the beer like in 'The Walnut Tree?'"

"There's no bad beer in Suffolk."

"Dear me, and yet they call it Silly Suffolk."

"The word in its old sense meant blessed or fortunate, Heather."

"Then it still holds good. I'm getting hungry. What's for lunch?"

"Cold lunch to-day. Have you ever tasted a haslet?"

"Never. I hope it's not a cocktail."

"No. I believe it's made of pork. But let's go in for lunch and you can sample a Suffolk haslet. Over it we can discuss this affair at Cobbler's Corner."

The two men entered the inn, and when lunch had been served and they were alone, Heather at once brought the conversation to the business on which they were both engaged.

"Now, Mr. Vereker, you've been here from the commencement of this affair. What d'you know?"

"Nothing much so far, but I'll tell you all about it, *ab ovo*."

"What's that?"

"You must ask them at Hendon. But to proceed. Some days ago, I believe it was on a Friday night, a man called Clarry Martin, who was on holiday in the village, disappeared. He belonged to Yarham, but lived and worked in London. Something to do with the motor business. Started as a mechanic and soon owned a large garage, show rooms, repair shop, etc. He was his own boss, and often came to Yarham to see his parents."

"You mean his best girl," interrupted Heather. "Parents are seldom good for more than one visit a year nowadays."

"Perhaps you're right. There's a best girl in the case anyway. Her name is Dawn Garford."

"Dawn, eh? A real daughter of Eve, of course."

"Possibly so. I'm glad to see you're in form, Heather, and as chirpy as ever. Well, Martin was very much in love with the young lady, and whether she returned his affection or not, I'm unable to say. But she encouraged him. However, he wasn't the only suitor she encouraged. There were several others, it village gossip is to be believed."

"Strange world, Mr. Vereker," commented Heather, lighting his pipe; "there's never enough of a good thing to go all round. So Mr. Martin got his back up with the lady and there was a row."

"Exactly; and Mr. Martin disappeared. One of the other suitors was Mr John Thurlow, and rumour says that prior to his death it looked as if he were going to draw the prize in the sweep. He was a retired Indian merchant and reputed to be wealthy. He was much older than the lady, but his wealth probably discounted that item. Last Monday night he also disappeared from his place, Old Hall Farm. On Wednesday morning, both the missing men were discovered, as you know, at Cobbler's Corner. They were dead."

"Thurlow with his head smashed in, and Martin shot through the shoulder. I'll see the local police inspector this afternoon and get his full report on the case. Was there anything that particularly struck you, apart from what you've told me?"

"I've left the most exciting bit till the last, Heather. On Monday night, Miss Thurlow and her uncle, both spiritualists, held a little séance in Mr. Thurlow's study. It was an experiment as far as Thurlow was concerned. They extinguished the lights, and, according to the niece's story, after a short period of silence, the room was suddenly filled with the strains of ghostly music. Thurlow was so astonished that he switched on the light. The music continued for a while and then died away. Miss Thurlow left her uncle in the study. She says she went into the garden to try and collect her thoughts before going to bed. Her trance state had upset her, and she feels that she was a bit distrait. So much so, that she doesn't remember how long she stayed outside. She thinks about an hour. Eventually, however, she came to her full senses and found herself in bed. She says she never heard her uncle come upstairs to his room, and finally she fell asleep. Next morning, the servant discovered the electric light in the study still burning and the window wide open. All the doors of the house were shut and locked. She went upstairs to her master's bedroom with his morning tea. The room was empty and the bed had not been slept in."

A frown had gathered on Inspector Heather's brow, and he began to rub his chin thoughtfully.

"You got the story of this séance business from the young lady?" he asked.

"Yes"

"Is she... is she loopy?" asked the officer in an impatient tone.

"Not in the least. She's a very sensible and charming young woman, in my opinion," replied Vereker with emphasis.

"If they're charming, they're always sensible, with most young men," commented Heather and asked: "but you don't think this spirit business had anything to do with Thurlow's disappearance and murder?"

"I'm not going to express any rash opinions at this stage, Heather. Miss Thurlow has asked me to come and see her, if I want to ask her any further questions. I'd like to get a little more information about this spirit manifestation. As you know, I've always been rather interested in the subject."

"God bless my soul, I'd forgotten that! Does the young lady call herself a medium by any chance?"

"I'm not certain. She impresses me as a genuine psychic, if there is such a thing, and I can only presume there is from what I've read."

"You mean Psyche, I suppose. This is a bad beginning, Mr. Vereker. I don't know what's the matter with the younger generation. A sensible man like you—apart from your painting—paying any heed to this kind of bugaboo! That's the word, pure bugaboo! Really, really, it's too bad!"

"Have you ever been to a séance with a genuine medium, Heather?"

"Yes, but it's many years ago now."

"What happened?"

"We arrested the genuine medium. You've heard of the Farrow case?"

"I've read of it. Spiritualists say it was a disgraceful business on the part of the police."

"That may be their opinion. I simply did my duty. Still, it's no use discussing that affair now. It doesn't affect the present case."

"And you're no wiser on the subject to-day?"

"I wouldn't say that, but I can't for the life of me see what this séance business has to do with Mr. Thurlow's disappearance and murder. What connection do you see?"

"None at present, but I feel that Miss Thurlow thinks there is, and I'm going to keep it in mind."

"Have you managed to get in touch with Miss Dawn Garford?"

"No. She left Yarham on the morning of Tuesday, the very morning that Miss Thurlow discovered that her uncle had vanished. She has gone down to stay with friends at Midhurst, in Sussex."

"That sounds more significant to me than raising spooks," commented Heather. "Do you know anything more about this Miss Garford?"

"Very little. Village gossip says she's in the habit of exceeding the speed limit. In a little place like Yarham, gossip's guarded. A wink says what it's unsafe to say. The worst of it is, you can't translate winks explicitly."

"Just so. How is she fixed financially?"

"Her late husband left her enough to live on."

"I thought you said she was Miss Garford."

"That's how she's known in Yarham. Her married name is Mrs. Button."

"Why didn't you tell me she was a widow? It's most important. They never hesitate to employ bodyline stuff to pull off an important match. How did she get on with the old boy's niece?"

"It seems they were quite good friends."

"Would her marriage to Thurlow have had any financial effect on the niece?"

"I can't tell you definitely. The rector, who was very friendly with the dead man, tells me that, by his will, Thurlow had left everything he possessed to his niece. His marriage might have altered that considerably."

"Almost a certainty. To put the matter very bluntly, by her uncle's sudden death, Miss Eileen bags the dough. It's an important point; it supplies a motive at once, and the spirit stuff may be eye-wash."

"I've been thinking a lot about that, Heather, but it doesn't seem to me at present to be of much consequence. Still, we must dig deeper. We've got a lot to learn."

"Were Martin and Thurlow friends?" asked the inspector after a pause.

"Certainly not after Martin found that Thurlow was his rival. But we mustn't jump to hasty conclusions. On the face of it, it looks as if Martin had been shot through the shoulder by Thurlow, and in return slammed Thurlow over the head with the iron bar. It's not as simple as all that. In the first place, the blow that smashed Thurlow's skull was delivered from behind, and must have been dealt with considerable force. The iron bar, called a fold-drift in these parts, because it's used for fixing up sheep folds, is a very heavy instrument. Martin certainly couldn't have swung it after being shot with a Webley .45. I've had a long chat with Cornard on the subject, and he's thoroughly mystified about the cause of Martin's death. The wound was not what you'd call a deadly one, though he may have died of subsequent shock. But there are other points which need clearing up. Cornard says that there are marks on Martin's wrists and ankles which show that he'd been bound hand and foot prior to death. As far as I can gather, your great expert, Sir Donald McPherson, will have to be called in to make an autopsy, and probably portions of the body will have to be submitted to the Home Office analyst, to see if poison enters into the business of Martin's mysterious death."

"Looks as if we're up against a first-class mystery, Mr. Vereker," remarked Heather, rising and preparing to leave the inn.

"You'll get a fuller account of the police findings from the local inspector, this afternoon, Heather. I'll expect you to stick to our rules, and not hide any vital information from me. I can't rise to brilliant intuitions out of a vacuum."

"I'll play the game fairly, Mr. Vereker. I daresay, when you were left at Cobbler's Corner by Godbold, you weren't idle. You've spotted a thing or two you've not told me about, but that's part of the contract. You've not said one word about this man, Ephraim Noy, who found the bodies. What about him?"

"Now, Heather, you're getting hot. The very name Ephraim is a deadly pointer, nearly as incriminating as Silas. He's a mystery even to the village. He lives entirely alone in his new bungalow, and is about as communicative as a brick wall. His vocabulary doesn't get much further than yes and no. No one seems to know where he came from, what he is or has been. Apparently he lives on investments, and is as free with his money as a Yorkshireman. Godbold was very suspicious about Ephraim's chance discovery of the bodies, and looked handcuffs at him straight away. When questioned by the constable, he said he had nothing further to say about the matter, which didn't concern him. If he were forced to make any further statement, he'd make it to a 'responsible officer.' Godbold exploded in choice Suffolk dialect, of which I couldn't understand one word, but it didn't upset Mr. Ephraim Noy."

Inspector Heather glanced at his watch, and as he left the room, remarked cheerily: "Au revoir, Mr. Vereker. I'll see you some time this evening. In the meantime, while I'm getting the facts of this business from the Suffolk police, I hope you'll work up a few of your best intuitions. You'll need them all, if I'm not mistaken. What are you going to do this afternoon?"

"You ought, as Oscar Wilde said, ask me what I'm going to think, Heather. My best intuitions come to me when I'm doing absolutely nothing at all."

"You might go and see this charming and sensible Miss Thurlow. You're better than I am at dealing with genuine psychics. In fact, all women are a bit of a puzzle to me."

"First time I've heard you say so, Heather. In any case, the man who says he knows all about women, never knows the first thing about himself. I forgot to mention that there's a very pretty cook up at..."

But the inspector had disappeared through the dining-room door before Anthony Vereker could finish the sentence.

Chapter Five

Shortly after Heather's departure, Vereker strolled lazily out of "The Walnut Tree" into the warm summer sunshine. He took the road skirting the village green and leading southwards to Hawksfield.

All this portion of Suffolk about Yarham is dotted with villages of a few hundred inhabitants, with isolated farms scattered between. The population is almost entirely agrarian, and the conditions of life can soberly be called truly rural. It has an insidious charm, detachedly somnolent and meditative, and Vereker was under its almost uncanny spell. There was no settled plan in his mind, and if he had any objective, it was almost subconscious. He had chosen the road because it was perhaps more picturesque than any of the others winding tortuously out of Yarham. He was aware that there was little likelihood of meeting anyone he knew, because one can traverse any of the roads about Yarham for miles at any time of day without passing more than half a dozen pedestrians, a farm waggon, and an occasional motor car. He felt an overwhelming sense of remoteness from the hurrying world, and was conscious of that absence of distraction which leaves a man starkly facing his own thoughts. Yes, Yarham was conducive to quiet thinking and sound sleeping.

He had not, however, walked more than a mile before he encountered Miss Eileen Thurlow. She had just emerged from a rough grassy lane which ran into the road at right angles. This lane, a primitive cart track called a "drift," was an approach to Church Farm, lying about a mile from the road and inaccessible by any other means. In summer these drifts are passable on foot, but in winter the pedestrian can only wade through them in gum boots. Thus many farms are completely isolated, and no traffic passes them except that of their own farm waggons and servants.

Miss Thurlow at once recognized Vereker.

"I was just coming down to see you," she said. "I've been expecting you to call at Old Hall Farm every day since your visit with Mr. Sturgeon."

"I've been going to do so, Miss Thurlow, but somehow or other..."

"You didn't like to trouble me in the circumstances. I understand. I've been wanting to talk things over with you alone, because I think you understand me. We're only half a mile from the Old Hall. Would you care to come along now to tea, or have you some other engagement?"

"I'm quite free and shall be glad to come. I hope you won't mind my asking you all sorts of questions."

"I want you to, and I'll answer them as best I can. I'm anxious to help you to clear up this terrible business of my uncle's death. The police seem unable to make head or tail of it, and Inspector Winter treats me as if I were an imbecile. When I mentioned to him that my uncle and I had a séance on the night he disappeared, the man was positively insulting. He asked me abruptly what 'the dooce' had that got to do with the business."

"You've heard that Inspector Heather of Scotland Yard is now in charge of the investigations?" asked Vereker.

"I read it this morning in the *West Suffolk Post*. I hope he's politer than his local colleague."

"He's a great detective, Miss Thurlow, and a particular friend of mine. I'm sure you'll find him very tactful even on the subject of your séance."

"I'm glad to hear it, because I'm certain that our séance is in some way connected with what followed."

"Will you try to explain how?" asked Vereker quietly.

"It's difficult to explain clearly, but I think there's a connection in either of two ways. But first may I ask if you believe in spiritualism, Mr. Vereker?"

"It's a subject on which I must plead ignorance. I've not had sufficient first-hand experience to say I believe in it definitely. From my reading, I'm inclined to think that the spiritualist has, on the whole, proved the soundness of his claims. Further than that I can't go."

"What I want to know is that you're not obstinately certain that it's all nonsense."

"I'm never obstinately certain about anything, Miss Thurlow," replied Vereker smiling.

"I'm glad. To resume; the séance may have had an indirect connection with my uncle's disappearance. After I said good-night to him, he may have left the house by the window, in search of something arising out of the séance. He probably thought the music had some material origin and was determined to find out..."

"Pardon my interrupting, but why did he leave by the window?" asked Vereker.

"We can only surmise that he did. Raymer, one of my maids, said that when she went downstairs next morning, all the doors were closed and locked. The study light was still burning and the window wide open."

"Your uncle possessed a revolver?"

"Oh yes, he always kept a loaded one in the top left-hand drawer of his writing desk in the study."

"Of course, it's not unusual to have a fire-arm for protection, especially in a lonely house, but was there any special reason for the precaution? Was he afraid of someone? Had he any enemies?"

"I'm not very sure on that point. He spent a portion of his early life in India. When quite a youngster, I once heard my parents discussing some trouble Uncle John got into out there. It had something to do with an Indian dancing girl, her husband who was murdered, and a temple of the goddess Kali. Not long ago I tried to get my uncle to tell me about it, because it sounded interesting, but he denied all knowledge of the story. For some days after I had revived the memory, he was in a very jumpy state of nerves. It struck me that he was afraid there might be some sequel to that affair even after the lapse of all those years. Just about that time, too, the man Ephraim Noy came to live in Yarham and called on my uncle. My uncle, however, said he didn't want to see him, and Noy went quietly away. I don't know why Noy called, or why my uncle refused to see him, but I've an idea that he knew Noy long before the man came and settled down in Yarham. Shortly after that visit, my uncle bought a revolver and put it in the drawer of his desk. He showed me where it was, and told me that if anything happened in his absence from the house, say a burglary, I was to take the weapon for self-protection if necessary."

"Did he show by any of his actions that he was afraid of Noy?"

"No. After the incident of his calling at Old Hall Farm, my uncle didn't seem to worry any more about him. Once, when his name cropped up in conversation, he merely said Noy was an unscrupulous and ungrateful brute, and the subject was allowed to drop. About the other connection which our séance may have with my uncle's tragedy, I find it very difficult to talk. But I'm going to mention it at the risk of your thinking me superstitious or of incurring your ridicule. If you're a spiritualist, Mr. Vereker, you must, of course, believe in evil as well as good spirits. Men are evil and good and their spirit counterparts are similar. By some chance he may have got in touch with an evil and vindictive spirit."

"But you surely don't think an evil spirit could kill a man, Miss Thurlow?" asked Vereker, amazed at this suggestion, and regarding his companion with sharply awakened curiosity.

"Why not?" asked Miss Thurlow with unruffled calm. "At a séance I've seen a heavy table, weighing sixty pounds, turned over as if it had been a toy, the medium being a fragile woman of sixty years. Then there's the Biblical example of the Gadarene swine. Spirits, like their human counterparts, may be irrational, insane, even murderous. As I've said, it's difficult to discuss the subject with people who've no knowledge of spiritualism. They simply think you're a candidate for Bedlam."

"Yes, I confess that's the general attitude," commented Vereker thoughtfully.

"Now Mr. Orton of Church Farm is inclined to agree with me that there may be something in the theory of an evil spirit. He is, of course, a confirmed spiritualist. I've just called on him, and he says that Old Hall Farm has always been associated with evil spirits. All the villagers know it, and the older ones can recount very strange things that have happened there.

"Don't you think that it's merely country superstition?"

"No, certainly not. People who live isolated lives, like the East Anglian peasantry, are in much closer touch with this hidden world or whatever you like to call it. There's a lubberfiend who plays all sorts of mischievous pranks at Mr. Orton's farm. Mr. Orton used to have great difficulty in keeping his men till he gathered his present staff, who are not scared by such things, and accept them as part of the many inexplicable things of life."

"Have you known Mr. Orton long?" suddenly asked Vereker.

"Ever since we came here. His farm belongs to my uncle's estate."

"What kind of a man is he, Miss Thurlow?"

"He's not a typical countryman. He's much better educated, has been abroad a good deal, and is very musical. He's a good farmer and a shrewd hard-headed business man, but rather reserved on the whole, especially where villagers are concerned."

"You get along well with him?"

"Oh yes. To put it bluntly, I think—I think he rather likes me," replied Miss Thurlow, smiling and blushing informatively.

"Was he on friendly terms with your uncle?"

"On the best of terms. He often came round in the evening to see my uncle and have a chat with him."

"Now I'm going to put rather a pointed question to you, Miss Thurlow. If you think me rude, just say so. Are the relations between you and Mr. Orton anything more than mere friendship?" asked Vereker, and furtively watched his companion's face to see the effect of his words.

Miss Thurlow's lips were suddenly compressed and then twitched as if she were suppressing a smile. A merry light stole into her large brown eyes and faded out as quickly.

"Nothing more than friendship at present, Mr. Vereker. I feel sure Mr. Orton admires me. A woman can always tell when a man admires her, though she rarely admits it from fear of being thought conceited. I've admitted it frankly, because I feel sure you think you ought to know. As for my feelings, well, at first he faintly repelled me. Now I'm quite certain I find him—er—likeable."

"Thank you. Now I've got over that difficult fence, I feel relieved. To return to the subject of spirits; have you ever seen a spirit, ghost, call it what you will, about Old Hall Farm?"

"No, but Miss Garford tells me that villagers have seen an apparition on several occasions on the road between Old Hall and the village."

"You're referring to Miss Dawn Garford?" asked Vereker.

"Yes."

"You're very great friends, I hear?"

"Not exactly. I'm friendly with her rather through force of circumstances. There are so few women in Yarham with whom I have anything in common. She's bright and amusing, and I enjoy her company."

"She lives with her aunt in the village, I believe?"

"Yes, when she's in Yarham, but she spends a great part of the year roaming about the home counties in her small car. She seems to have numerous friends and is apparently very popular. I don't see very much of her altogether."

"Your uncle was fond of her?"

"You're an encyclopaedia of village gossip, Mr. Vereker," exclaimed Miss Thurlow with a laugh. "Well, Uncle John was always very gallant in a charming, old-fashioned way where a pretty woman was concerned. He may have been more serious than that with Dawn. People seemed to think so. I didn't, but then he probably concealed his feelings from me. Besides, I'm not at all observant in such matters."

"Let us suppose his intentions were serious, Miss Thurlow. Would his marriage to Miss Garford have affected you greatly?"

"No, I don't think so. Uncle John had made me his sole heiress by his will. That would certainly have been altered if he had married."

"Would you have suffered considerably from a financial point of view?"

At this remark, Miss Thurlow laughed heartily.

"Is that a leading question, Mr. Vereker? If I answered yes, you'd begin to think it confirmed some suspicion in your mind that I might be interested in my uncle's death."

"No, it's not a leading question, and your surmise isn't quite accurate," replied Vereker, rather embarrassed by this direct and disarming thrust.

"In any case, I'm not going to answer the question as you want me to, or shall I say, expect me to. If my uncle had married and altered his will, I shouldn't have inherited the whole of his estate. I wouldn't, however, have cared very much, because I'm a woman of very simple tastes. I'm not fashionable, I don't dress expensively, I don't travel, I can do without a car. I think I'll surprise you when I say I could live in the greatest comfort in the country on two hundred a year. I have that now. Still, don't get it into your head that I'm not fond of money. I certainly am."

"I apologize, Miss Thurlow. I didn't think you were such a philosopher," said Vereker with a genial smile, "but still my question had quite another aim in view than wringing such a confession from you."

"May I ask what you were driving at, Mr. Vereker?"

"I shan't tell you. A detective, like a conjurer, must keep his methods to himself. But about Miss Garford. How did she stand in relation to Mr. Clarry Martin?"

"I'm not sure. It was a subject on which she was always extraordinarily reticent, though I tried to chaff her into telling me. I'm fairly certain Martin was very much in love with her, but I don't think she was with him. There was something else other than love between them. They shared some secret, I feel sure. I can't tell you why I feel sure, but there's a strain of the clairvoyant in me; I have confirmed that on many other occasions. Now, Mr. Vereker, if you're a detective, here's where there is a baffling little mystery for you. It has probably nothing to do with the case on which you're engaged, but it might pay you to probe into it."

"It may be quite important. In any case I shall leave no stone unturned, Miss Thurlow," replied Vereker, thankful for the information.

By this time, they had reached the gates of Old Hall Farm, and as Vereker was apparently lost in his own speculations, the conversation languished while they walked up the gravel drive leading to the house. Anthony Vereker's eyes, however, were busily occupied in looking about him. The old, fourteenth century building with its wide sweep of surrounding lawn, its broad herbaceous borders, bright with flowers all bathed in summer sunshine; the surrounding woodland, motionless in the breathless air; the trim walks and beautifully shorn hedges were all eloquent of sane living and affluent refinement, rather than suggestive of evil spirits, mysterious happenings, and a terrible tragedy. To Vereker there was always something intensely satisfying about this type of English country house, and as he was admiring its air of gentle well-being, he could not help coupling it with its recent owner, John Thurlow. Whatever might be said of the acquisitive characteristics of the financial or merchant type, that type was certainly sensitive to beauty. Or was it merely the following of a tradition, a sheep-like treading along the paths laid down by a finer and more cultured generation?

"I see you like Old Hall Farm," said Miss Thurlow, interrupting his thoughts.

"You're quite right; it's very beautiful," replied Vereker.

"I can scarcely realize it's now my own," continued his companion musingly.

"You intend to stay on here?"

"Certainly. I wouldn't dream of selling it. I love the place," said Miss Thurlow emphatically, and they passed through the main door into a small entrance hall, in the centre of which was an antique gate-legged table furnished with a large cut-glass bowl of yellow roses.

"We'll have tea in my uncle's study," remarked Miss Thurlow. "I feel sure you want to see that room."

"You've guessed my thoughts again, Miss Thurlow. I'm convinced you're telepathic."

Miss Thurlow smiled with an air of satisfaction and led the way into the room which Vereker was so eager to see.

"Now, Mr. Vereker, you must excuse me for a few minutes. Take a comfortable chair, or wander round and have a good look at everything. You'll be interested in those early English watercolours for one thing, and if you have any gift of psychometry, you'll probably learn more about the place than I could tell you."

With these words and the promise that she would return as quickly as possible, she left the room.

On her departure, Vereker at once surveyed the charming oak-wainscoted room, and making a circuit of the walls, tapped them all gently with the knuckles of his right hand. He examined the joints in the wainscoting with particular care. Satisfied with this scrutiny, he then opened and closed the door leading out into the garden and inspected the lock. Then, rapidly crossing to the large window by which John Thurlow was supposed to have left the house on the night of his disappearance, he produced a magnifying glass and scanned every inch of the solid oak frame and the metal catch. He was busy over this task, when he was startled by the presence of Eileen Thurlow behind him, for in his preoccupation, he had not heard her re-enter the room.

"This is the window by which your uncle left the house on the night of his disappearance?" he asked mechanically.

"I only presume he did," replied Miss Thurlow.

"But he must have done so, if all the doors were locked."

"That's the matter-of-fact explanation, Mr. Vereker, but who can say? Sir Arthur Conan Doyle, I think, put forward a theory that Houdini had some power of dematerializing and then materializing again to perform some of his amazing tricks. Houdini professed to be a conjurer and was hostile to spiritualism probably to keep his secrets inviolate. My uncle may have stumbled suddenly on some knowledge of the kind on that occasion."

"It seems rather a far-fetched explanation," remarked Vereker with a sense of uneasiness. He began to feel that Miss Thurlow was deliberately trying to be incomprehensible.

"I merely suggest it as a possible alternative, because it seems ridiculous for the owner of a house to climb out of the window when there's a door handy," replied Miss Thurlow.

"I agree, but I'm going to use up every matter-of-fact explanation before proceeding to something highly improbable. The difficulty I'm confronted with is that I can't for the life of me see why he should go out by the window when there was a door handy."

"The alternative theory is highly improbable to you, because you've not accustomed your mind to it yet, Mr. Vereker. For instance, do you believe a table is solid?"

"Scientifically I know it's not, but I know I can't put my hand through it," replied Vereker smiling.

"Exactly, but that's simply because you don't know how. Neither the table nor your hand is solid; they are merely, so scientists assert, composed of ions and protons of electricity. The matter-of-fact man will accept this wonder, but he won't accept any spiritualist theory. It seems rather inconsistent to me."

"Well, we won't quarrel on the point," continued Vereker. "For the present, I'm going to assume that your uncle left by the window. For the sake of argument, we'll say he chose that course, because it was quicker than unlocking the door."

"I hadn't thought of that explanation," remarked Miss Thurlow with a note of surprise. "Of course, he might have been in a desperate hurry."

"That's so, but we want to know why. If we could just get hold of that why, we'd have made one step forward in our solution of the problem."

"Ah, well, here's the tea," exclaimed Miss Thurlow, as a maid brought in a tray and laid it on a small table in the centre of the study. "A cup of tea ought to brighten you up to making brilliant deductions," she added with a laugh.

"Your uncle didn't belong to the hatless brigade, Miss Thurlow?" asked Vereker, after a pause.

"No. He often sat about the house with a cap on. Said he believed in keeping his head warm. But why do you ask?"

"He was hatless when his body was found, and I shall be glad if you can check up whether one of his hats or caps is missing."

"I'll do that immediately after tea. I ought to have thought of it before, but, there, I'm not a detective."

"Then there was an iron bar, called a fold-drift, found lying between the bodies of your uncle and Martin. I believe this tool is generally used for making post holes for light fencing. Did it belong to Old Hall Farm?" asked Vereker, helping himself to blackberry jelly.

"I'm certain it didn't," replied Miss Thurlow emphatically. "Inspector Winter asked me that question. I spoke to Runnacles, our gardener, about it and he said he had never seen one about the place, though it's possible there may have been one in one of the out-houses."

For some moments Vereker sat lost in speculation. Suddenly looking up, he asked: "Have you a wireless set, Miss Thurlow?"

"No; my uncle had an unreasonable dislike for radio. He always called it a 'damned annoying contraption,' and said it was the refuge of an age that had neither conversation nor good taste."

"He also disliked gramophones?"

"Yes, but now I guess what you're getting at, Mr. Vereker. You're seeking a simple solution of the strange music I've often heard in this house and that my uncle and I both heard on the evening of his disappearance."

"No; I'm only eliminating simple explanations," replied Vereker.

"I've eliminated the only possible one already," continued Miss Thurlow. "My uncle thought it might be the church organist practising. The church is nearly a mile distant. We can never hear the organ, even when there's a service, and on that night the church organist, Mr. Veevers, wasn't practising."

"That seems pretty conclusive," commented Vereker and asked: "When did you first hear this strange music, Miss Thurlow?"

"About two months ago. On the thirty-first of May, to be precise. The date is fixed in my mind because it was then that I first detected that I possessed psychic powers."

"You're sure it's not a kind of aural illusion?"

"How can it be when my uncle heard it, too. Look here, Mr. Vereker, to settle any doubts there may be in your mind, I suggest that one evening we have a little séance on our own. I feel sure I can get a repetition of that spirit music. Personally, I'm convinced, but Pm dying to convince you. Are you game?"

"Certainly, Miss Thurlow. I was eager to ask you if you'd consent to another experiment, but didn't like to do so."

"We'll say that's settled then. We'll make arrangements later, and if you'd care to bring a sympathetic friend along with you, all the better. Do you think Inspector Heather would like to join us?"

"I couldn't say, but knowing the inspector as I do, I'm sure he'd make an intractable member of the circle. He has already told me since his arrival that he thinks spiritualism's a kind of bugaboo."

"Then we'd better leave him out, but you must use your own discretion after talking the matter over with him. Now, I've an idea you'd like to make a thorough examination of the house, and I've a suggestion to make. I shall have to go up to town in a day or two to see my uncle's solicitors and visit my dressmaker. I shall be away for two or three days, and while I'm absent, I'd like you to come and stay in Old Hall Farm. You can then explore the place from top to bottom. The house staff will be at your service, and Runnacles will do anything you want done outside."

"This is very generous of you, Miss Thurlow. I don't know how to thank you," remarked Vereker sincerely.

"You can thank me after the horrid business is all over and done with, Mr. Vereker. I want to help you in every way I can, and I feel somehow that you'll be more successful than the police in the matter. There's another thing that may help you indirectly. I'll leave the keys of my uncle's desk with you, and you can glance through his diaries and papers. I don't know whether you'll find anything in them bearing on this mystery, but one never knows."

Vereker again thanked Miss Thurlow very warmly, and a little later, took his departure. Before leaving, he learned from his hostess that one of her uncle's caps was missing, a fact which definitely settled that John Thurlow, on the night of his disappearance, had put on a cap before setting out from Old Hall Farm.

On returning to "The Walnut Tree," Vereker found Benjamin Easy sitting in the empty tap-room, smoking his pipe in that lugubrious meditation which was his habit when there were no customers in his inn. Vereker, taking a seat, ordered a pint of beer to dispel the landlord's depression, and on his return with the brimming mug, asked him if he knew Mr. Arthur Orton of Church Farm.

"Don't know much about the gentleman," replied Ben, puffing at his pipe with awakening animation. "He seems to be well-off. He farms well, but a man with capital can allus farm well if he likes. That don't say he makes a fortune out of it. One thing I like about him. He's the fust farmer I've met who don't grumble about farming."

"Is he a bachelor or a widower?" asked Vereker.

"He has a housekeeper," replied Easy.

"Well, I didn't expect him to manage his house himself, Ben," commented Vereker.

"Perhaps you didn't," replied Ben, and was portentously silent.

"Ah, I see. You mean that there's something between the two."

"They say she has a mind to make him her husband, but one never can be certain."

"Does he ever come in here?" asked Vereker.

"Very seldom and then doesn't help me much to pay my way."

"He's abstemious, eh? You don't seem to like the gentleman, Ben."

"Can't say as I do or I don't. Never had much to do with him. They say he drives a hard bargain."

"What do his men think of him?" asked Vereker.

"Ah, now you're asking something. He's a hard master, and his men come and go, all except Joe Battrum and Sandy Gow. They say he's all right, especially Gow, but he's a Scotchman and as tight as his boss."

"Have you heard that Church Farm is haunted, Ben?" asked Vereker with a smile.

"Haanted be damned!" exclaimed Ben vigorously. "On that score I think Orton be crazed. He believes in ghosts and all that. So do Joe and Sandy, but I think they do it to oblige the master, so to speak."

"Then you don't believe Church Farm is haunted, Ben?"

"My father farmed it for twenty years, and I was brought up there. We never saw no ghosts. Still, it's a rum old house, and if there be such things as ghosts it ought to be haanted. The only thing that haanted us was how to pay the rent to the old squire."

"Have you heard anything about Orton and Miss Thurlow?" asked Vereker at a venture.

"Lor bless me, yes. He's setting his cap at the young lady, they say. He wants to marry the farm, I reckon. Still, I don't know. He's very thick with young Miss Garford, too. She's allus running up to Church Farm. There's summat queer about it all, especially with Miss Garford."

"In what way, Ben?" asked Vereker, glancing up at the landlord's furrowed brow.

"Well, his housekeeper don't seem to mind Miss Garford. Don't strike me as reasonable. Most housekeepers would be jealous."

"What sort of a woman is the housekeeper?"

"A nice looking gal, and what's more they say she's boss."

At this juncture a heavy step sounded outside the door of the inn, and a few seconds later, the burly figure of Inspector Heather entered the room.

"You've come back at the right moment, Heather. I suppose yours is a pint of bitter as usual?" said Vereker.

"I'll need more than that, Mr. Vereker," said the inspector with an unusually grave air. "This is the damnedest case I've ever had anything to do with. I'm getting depressed already. Still, I've found that the fifth pint always completely alters my point of view, so I mustn't get disheartened. I'll start with one at your expense."

Benjamin Easy rose and left the tap-room to get the necessary drink, and on his departure, the inspector laid his hand on Vereker's shoulder.

"I think we'd better retire to your sitting-room. This place will begin to fill up shortly, and we'll have to move in the middle of an interesting discussion. What d'you think?"

"It would certainly be better, Heather," agreed Vereker, and when the inspector had drunk his beer, they left the tap-room and ascended the stairs to Vereker's private sitting-room.

Chapter Six

"Now, Heather, shake yourself and tell me all you know. You've heard something from Inspector Winter that puzzles you, and you're not happy."

"To tell the truth, I'm not feeling very clever to-day. Too much work of late. There's the Barton murder case still in the air. We came to a full stop in our investigations. And now this one looks as if it's going to turn nasty. It's enough to drive a man to drinking grape-fruit!"

"You badly missed my help on the Barton case. I've a lovely theory about it which meets all the difficult points. Pure deductions of course, but I love pure deductions. Like pure mathematics, they never disillusion you."

"What I don't like about pure deductions is that they never hang a man. But to get to the case we're on. There are several rum points about it. First, it seems impossible that Martin died from the effects of his bullet wound. Second, the wound shows that he was shot from behind. Third, it's evident that he was bound hand and foot before he died. Fourth, the police surgeon is almost certain that the bullet wound was inflicted after death."

"The last point is always a bit problematical, but if it's the doctor's opinion, that's something to go on," remarked Vereker, lighting a cigarette.

"Can you tell me why Thurlow should want to shoot a dead man?" asked Heather lugubriously.

"One good reason is that the dead man couldn't shoot back. Are you satisfied that Thurlow fired the shot?"

"Looks darned like it. His right hand gripped the revolver firmly, and only one cartridge had been discharged. We couldn't find the bullet, though we searched every inch of the ground for hundreds of yards around."

"A shocking waste of time, Heather!" declared Vereker emphatically.

"Why a waste of time? We want the bullet to prove that it was discharged from Thurlow's revolver. It's important."

"You didn't let me finish what I was going to say. It was a shocking waste of time searching for the bullet at Cobbler's Corner."

"I agree. And there's another question requires an answer. Where are the ropes that bound Martin's wrists and ankles?"

"I reckon they'll be somewhere near the bullet, Heather."

"You mean that someone took the trouble to find the bullet and remove the cords? Who would do that and why?"

"It's evident that someone removed the cords. About the bullet, I've got a little theory. As it's pure theory, it won't interest you at this stage."

"I don't want theories, Mr. Vereker. Give me facts!"

"Well, there are two facts about the case which ought to prove useful to you. One concerns Thurlow's patent leather evening shoes. You've noticed them, of course. The second is that when his body was discovered, it was hatless."

"It simply says he left Old Hall Farm in a hurry. He probably heard someone moving about outside his study and went out at once to investigate."

"Against your inference, is the fact that he always put on a hat or cap when he went outside, and one of his caps is missing. Miss Thurlow has confirmed the last point. Even if he'd heard someone outside, too, he'd hardly have been in such a hurry as to jump through an open window to get at the prowler, when there was a door handy through which he might have passed with dignity."

"That window jumping is certainly puzzling. I can't explain it."

"It seems so illogical to me, that I've decided he didn't pass through the window."

"Then how did he get out? The maid, Raymer, says all the doors were locked when she came down in the morning. If she told the truth, he must have gone through the window."

"We've only got the maid's word for it that all the doors were locked. She came to that conclusion after she had discovered that her master was missing, which was some time after she came down. She may be quite sincere in her statement, but memory's a fantastic thing at times, as you know from the evidence of perfectly honest witnesses."

"That's true, but what struck you as strange about Thurlow's evening shoes?"

"He'd been walking over chalky ground. There was chalk sticking to the soles. I didn't mean to give that clue away, but I must play fair."

"I noticed the chalk, but I suppose there's chalk somewhere about the district."

"There certainly is some twenty feet below the top soil. We must find out where it's lying on the surface. That'll give us the direction he took after leaving Old Hall Farm. But, Heather, if you can explain to me how he could chase a man, presumably Martin, from Old Hall Farm to Cobbler's Corner, a mile away and more, and pass through Yarham village without being seen by anyone, then call me a born idiot!"

"It doesn't seem feasible, but anything can happen in Suffolk, if you ask me. As for being seen by someone in the village, as a matter of fact, he was seen in Yarham at about eleven o'clock."

"I'm glad I've squeezed that out of you. I hadn't heard it. Who saw Thurlow, revolver in hand, in full cry after his man?"

"Orton and his man, Joe Battrum, saw him get into a car on the road skirting the village green, at eleven o'clock on the night he disappeared."

"This is all very confusing, Heather. Was he wearing his cap?"

"Yes, but he hadn't got a revolver in his hand, and he wasn't chasing anyone. He was apparently waiting for the car, because he was quietly pacing up and down the road just near the war memorial. He didn't seem to be excited about anything. Battrum says he bade Mr. Thurlow good-night. Thurlow returned the greeting and said it looked as if the rain the farmers were praying for was as far away as ever. What do you make of that?"

"It convinces me that he didn't get out of the window at Old Hall Farm."

"What has the window got to do with it?" asked Heather.

"Let me explain. If Thurlow was seen in the village, pacing up and down the road at eleven o'clock, it appears that he was waiting for the car that eventually picked him up. Therefore he had an appointment. Knowing that he had an appointment, he'd give himself time to keep it; and even if he'd cut things fine, he wouldn't have left the house by the window. It also clearly shows that he heard no prowler outside while he was sitting in his study, and that there was, therefore, no chase."

"You're improving, Mr. Vereker. That's just how I've figured it out. He had plenty of time to get his revolver, put on his cap, and then walk straight through the wall of the house without bothering to unlock the door."

"Those locked doors are a bit of a snag, Heather!" exclaimed Vereker with a laugh. "Miss Thurlow, who is a spiritualist, gets round the difficulty with consummate ease. She hints that it's possible for a human being to dematerialize, pass through a brick wall, and then re-assemble his component parts outside!"

"Great Scott, and I've got to interview and question the young lady yet! Of all the damned nonsense..."

"Now, now, Heather, don't lose your wool. Try and get a prettier solution if you can. But to return to Mr. Clarry Martin; what does the doctor think he died of?"

"He doesn't know. Says the post mortem shows no sign, and nothing very characteristic except dark venous blood. It looks like apoplexy, but he wouldn't be sure. To all appearances, the man died without a struggle, which seems extraordinary in conjunction with the fact that he was bound hand and foot."

"He might have died of shock, but I think we can rule that out. He was, as far as I can judge, a strong, healthy man. Miss Thurlow is again helpful on the subject. She thinks that an evil spirit may have killed her uncle. Possibly the spirit accounted for Martin, too. A spirit would kill a man in a mysterious way, I should say."

"Spirits be damned, Mr. Vereker!" exclaimed Heather.

"I agree. Beer is best! But there's one more point that's intriguing. Thurlow disappeared on Monday night; Martin, the previous Friday. Their bodies were found at Cobbler's Corner on Wednesday morning. What were the two men doing in the interval? I'm presuming that the bodies were not at Cobbler's Corner on Tuesday morning."

"Mr. Ephraim Noy says he crossed that bit of waste land on Tuesday afternoon, and they were not there then. Again, when Martin left his parents' house on Friday evening, he was carrying a small attaché case. That attaché case must be searched for as well as Thurlow's cap."

"This fellow Ephraim Noy gets more important every moment. According to Miss Thurlow, her uncle evidently knew Noy before the latter came to Yarham. It was shortly after Noy's arrival in the district that her uncle bought a revolver. This seems significant to me, Heather."

"Thank heaven, she didn't drag out her spooks to explain that point," remarked Heather with relief. "I was afraid you were going to give me another visitation. I don't like this marked enthusiasm for spectres, Mr. Vereker; looks uncommonly like a red herring. Are you certain the lady isn't anxious to mislead us?"

"Almost certain. She's genuine enough, I think, though certainly a strange mixture. But I'm going to keep my eye on Ephraim Noy."

"That's advisable. He's a dark horse. Nobody here seems to know much about him from what I can gather. But I'm not too comfortable about Miss Thurlow. She's an enigma and I never trust enigmas."

For some minutes the two men sat in silence, and then Heather suddenly exclaimed in a tone of exasperation: "My memory's going, Mr. Vereker. It's about time I retired and settled down to breeding Rhode Island Reds."

"Perhaps another pint would help it," suggested Vereker amiably.

"Now, I'd even forgotten that!" remarked Heather as he rose and left the room. He returned with two mugs of beer.

"What were you trying to remember?" asked Vereker, when the inspector had again settled down in his easy chair.

"I was trying to recollect where and in what connection I'd met the man Runnacles before. I've been ransacking my brain ever since I set eyes on him."

"Runnacles? You're surely not going to put Runnacles in your list of suspects?"

"Ah, that's where experience is so much better than intuition, Mr. Vereker. I've met the man Runnacles before, but where and how, I can't remember. He has been through our hands. It'll come back to me before to-morrow morning."

"In a detective yarn you could put your shirt on Runnacles as the villain, for he's the Most Unlikely Person, but we're not dealing with fiction, Heather. A simple, honest gardener, a prisoner of the flowers, a high priest in the temple of Flora!"

"You mustn't harbour any illusions about gardeners, Mr. Vereker. There's the making of a villain in every good horticulturist. A man who can plant bulbs in the autumn and wait till the spring of the following year to see them bloom, is a determined and ruthless fellow. He can wait for revenge cunningly and patiently. And if you think a gardener's boss eats the best melons and peaches, and that the boss's vegetables can't be conjured into cash on the quiet, you're a harmless and credulous idealist!"

"You're not joking about Runnacles, Heather?" asked Vereker seriously.

"No. When I remember his past connection with me, I'll let you know so that you can keep your weather eye on him."

"Good. Now you've not said a word about the iron bar, or fold-drift, which was found between the dead bodies, and which was certainly used to smash Thurlow's skull. The police will have examined it carefully."

"How d'you know it was the weapon used, Mr. Vereker?"

"While I was in charge at Cobbler's Corner, I examined it very carefully without touching it in any way. There was blood and hair adhering to one end of it. I should say the hair was Thurlow's. But what I want to know is, were there any finger prints on it?"

Inspector Heather allowed himself to smile as mysteriously as his good-natured face would permit.

"No, not a finger print on it," he replied.

"This is dramatic evidence, Heather, most dramatic! Thanks for the information, and in return I must tell you that the business end of the bar was covered with chalk. It had certainly been thrust into chalk."

"I had taken a note of that, but don't see where it leads to."

"I hope it'll help to lead us to a solution of the crime, but perhaps that's being a bit sanguine at the present moment. That iron bar drives me back to the subject of spirits, Heather. This afternoon, Miss Thurlow invited me to a stance with her. She wants to convince me that the spirit music she spoke of at our first meeting, was not sheer bunkum. I've promised to attend. At the same time, she suggested that perhaps you'd like to be present, too."

"What?" roared the inspector. "Spirit music? I'd rather listen to a spoon slapper. Never, sir, never! The police attended a stance on one historic occasion in a south coast town. It was in connection with a murder. I heard all about it, and that was enough for me. I leave stances to people with more leisure than intelligence."

"I hinted that you were an unbeliever and might prove a hindrance to any manifestation, so Miss Thurlow left the invitation to my discretion."

"Then you can exercise it at once against me. No doubt you've done so already, because, if you're going to sit and hold the charming medium's hands, you don't want me to start giggling when the lights are switched off. Dear, oh dear, this case is getting me down. At every turn of my investigation, I'm confronted with a gibbering spook!"

"Then there's something else about spooks that you haven't divulged yet, Heather," remarked Vereker. "Out with it like a man."

"There is, but knowing your weakness, I couldn't for the life of me keep it to myself. In one of the pockets of Martin's jacket was found a piece of paper. It was evidently part of a note written to him. The remainder of the note probably went to light his pipe. I made a rough drawing of the fragment. I'm sure you'd like to see it."

With these words, Inspector Heather produced from his pocket-book half a sheet of notepaper and handed it to his companion. On that half sheet of paper was the following sketch:

Vereker examined the sketch carefully, read the inscription on it, and burst into hearty laughter.

"It's no use trying to dodge 'em, Heather. You can't evade ghosts in any case, and it looks as if they're going to play a big part in this mystery. The air here is full of them."

"What do you make of it, Mr. Vereker? It conveys absolutely nothing to me. Looks as if we'd wandered into Pandemonium instead of Suffolk."

"It's a fragment of a note from a pal to Martin ..." commenced Vereker.

"You don't mean to say so," interrupted Heather ironically.

"A fragment of a note," continued Vereker, "from a pal to Martin, telling him all about a spiritualistic séance that he had attended. Let's reconstruct it at a venture. It strikes me as rather a simple exercise in guesswork.

"'Dear Clarry. The spirit taps at our séance began as soon as the lights were extinguished. The curtains of the cabinet blew out straight, though the windows and doors of the room were sealed. Finally a waste-paper basket, on the table near the cabinet, was lifted and thrown on the floor; a hand-bell was rung; and a soap box was broken over the head of an unsympathetic member of the circle!'"

"God help us!" exclaimed the inspector.

"That's just a preliminary scamper, so to speak, Heather. I'll be able to sub-edit that and fit it into a scheme of things."

"This is not criminal investigation; it's a jig-saw puzzle," commented Heather, and consoled himself with a draught of beer.

"But you don't mean to tell me that this fragment of paper hasn't revealed something to you already?" asked Vereker seriously.

"Nothing as yet. It may be in code. That's my impression, and till we get hold of the code, it'll simply remain damned nonsense."

"Of course it may be in code, Heather, but I don't think so. A message between two persons would almost certainly follow one of the ordinary systems of what is called cryptography, or cipher writing. Most systems are based on two methods, namely, the transposition of letters, and the substitution of letters. A key-word is all that is necessary for the receiver to decipher the message. This note is in actual words and not in groups of letters without meaning, except to the initiated. It might, however, be in what is called lexicon cipher. The correspondents have copies of the same dictionary, of which the pages are divided into two columns of words. The key to a word in the letter is the word opposite it in the adjacent column of the dictionary,"

"I don't know anything about the subject, but what about Bentley's code, which is used by commercial houses?"

"Yes, Heather, I know, but Bentley's is a code for saving telegraphic and cable expenses. Anyone with a Bentley in his pocket can decipher the message. No, I'm almost certain it's a straightforward message in intelligible English. What we want is the remainder of the message."

"Well, that's something to be thankful for. But what d'you make of it? You seem to be an expert in these matters."

"So far I can make nothing of it, except that there's something shady about it."

"Shady's the right word!" commented Heather with a twinkle in his eyes.

"You're brightening up under the effects of our Suffolk brew, Inspector. But I wasn't punning. Apart from spirits, there's something distinctly shady about that note, and we must bear it in mind."

"What is there about it that strikes you as peculiar?" asked Heather.

"Before answering you, I must ask if your sketch of the fragment of paper and the writing is facsimile."

"Yes, as near as I could get it in a hurry."

"Well, even if it's not in code, it shows that the writer wrote his note in block capitals. Either he was determined that there should be no difficulty about reading his message, or he was attempting to conceal his ordinary handwriting. I'm inclined to think the latter."

"That's a toss-up. Why should he want to conceal his handwriting?"

"I know no more than you; just an intuition again. But there are a few things I'd like to be clear about, Heather, before I start serious work to-morrow morning. First, has the doctor expressed his opinion about the times when death occurred to the two men?"

"Not definitely, but he thinks that Martin had been dead about three days, and Thurlow about twenty-four hours prior to the alleged time of their discovery by Noy. Mark the word, alleged!"

"Good. About the case Martin was carrying when he set out from home on the previous Friday; was the case empty? If not, do you know what it contained?"

"No, and I don't suppose we'll find out till we find the case."

"His parents didn't know where he was going?"

"So they told Inspector Winter. Martin said he might be rather late returning home and they were not to sit up for him, but he didn't say whom he was going to see, or what his business was. He was always rather secretive, and his parents never pressed him with questions."

"I must probe a little further into these details; they look promising. I've told you, Heather, about the chalk sticking to Thurlow's shoes. Well, there was a considerable amount of clay adhering to Martin's boots. The weather has been very dry, and yet that clay was certainly very moist when the man trod in it. I detached a small fragment from the arch of the boot, between heel and sole, and I've examined it very carefully."

"What secret did it give up?"

"The fragment was composed of clay with traces of chalk, but imbedded in the mixture was one barley-corn."

"I hope you christened it 'John,'" said Heather with a grin, "for there are acres of barley about."

"I certainly will; it would be appropriate. I'm glad to see you cheering up, Inspector. But to continue; was there anything about the state of the men's clothes that struck you as remarkable?"

"They were filthy. Anyone would think that both had been rolling about in pig-wash."

"Exactly, and there was no evading the curious smell of that pig-wash, or whatever it was. That fact might suggest that there had been a desperate struggle, but from the nature of the wounds and the absence of any other sign of a scuffle, I don't think we can infer that either had struggled before being killed. On the elbow of Martin's jacket, moreover, there was some yellowish substance which might be informative, if we could make out its nature."

"Come now, Mr. Vereker, own up. You've guessed what that stuff is."

"I've a shrewd idea, but your laboratories at Hendon will certainly put you wise on the point, unless you know already."

"No, I don't, but talking of Martin, there's one important thing I've forgotten to mention. The doctor says he had punished quite a lot of whisky, and may have been drunk when he passed out."

"Ah, that's significant. It would account for the absence of any sign of a struggle before he died. It might also account for his getting his clothes in such a mess. The explanation doesn't apply to Thurlow. He was, I hear, practically a teetotaller. But who was the last person to see Martin? I hear that he was seen with George Mobbs, the baker, outside this inn about ten o'clock at night. They had evidently met earlier, spent the evening here, and then Martin had gone about his business. Nobody seems to have seen him after that. Where did he go to?"

"Don't ask me," murmured the inspector.

"There's only one explanation, Heather," continued Vereker with a furtive smile. "He, too, must have vanished into thin air—dematerialized."

"What with spirit rapping and ghostly music and soap boxes smashed and decomposition, or whatever you call it, I'm getting tied up in knots!"

"That's because you're a shocking materialist, Heather. You really must change your whole mental attitude to this business. The case is a special one, and you must adapt yourself to it. It would do you good to read my old friend Emerson's essay, called 'The Transcendentalism'. I always keep one of Ralph Waldo's volumes in my pocket; it makes a splendid pillow book. Listen to what he says. 'The materialist, secure in the certainty of sensation, mocks at fine-spun theories, at star-gazers and dreamers, and believes that life is solid... the idealist, in speaking of events, sees them as spirits...'"

"One minute, Mr. Vereker, I'll just finish my beer," interrupted Heather, and putting his empty mug down on the table, added, "I'll see you sometime to-morrow. Good-night!"

"Good-night," replied Vereker, laughing, and on Heather's departure, closed his volume of Emerson, thrust it into his pocket, and produced an ordnance survey map of the Yarham district.

"Now let's have a look at the geography of the place!" he said to himself, as he spread out the map on the table and began to study it with concentration. "Lovely things, maps! They'll completely oust fiction in the near future."

Chapter Seven

Next morning, Vereker breakfasted alone. Before going to bed on the previous night, he had made a close study of the map of the district and noted carefully all the roads, lanes, and field-paths in any way connected with the thoroughfare that swept round and enclosed Cobbler's Corner. After that survey, he had decided to revisit the scene where the bodies had been discovered, and explore the surrounding district on foot.

The morning was fine, with an almost cloudless sky and a gentle breeze that promised to temper the sultriness of a perfect summer day. Vereker ate his breakfast with gusto. There was an alertness and excitement in his manner, and a brightness in his eye which declared he was in that cheerfully aggressive mood that an intricate problem always roused in him. There was something in the very air which seemed to promise good fortune.

Lighting a cigarette, and picking up a stout ash stick, he set off, and, after half an hour's walk, arrived at the small stretch of waste grass land, which for some reason unknown to any of the inhabitants of the parish, was called Cobbler's Corner. Not a soul was in sight when he arrived, and the hard, drought-baked ground, with its covering of coarse, sere grass bore no impression of the tread of the numerous villagers who had crossed and recrossed it on the previous day after the police had finally left the scene. Measuring the distance from the road as he paced, he proceeded rapidly to the spot where the bodies of John Thurlow and Clarry Martin had lain. Coming to a standstill, he glanced about him, his eye roving from one point to another in casual observation. Then drawing his map from his pocket, he took his bearings with reference to the village and to Old Hall Farm. They lay almost in a direct line to the south. He noted a field-path that left the road, crossed the meadow opposite the angle of Cobbler's Corner, and made its way to the outskirts of the village, effecting a very appreciable short cut. That field-path was reached by climbing over the gate on which Ephraim Noy had sat when Vereker first came on the scene, the day before.

The sudden recollection of Ephraim Noy at once made him turn round and look up the road running north. That road presented a fairly stiff gradient from Cobbler's Corner, and just above the summit, through surrounding foliage, could be seen the red asbestos tiled roof and the upper portion of a window in the gable of Noy's bungalow. It was barely a hundred yards in a direct line from the point at which Vereker stood.

The sight of Ephraim Noy's bungalow immediately filled Vereker with a lively curiosity to see the place and its owner. After another careful scrutiny of the ground around him, he passed through a gap in the hedge into the adjoining meadow and made a straight line for the bungalow. As he paced up the steep, grassy slope, he was smiling to himself, for he was carrying out a rapid mental adjustment which always secretly amused him. He was putting on the armour of the journalist, assuming the "hide of brass" which is essential to a successful interviewer. With some, it is a natural shield against the onslaught of a hostile personality; the arrows of insolence glide off it without inflicting any hurt. With Vereker, naturally sensitive, that impervious defence had to be forcibly created by cold reasoning and vigorous self-exhortation. By the time he had reached the fence and recently planted hedge which divided Noy's demesne from the meadow, Vereker had prepared himself to meet the most frigid rudeness with unshakable imperturbability.

The first object that interested him and brought a sharp exclamation of surprise to his lips, as he stood surveying the bungalow and its surroundings, was a large heap of greyish white earth, some seven feet high, that lay a few yards from the back entrance. Just visible over the piled-up earth, could be seen the top of a heavy wooden tripod, to which was attached a pulley and rope. Working his way round, Vereker came to a point from which he could see that this tripod stood directly over a shaft which descended into the earth. He at once knew that these were the outward signs of the operation called "sinking a well." Without further hesitation, he calmly stepped over the young privet hedge, barely three feet nigh, and crossed over the still undisturbed meadow grass which formed the bungalow's back lawn, to the mouth of the shaft. The shaft was from five to six feet in diameter, and he could clearly see its bottom some forty feet below. He glanced at the section of earth through which the shaft had been sunk, and noticed the heavy surface loam, under which lay a bed of clay superimposed over the basic chalk. This was the first chalk he had seen in the district, for in this part of the county the long westerly chalk slopes pass well beneath the London clay and crag. At once there flashed across his memory the fact that John Thurlow, just prior to his murder, must have trodden on chalk, and he carefully examined the chalky earth that had been excavated from the well and flung up in an unsightly heap near its mouth. Vereker's close inspection of that chalk debris yielded no information, and approaching the well, he was just considering a descent by the rope attached to the pulley, when he heard a footstep on the gravel path behind him. Swinging round on his heel, he came face to face with Mr. Ephraim Noy, who, with his hands behind his back and an ugly frown knitting his brow, eyed him up and down with marked displeasure. At this close view of him, Vereker was immediately struck by the remarkable resemblance of Ephraim Noy to "Uncle Sam," Punch's pictorial personification of the United States of America. The likeness was so close that Vereker was obliged to smile, and he was wondering who had given the original artist the idea for that caricature, when its counterpart spoke.

"Well, young man, may I ask how you got in here?" he said with ironical politeness.

"Just stepped over your hedge at the back," replied Vereker bluntly.

"Would you mind just stepping back over the hedge to oblige me?" asked Mr. Noy.

"Certainly," said Vereker with a rapid investment of himself in his journalist's hide. "I'm sorry if I happen to have annoyed you." He was about to say, "Mr. Noy," but the sound sequence reminded him of a music hall song in which a certain Mrs. Moore is urged to desist from drinking any more, and he deftly substituted, "Sir." After a pause he continued: "But I'm rather interested in the geology of the district and couldn't resist having a look at your well shaft."

"I don't see anything very interesting in a well shaft," remarked Mr. Noy with an air of being mollified much against his will.

"To the owner, I suppose the sole interest is water," commented Vereker, "but I was wondering at what depth the chalk passed under the London clay."

"You mean Suffolk clay. London's seventy miles away from here," remarked Mr. Noy, looking at Vereker with an alienist's glance in his eye.

"Of course it's Suffolk clay, but the bed is known to geologists as London clay."

"Very interesting, I'm sure. He must have been a Cockney who called it so," commented Mr. Noy, and then with a swift change of tone asked, "Were you the gentleman who took charge for Constable Godbold at Cobbler's Corner while he ran into the village to telephone, yesterday morning?"

"Yes, and I believe you're Mr. Ephraim Noy, who discovered the bodies of Mr. Thurlow and Mr. Martin. You were sitting on the gate leading into the meadow when I came on the scene."

"You're right; my name's Ephraim Noy. And yours?"

"I'm an artist by profession," replied Vereker guardedly, "though on this murder case I'm acting as a special correspondent of the *Daily Report*."

"Oh, a newspaper man! I see, I see," remarked Mr. Noy with undisguised relief. "You weren't long in getting on the spot. Talk about a vulture's eyes for a carcase!"

"Where there's a carcase, there's a news story, Mr. Noy," said Vereker, with a supreme effort at amiability.

"Naturally. But you mentioned the word murder. Have they decided that this is a case of murder?"

"I believe the police think it's a case of one murder, perhaps two."

"They love to get the Press screaming about mystery, so as to make the subsequent solution redound to their credit as investigators. I see nothing very complicated about it. Two men, ostensibly rivals in love, meet and fight to the death. Seems simple enough to me, almost as simple as they were to scrap over a pretty face."

"I don't think it's as simple as all that," remarked Vereker, scrutinizing Mr. Noy's face.

For a moment Mr. Noy's hawk-like glance met Vereker's gaze, hovered uncertainly, and then fell to admiring his own boots.

"You pressmen are nearly always hand in glove with the police," he commented with a cynical air. "They flatter you by letting you partly into the know, and then you gratefully pat them on the back for helping you to write up your news story. I suppose it's the way of the world; a variation of the crocodile and the crocodile bird. But as far as policemen are concerned, give me old Godbold as in the running for the post of village idiot."

"You were rather rude to him, yesterday," said Vereker in defence of his friend. "Godbold's not a bad fellow."

"He simply asked for it. Strutting about with the importance of a Lord Chief Justice, and then spoiling the part by wetting his pencil point with spittle before jotting down his notes. When the inspector arrived, I thought we'd get a bit of a hustle on in the grey matter, but he ran Godbold a dead heat. They simply wouldn't let me tell my story in my own way. Treated me as if I was bughouse— that is cracked. So I shut up, and they got no information out of me at all in the finish."

"Was there anything vital that you withheld?" asked Vereker, with as casual an air as he could assume.

"Who's to say what's vital and what isn't in a case like this? If the affair was, say, a double murder and not a fight, the most ordinary information might prove just the goods."

"I think you must dismiss the theory of a fight as a solution, Mr. Noy. If Thurlow had shot Martin, it's difficult to see how the latter could have brained his opponent with that iron bar. If Martin got his blow in first, then Thurlow certainly couldn't have fired his revolver at Martin."

"That's the ordinary way of looking at it, but in such cases you never can tell how things just happened. The blow may have been delivered and the shot fired almost simultaneously."

"True, but most unlikely. Again, it's clear that Martin, prior to his death, was bound hand and foot, and the doctor's of the opinion that the bullet wound was inflicted after death."

"Ah, so that's what they've discovered!" exclaimed Ephraim Noy with considerable surprise. "Amazing! Amazing!" Thrusting his hands into his pockets and looking steadily at Vereker, he added gravely, "I wouldn't say but what they're right. It seems to bear out a little theory of my own."

Vereker, at this juncture, glanced at his watch, as if to convey to Mr. Noy that his time was limited and extremely valuable. If Mr. Noy were eager to tell his tale, this manoeuvre would immediately put him in the inferior position of a man to whom a favour was being granted. If he were merely wasting time by flinging out intriguing hints, without any intention of being communicative, it would show him the futility of his conduct.

"Perhaps you're in a hurry to get away?" asked Mr. Noy, with the first sign of any deference to his unexpected visitor.

"Well, not exactly in a hurry," fenced Vereker.

"Because, if you can spare the time, I'd like to tell you something bearing on the case, something that's really important. If you're a pressman, you'll be able to make use of it. After you've squeezed the juice out of it, you can pass it along to the police. They'll come to me to corroborate the story, and I'll see that Inspector Winter treats me with more respect than he did yesterday. But I'm tired of standing here in the sun. Let's go into the bungalow and sit in the cool."

With these words, Ephraim Noy led the way into the very simply but elegantly furnished sitting-room of his bungalow, pushed a cane chair over to his guest, and handed him a box of cigars.

"Like cigars?" he asked. "Believe they're good, but I don't smoke 'em myself."

Vereker helped himself to a cigar and lit it while his host charged an out-size in briar pipes.

"Now, Mr. Vereker," said Ephraim Noy at length, "when I came upon the bodies of Mr. Thurlow and Mr. Martin at seven o'clock yesterday morning, there was one thing that immediately struck me as peculiar."

"Excuse the interruption, but were you making your way to the village?" asked Vereker.

"Yes. I was going to catch the eight o'clock coach that runs through Yarham to Sudbury. I'd run out of baccy, and the brand I smoke isn't sold in Yarham. I can get it in Sudbury, and that was my destination. I left myself plenty of time, because I hate to waste time hustling. I strolled down the hill and was cutting across Cobbler's Corner, when I came upon the bodies."

Mr. Noy paused dramatically.

"And you observed something that struck you as important," remarked Vereker, eager to eliminate any play of his host's sense of the histrionic.

"Yes, and it was simply the way the bodies were lying. They looked as if they had been carefully placed there. When I observed their wounds, it at once struck me that, if there had been a fight, the combatants would have looked crumpled up, so to speak."

"Exactly what I noticed myself, Mr. Noy. But this statement of yours doesn't tally with your first idea that there had been a fight to the death between two rivals," observed Vereker pertinently.

The comment evidently took Mr. Noy by surprise, but he countered it after a moment's hesitation with the remark: "I was simply testing your intelligence, Mr. Vereker."

"You were wasting your time," observed Vereker with a suspicion of tartness. "I'm simply lit up with intelligence."

"Then what I'm going to tell you will interest you," continued Mr. Noy with smug serenity. "On the previous night, that was Tuesday night, between ten and eleven, I was sitting reading. The night was perfectly still, and I was interested in my book, when I heard a motor car down below at Cobbler's Corner. I read on, expecting the car to come up the hill and pass this shack. It didn't, so I glanced out of the window there and saw its lights in the hollow. It turned and went back up the hill to Yarham. At the moment, I thought the driver had discovered he was on the wrong tack and had decided to correct his mistake. Next morning, in the light of my discovery, the incident struck me as most important. Do you get me?"

"It may be of the utmost importance, Mr. Noy, and, of course, it may have nothing to do with the tragedy," remarked Vereker judicially. "Did you tell the police about this?"

"No. We began to insult one another before I reached the climax of my story. I lost my temper and shut up. A couple of years ago, I came here to Yarham to pass my days in peace and quietness, and now by some rotten luck I'm dragged into the thick of this miserable police investigation. I was quite willing to give any information I could on a subject that interested me no more than the exploits of Jack the Ripper. I began to tell them what I knew, and I was cross questioned by a set of mutts, as if I was a big noise in the outrage. Damn it all, there's a limit to a man's patience!"

"The police are very trying at times," agreed Vereker, and remarked, "I bet you got a dreadful shock when you discovered that one of the dead bodies was that of Mr. Thurlow, didn't you?"

The question asked casually, but with intention, at once arrested Mr. Noy. He nearly dropped the briar pipe that he held lightly in his hand, but managed to recover it and his composure with commendable adroitness.

"To stumble over a couple of corpses on a fine summer morning isn't what you'd call having a lucky break, but why do you ask?"

"Because I thought you were an old friend of Mr. Thurlow," commented Vereker, looking straight at his host.

"No, I knew no more about Mr. Thurlow than I did about Mr. Martin," replied Noy with a shifty look in his eyes. "I knew them both by sight, if that's what you mean."

"I was under the impression that you and Thurlow had known one another long before you came to Yarham."

"Then you're up the wrong street," replied Mr. Noy, and rose to signify that he wished the interview to be considered at an end. "What put you on this line?" he asked as if the question was an afterthought.

"I don't know what gave me the idea," replied Vereker with studied carelessness. "I must have misconstrued some remark I'd heard in the village. In any case, it's of no importance."

"None whatever," agreed Mr. Noy readily, and added: "Well, I must get on with my work outside instead of shooting hot air. I'm expecting the men who are sinking my well to arrive at any moment. We're down forty feet already and not a goddam sign of water. I had a simp's faith in water diviners when we commenced the job, but I'm on the verge of thinking it's merely a profitable form of spoofing fools."

"You must give it a fair trial, Mr. Noy. Water divination is practised throughout the county professionally, and the average East Anglian doesn't part with his hard won cash for mere superstition," said Vereker.

"Your faith is most encouraging, Mr. Vereker," said Mr. Noy complacently, and as he showed his visitor to the door, added: "Next time you pay me a call, please come in by the front gate. It'll save my temper and give my privet hedge a chance of establishing itself."

Vereker bade him good-day and, lost in thought, made his way slowly back to Yarham. There was something about Mr. Ephraim Noy that he found forbidding. His manner was unpleasantly aggressive, and what in a more genial man might be called bluffness, in him verged dangerously on churlishness. Vereker had met his type before; lonely, secretive, ill-natured, with a passion for stripping life of any pleasant illusions. His attitude to his fellows, too, was tinged with an arrogance which made him intolerable. Perhaps some past experience, some grave injustice, or deep disappointment had embittered him and distorted his outlook on life. There was one thing, however, about the short interview which roused all Vereker's suspicion and impressed him with a sense of its importance in the circumstances. Ephraim Noy was a liar. He had certainly lied when he disclaimed any past knowledge of John Thurlow. This was a significant pointer, and Vereker decided that he must probe discreetly into the past history of Mr. Ephraim Noy. It was a subject that might prove highly informative.

Chapter Eight

At eleven o'clock on the morning following Vereker's interview with Mr. Ephraim Noy, Runnacles, the gardener at Old Hall Farm, called at the inn with a note from Miss Thurlow. In it she informed Vereker that she had definitely decided to go up to London for a few days. Prior to her departure, she would like to carry out the experimental séance which they had discussed together on their last meeting. Could he call that evening about eight o'clock, and if Inspector Heather were willing, would he bring that officer along with him.

Vereker, knowing Heather's attitude to the subject of spiritualism, felt that it would be idle to discuss the invitation with him again, and had finally decided to go alone, when he suddenly heard a loud and familiar voice in the entrance hall of the inn below.

"Algernon, where the blazes are you? Come out from behind that arras!"

Recognizing Manuel Ricardo's voice, Vereker at once rose from his chair and hurried downstairs to meet his friend.

"Hello, Ricky, this is most opportune!" he said. "You're the very man I want. Come up to my room. I've got something important to discuss."

"What a lovely old tavern, Algernon!" said Ricardo, glancing around him. "I suppose they drink nothing but sack here. What about a gallon or so to start with?"

"I'm just having a morning coffee. That'll refresh you after your journey."

"From sack to coffee's a bit of a descent, but as I'm your guest, and we have the whole day before us..."

"Now, Ricky, I want you to be serious. There's no time for fooling," said Vereker as they entered his private sitting-room. "In the first place, what brought you down here in such a hurry?"

"In the first place, I'd nothing better to do. Also, an evening paper, reporting on the Yarham business yesterday, labelled it 'The Spirit Murder Mystery.' A lovely headline that! I promptly read the report and found that spiritualism came into it. You know that I'm writing up my many and varied experiences on the subject, and I thought I'd gather my brightest chapter down here."

"Excellent! We're going to attend a little séance together to-night at Old Hall Farm. Have you read up the case?"

"I've read all that's been divulged. Besides, I had a long chat with the landlord immediately I arrived. He served me up the story of the murder with my beer, as if it were part of the hospitality of 'The Walnut Tree.' I've got the hang of things in a general way, and I'm eager to assist in the unravelling."

"Knowing your interest in the occult, I thought you'd turn up sooner or later. Of course, you're a firm believer in spirit manifestation?"

"Look here, Algernon, there's no necessity to go into all that with me at this date in history. I've attended innumerable séances. I've seen spirit forms materialize, I've heard direct voice manifestations, I've touched ectoplasm, I've been present when wax moulds were taken of a spirit's hands... we'll take all that as read. But what earthly connection has it with this wretched crime?"

"I'm glad you're serious about the subject, Ricky," said Vereker gravely. "Your experience in these matters ought to be helpful.

As for the connection between spiritualism and this case, we've got to find that out. That it has some connection, either direct or indirect, I'm almost certain. On the very evening of Thurlow's disappearance, he and his niece had an experimental séance. They both heard the sounds of organ music in Thurlow's study at Old Hall Farm. There is, up to the present, apparently no material explanation of the phenomenon. We're going to try and revive that phenomenon to-night. You and Miss Thurlow and myself. You're not easily deceived in such matters and you've your experience to back you up. If we're fortunate, we may learn something vital. I want you to be absolutely on the *qui vive* for any kind of fraud. Not that I think Miss Thurlow would stoop to trickery for one moment, but she, in turn, may be the victim of some kind of bunk."

"This sounds promising, Algernon. None of your miserable cases has interested me so deeply before. Old Heather will be breathing fire like a dragon, I'll bet."

"Rather! He set aside the séance as wholly irrelevant. Then, in the midst of his ferreting, the subject of spirits turned up again as if to rattle him."

"How?"

"A piece of paper, evidently a portion of a note, was found on Martin's body. I've got a copy of that fragment. Tell me what you think of it," replied Vereker, producing from his pocket the copy referred to and handing it to his friend.

Ricardo glanced at the sketch and read aloud to himself: "'Dear Clarr... the spirit taps... soap box broken...'"

"'Clarr' refers to Clarry Martin, I presume?" he asked.

"Yes, Clarry is the man's Christian name. It may be a version of Clarence, but I don't know."

"Of course, rapping sounds are one of the commonest of occurrences at stances," continued Ricardo. "Most manifestations are prefaced by these curious raps, sometimes on the table, but frequently from all parts of the séance chamber. The thing's as old as the hills. I daresay the Witch of Endor often called them forth, though she seems to have been a direct voice medium."

"The writer calls it taps, but I suppose it's the same thing," commented Vereker.

"Undoubtedly, but I can't for the life of me guess what's hidden in the soap box," continued Ricardo.

"No, nor can I at the moment, unless it's soap. Possibly it was one of the properties used in the demonstration, but that little conundrum can wait. It may have nothing to do with our case."

For some minutes Vereker was lost in thought, and then his eyes suddenly lit up as if he had struck on some new and illuminating train of speculation.

"Now, Algernon, you've been on the scene of action from the beginning. Give me some idea of what you think has happened. Do you think the two men killed one another?" asked Ricardo, breaking the silence.

"No, that seems an impossibility, and Heather, too, has dismissed the theory as untenable. The iron bar with which Martin apparently killed Thurlow, hasn't a single finger print on it. The doctor thinks the bullet wound in Martin's shoulder was inflicted after death. There were no signs of a struggle at Cobbler's Corner. A man called Noy, who lives in a bungalow close to the spot where he found the bodies, told me that he heard and saw a motor car at that spot at about eleven o'clock the night before."

"I take you, Algernon. You've figured it out that the bodies were planted there, so to speak."

"I do, and that it's possibly a double murder, committed somewhere else. I don't know Heather's findings, but I daresay he has tumbled to this too. The fight theory won't hold water."

"In any case, you must keep Heather in the dark, or he'll be first past the winning post, Algernon. Good job I'm not his rival. I'd fake false clues for his utter confusion, even at the risk of imprisonment for obstructing the police in the execution of their duties."

"I think I'll score this time, Ricky," replied Vereker with unmistakable eagerness. "If I win, that puts me one point ahead. But you've got to help me as you've done before. Heather naturally has an army of assistants and experts at his beck and call. You're the only helper I've got. We don't start fair, so to speak.

"Tell me if you're going to cry about it, Algernon, and I'll lend you my handky. You ought to know by now that his Boeotian myrmidons are no match for my brilliant wits. We'll leave the whole bunch of pachyderms panting in the rear," assured Ricardo with jocular confidence.

The conversation then reverted to the subject of spiritualism, on which Ricardo was well informed. The morning passed swiftly as he deftly traced out for Vereker's information the history of the movement from its disconnected beginnings to its present day world-wide ramifications. Interested as Vereker had been in the subject, his knowledge of it was fragmentary, and centred chiefly on the records of specific mediums who had, at various times, become notorious through "exposures." As Ricardo, with the eagerness of the enthusiast, described to him the work of Dr. Chiaia, of Professors Lombroso, Morselli and Porro in Italy; of Professor Butlerof in Russia; of Professor Richet and Dr. Geley in France; of Professor Zöllner at Leipzig; of Dr. Alfred Russell Wallace, Sir William Crookes, Sir Oliver Lodge and Sir Arthur Conan Doyle in England, he grew more and more interested, and began to look forward to the proposed séance at Old Hall Farm with increasing ardour and a more tolerant outlook.

After lunch, Ricardo, left to his own devices, decided to visit Yarham Church, a flint and stone building in the Perpendicular style, famous for its painted central roof and carved oak benches with their quaint poppy heads. He had hardly left the inn, when Inspector Heather returned and at once sought out Vereker.

"Well, Mr. Vereker, I see your assistant has arrived. What errand have you sent him on?" he asked.

"None. To start with, he has gone to admire church architecture."

"I thought feminine architecture was more in his line. He's an amusing cuss. I never know whether he's joking or serious. Got any facts since I saw you last?"

"One or two, but you're the fact merchant. Now spill the beans."

"I've been getting a little information from Mr. Thurlow's solicitors. I've seen a draft of the gentleman's will, which will be proved shortly."

"You're on the money-motive hunt. Is there anything you can tell me without prejudicing your chances in our little game?"

"I may as well let you know, because there's nothing to hide, and I mustn't be too hard on a mere amateur. By the terms of his will, he left ten thousand pounds to Miss Dawn Garford, nice little legacies to the maid-servants, if still in his employ, a pension of two pounds a week to Runnacles, and the residue to his niece, Miss Eileen."

"Was he a wealthy man?"

"Simply lousy with money. His estate, when published, will come as a thumping surprise to all his friends and acquaintances. He was known to be comfortably off, but he was secretive about money matters. He was always pleading poverty, in the way a virtuous man pretends to be a frightful devil. Altogether, his property runs into nearly half a million. A very large portion of it is in American securities."

"So the money-motive gives you Miss Thurlow as the principal suspect, Miss Garford as the second, Runnacles as the third, and the servants as 'also ran.' Nothing very startling about that will, Heather. What's your opinion?"

"It certainly doesn't tell us much so far."

"Unless you're still convinced that Runnacles could bump off his boss for a pension of two pounds a week."

"Now you've mentioned Runnacles, I've placed him since I saw you last. Rum fellow this gardener; he has done time."

"Many people have done that without qualifying for the hangman's rope. To revive an old joke, was it for pinching chrysanthemums?"

"In his younger days he was fond of poaching. As a sport it's quite exciting, and I've a weak spot for poachers. But it generally winds up in a row with keepers. Runnacles got his term for a very savage attack on a keeper, near Thetford on the Norfolk border."

"That's a bad reflection on his sportsmanship. He couldn't stand being licked at the game. What was he doing on the night of Thurlow's disappearance, Heather?"

"His wife says he was at home all that evening and the next."

"Of course, a man who resorts to violence once is generally capable of doing it again. How did he get on with Thurlow, his employer?"

"Very badly for some time now. Last year, he was found out in some petty business of disposing of his boss's fruit to a local greengrocer, and Thurlow warned him that a repetition meant the sack. He has never been the same man since. I think he has been brooding over it, wondering whether he had been cut out of Thurlow's will. He knew he was to benefit, and it's a stupid thing to let anyone know you've left him money. It's putting temptation in his way."

"I feel that the case against Runnacles is a bit thin, Heather. Anything more sinister that you're keeping back?"

"I haven't dismissed Runnacles altogether, because there seems no definite line to take in this business at present."

"You've definitely chucked the idea that Thurlow and Martin fought and killed one another?"

"I never entertained it. Circumstances put that out of court at once. And yet it's not a robbery murder. Thurlow and Martin both had their watches and money intact. It's a murder for revenge, or they were killed to stop their mouths. I'm rather inclined to the latter view myself."

"You're going to trace the iron bar to its rightful owner, of course?" asked Vereker.

"I don't think. Lord bless us, Mr. Vereker, every farmer round here has one of these tools, and there are dozens of them in the cottages of Yarham. There's nothing distinctive about such an instrument; no maker's name even. The village smith has made hundreds in his time, and couldn't identify any for certain as his handiwork."

"I was afraid it was useless without a finger print. The man who wielded that bar was hardly a yokel. It's not likely that a yokel would have thought of finger prints as a dangerous legacy to leave on a fold-drift."

"That's a good pointer in a general way, but what with thrillers and crime films, it's dangerous to attach too much weight to it. The present generation knows more about finger prints than it does about philosophy. It shows clearly, however, that there's a bit of theatrical fake somewhere. Someone wiped that fold-drift, I should say."

"By the way, have you questioned Mr. Ephraim Noy, Heather?" asked Vereker after a pause in the conversation.

"Yes," replied Heather, "and he gave me the same bit of important information that he gave you."

"Ah, you've made that startling discovery!" replied Vereker with a smile.

"I don't know so much about a startling discovery. The man's a bluffer. What did you make of him and his yarn about that motor car?"

"I'm a bit puzzled about Ephraim Noy. The car story lends itself to the theory that the bodies were planted. We've both settled that point to our satisfaction. On the other hand, Ephraim may be a subtle strategist. He may be trying to hide his own participation in this business, for all we know. It would be a daring and clever bit of bluff, and I think he's capable of it."

"I, too, jumped to that, and I'm going to rake into his past history. He has been in America, I know, which reminds me that Thurlow's solicitor put me on another suggestive line. Thurlow has had large American business dealings, or to be more precise, has had a hand in some big Wall Street gambles. 'The game of stock gambling breeds undying hatreds, gives birth to implacable enemies.' Those were his solicitor's words, and he hinted that possibly someone, crazed with the loss of his dough, had come and bumped off the man he blamed for his ruin. I don't know exactly what it means, but it had something to do with 'stock washing.'"

"This solicitor's a bit too dramatic for me, Heather. If I see that this case is going to widen till it swallows the continent of America, I'll fling up the sponge and leave you to the job. Of course, it's feasible that murder can spring out of stock gambling, but I'm almost certain that it didn't on this occasion. Any other clue? that you've picked up?"

"Some threads of rope fibre adhering to Martin's clothes. They've gone to be examined by one of our experts. They may, by some odd chance, tell us something worth knowing about the rope with which Martin was evidently bound before his death. One never knows!"

"This detection's developing into a dull business, Heather. It becomes more and more like exercises in simple addition. Science is knocking all the imagination out of it. Little bit of rope, plus finger prints, plus marks on bullet, plus a spot of blood belonging to a certain blood group; sum total, the gallows! But now you've mentioned the man Martin, tell me, have you found out anything about his actions previous to his disappearance? He was seen speaking to Mobbs, the baker, outside this inn, that evening. You've questioned Mobbs, I presume?"

"I have."

"Did he know where Martin was going? He was carrying an attaché case, and that looks as if he were bent on business."

"Yes, but the inquiry didn't prove very profitable, Mobbs said Martin was going to see Arthur Orton at Church Farm. Orton had bought a new motor lorry through Martin, and something had gone wrong with the rear axle. Martin was going to have a look at it and was carrying tools in his attaché case."

"What time was this?"

"Just after ten, when 'The Walnut Tree' closed."

"That's one bright fact. Did he see Orton?"

"Yes, and put the defect in the rear axle right something simple about lubrication, I believe. Having finished his job, he had a drop of whisky with Orton and his housekeeper, said good-night and vanished into the blue."

"No one else saw him after that?"

"Not that I can discover, but I'm making further inquiries."

"By the way, Church Farm's a good mile from the village, isn't it?"

"More than that, nearly two," replied Heather listlessly.

At this moment, Vereker tried to catch the inspector's eye, but Heather seemed all at once to be lost in a brown study.

"Have you made a deep study of that barleycorn, Mr. Vereker?" he asked at length with a smile. "Has it spoken and hiccupped the whole show away?"

"When you begin to be funny, Heather, I know you're trying to side-track me. I've been very interested in that barleycorn. I've examined it carefully under a magnifying glass, and it's a very characteristic barleycorn, but since you're inclined to be facetious about my bit of orthodox detection, I'm not going to tell you what I've discovered."

"There's only one use for barleycorns and that's beer!" exclaimed Heather with one of his explosive laughs.

"What about barley water for infants and invalids?" asked Vereker.

"I'm not an infant, and I've never been an invalid so I can't speak with authority," replied Heather, and after some desultory conversation, sought the seclusion of his own room to "think things out."

For some time, Vereker sat in his easy chair, reviewing all that he had learned about "The Spirit Murder Mystery," as the daily Press had now labelled the case. The more he pondered on it, the more baffling and elusive the whole affair seemed. Up to the moment, there were no salient points on which he could hang tentative theories, and he could see that Heather was experiencing a similar difficulty in his more orthodox methods. Martin and Thurlow had both disappeared mysteriously, and of what had happened to them between the times of their vanishing and the discovery of their dead bodies, very little had so far been learned. There was an exasperating lack of witnesses, witnesses who might have been able to fill up this destructive gap in the time table of investigation. The difficulty arose partly from the locality in which the tragedy had occurred. The population was sparse, and by nightfall most of the villagers were in their cottages. Before ten o'clock nearly everyone was in bed, except the dozen or so men who frequented the village inn. Even the latter were only abroad in full force on a Saturday night. Against this drawback was the factor that the countryman is an acute observer. Nothing in the shape of human activity escapes his inquisitive eye, and had anyone encountered either Thurlow or Martin, even in the dark, after he had been reported missing, the incident would have been mentally registered.

This absence of material on which to work was depressing, and Vereker felt that little good could come from further speculation. Rising from his chair, he glanced at his watch and descended to the bar parlour of the inn. He found this room, with its spotless deal table and benches, its uneven brick floor, its oak mantelpiece with loudly ticking clock, its chintz curtained windows looking on to an old-time flower garden, a peculiarly attractive room. At the moment it was deserted, except for a grey-haired but burly looking villager in a loose jacket, breeches and gaiters, and heavy boots. His waistcoat was open, except for the two top buttons, and disclosed that he wore a broad leather belt as well as braces. His shirt was certainly not immaculate; his throat seemed restricted by an old and disreputable silk scarf; and his cap had been dragged into a quaint and distinctive irregularity by its owner's forceful method of pulling it firmly on to his rather massive head. He had been sitting smoking a pungent smelling shag in that ruminative placidity which is characteristic of his class when at ease, but on Vereker's entry, he lost some of his detachment, and commented on the weather as he measured up the newcomer with a swift, comprehensive glance. Vereker made an obvious remark about the loveliness of the day with an excellently simulated heartiness, and added that the warmth created a generous thirst. The villager, thereupon, emptied his pint mug and replaced it noisily on the table. Whether this action was a frank hint or entirely unpremeditated, Vereker was at a loss to guess, but he at once suggested that the stranger should allow his mug to be replenished. The invitation was accepted without undue alacrity, and after Benjamin Easy had left the room, Vereker soon found that the stranger was eager to talk.

He commenced on the subject of beer, of its present inferior quality and high price, of past and better brews, and from that swung round, after some divagation, to the topic of poaching. Having, with unerring intuition, made sure of the possible outlook of his companion on the morality of poaching (the term "stealing game" is not permissible), he admitted that he had been an inveterate poacher all his life, and on learning that Vereker was connected with the Press began to expand generously. A "writer bloke" had already published a book on some of his exploits, but by some error of judgment, had only "put down" the tamest of them, and so forth. It was during this phase of their conversation, that Vereker, prompted by an association of ideas, suddenly asked:

"Do you know a man called Runnacles in the village?"

"Known him all my life."

"What sort of a man is he?"

"Toughish sort of chap, is Jim Runnacles. As clever a poacher as the next one, but you can't trust him. He'd shop his best pal, if it was going to pay him to do it. And when you see him next, ask him if he knows Barney Deeks, that's me."

Barney Deeks winked, and by a subtle grimace informed Vereker in a general way that, at some time or other in the past, things had happened which would certainly prevent Jim Runnacles forgetting him. It did not take Vereker long to find out that Barney and Jim had been deadly enemies for many years, and the story of Runnacles' attack on the gamekeeper was retailed with added detail, much to Runnacles' dishonour as a poacher. Then came a piece of unexpected information, which showed Vereker that, in the art of sleuthing, time apparently wasted is often well spent. Barney Deeks had heard that the police had been inquiring about Jim Runnacles' movements on the night that John Thurlow was murdered.

"He told the cop he had been at home all evening," remarked Deeks with surprising vindictiveness. "His missus backed him up. It's all a damned lie. I saw him on the road above Cobbler's Corner, about eleven o'clock that very night. If I was a dirty tyke like Jim Runnacles, I'd go round and split on him, but that kind of thing's not in my line."

"But why should the police want to know about Runnacles' movements?" asked Vereker.

"That's more'n I can tell you, sir," replied Deeks, as if the subject was beyond his depth and interest.

At this moment Ben Easy appeared at the door of the bar parlour, glanced at his watch, and fixed his eye ostentatiously on the clock. It was closing time, and, drinking up his beer, Deeks bade Vereker good afternoon and took his departure.

"This discrepancy in the gardener's story ought to wake old Heather up!" said Vereker to himself, and retired to his own sitting-room.

About an hour later, he heard footsteps hurrying up the stairs, taking the steps two at a time, and next moment, Ricardo noisily entered the room.

"Well, Ricky," said Vereker, turning to him, "had a good look at Yarham Church?"

"Most interesting hour I've spent for a long time. After examining the church's exterior, I cast an inquiring eye at some of the oldest gravestones. Doesn't sound a hectic sort of pastime for a summer's day, but it's a thrilling change from the cinema, and the shade of those primeval yews is delightfully cooling. I took a seat, well out of view of any chance visitor, on one of those old tombs that look like sarcophagi. It was perhaps rather disrespectful to the occupant, but time can play two diametrically opposed tricks; it can create reverence, and it can equally well banish it. I was getting into a sort of Gray's Elegy atmosphere, when I heard a most musical feminine voice on the other side of the dense yew behind me. The voice was jabbering volubly to a male companion who seemed to be sparing of his words. And what d'you think was the topic of her conversation Algernon?"

"The Absolute," suggested Vereker.

"No, Sir Anthony," replied Ricardo with a smile; "it verged on the dissolute. She was talking about night clubs and road houses. I don't think I'd have troubled to listen, only she mentioned Poppy Knatchbull, who runs the Blue Bottle Club in London, so dangerously and profitably. Now, there's only one Poppy Knatchbull, so I pricked up my ears. At this point, she dropped her voice to a whisper—and I was horribly disappointed. I learned nothing more of Poppy. On resuming in her normal tones, she mentioned three road houses very well known to me, and I became intensely interested in the speaker. Now what has this Arcadian Phyllis to do with road houses and night clubs? She'd shine there by contrast, but there's something more than that behind it."

"Your knowledge of road houses seems extensive and intimate, Ricky," remarked Vereker.

"It dashed well ought to be. Three or four years ago I wrote up some lurid stuff on road houses for the *Daily Report*. A job entirely suited to my temperament! The illicit pleasures of mankind interested me at the time more than their upward march towards—er—shall we say, civilization? Scotland Yard's war on the night life of London had driven the gay night-lifers into the more tolerant air of the country. Gambling, all-night drinking, bridge with high stakes, poker, roulette, dancing with pretty, young 'dance hostesses,' and so forth, were and are the attractions secretly provided by ye olde hostelries."

"I can't understand your interest in that raffish life, Ricky," ventured Vereker.

"My dear Algernon, I was a special correspondent of the *Daily Report*. It was my work, and I had to serve it hot with mustard sauce. As a journalist, I have to look at man in the round and leave reformers to think of him in the flat. Besides, I was spending my employers' money lavishly!"

"Let it pass as a virtuous defence and proceed, Ricky."

"In any case, the exodus from London was, in some ways, an improvement. It knocked the cheap and sordid element out of the picture. The good old country inns, tucked away off the main roads, have profited. The questionable proprietors of London's dens have been supplanted by sturdier, if not honester, hosts. The surroundings are genuinely antique and the air fit to breathe, the liquor, good and the food, generally excellent. Lastly, only people with means and motor cars can get out to these places of jolly entertainment."

"What has money to do with the moral side of the issue?" asked Vereker, gravely.

"Good Lord, Algernon, the authorities must safeguard the poor! That's why a betting slip in the street is vice and a telephone message from a swagger club, virtue. But to return to my subject.

I became devilishly interested in this butterfly among the tombs and rose from my seat so that I could skirmish round and get a look at her. At that moment, an accident happened. I sneezed in spite of a painful effort at hush-hush. I believe it's a world-wide custom to say 'God bless you!' when a person sneezes. The lady exclaimed: 'Well, I'm damned!' and next moment came round the yew with the lightness of a gazelle. By this time I was busy trying to read the inscription on the sarcophagus. Seeing she was eager to find out who I was, I turned my back gracefully on her. She took the hint and vanished. After she had given some instructions to her male companion, I saw her tripping away down the gravel path to the gate."

"What was she like?" asked Vereker with roused curiosity.

"Venus Epistrophia. I cursed myself bitterly for having turned my back on her. As she reached the gate, she turned and called back to her companion, 'Don't forget. At the "Fox" next Monday!' The male replied: 'Right-ho, Dawn!' and a few minutes later, I heard her car purring away into the wilderness. My brief glimpse or her face told me she was my kind of pet."

"So her name was Dawn," commented Vereker excitedly.

"By jove, Algernon, I hadn't thought of that. Dawn, eh? It suited her; she was Aurora!"

"What about her companion?"

"I'm coming to him. After yodelling round a bit, I saw him enter the church and followed. We got into conversation. He saw me gazing with rapture at the saints in a stained-glass window, while my earthly thoughts were following that vanished motor car with the seraph inside it. He discoursed at length on the history of the church, and, noticing that I was a bit absent, asked; 'Am I boring you?' When a man asks if he's boring you, he generally knows that he damned well is, but I professed complete absorption in his quatsch, as the Germans call it. Good word that, quatsch! Before long, however, he came to the *piece de résistance* of his lecture. It was a crypt, or underground vault, which the rector, the Rev. William Sturgeon, is exploring. My companion, who seemed upset by the rector's activities, informed me that Sturgeon was a queer old fish. 'Definitely so, I should say,' was my reply, but his sense of humour soared above it, and he went on to say that Sturgeon had got it into his stupid old Suffolk head that King John's treasure was buried somewhere in an underground passage, leading away from that crypt. I suggested that the Wash was the place for a Sturgeon to hunt for King John's treasure, but again he overlooked my point with annihilating calm."

"Perhaps he has a keen sense of the ridiculous," suggested Vereker quietly.

"I began to suspect it, so I shut up."

"How far has the padre got with his excavations?" asked Vereker, after a pause.

"He has partially knocked down the thick brick wall plugging the entrance to the magic tunnel, and had screened off his untidy work with a heavy curtain."

"Who was the man you were talking to?" asked Vereker eagerly.

"The verger, who appeared in the last scene of the drama, called him 'Mr. Orton,' and he's evidently one of the church council."

"I've heard a lot about him. He's a farmer in the district and was a friend of old John Thurlow. What did you make of him, Ricky?"

"Didn't strike me as a farmer. I put him down as a rather cultured man with a pedagogic complex. I may be wrong. He dogmatized under cover of the expression, 'of course, that's only my opinion.' We gradually drifted into an argument about modern music. I finally shut him up by saying that every man was entitled to his opinion, but that a kind deity ought to prevent some people from expressing theirs. He then got heavily sarcastic about the impertinence of the rising generation and left me to the mercy of the verger. The verger was more interesting. From him I got a long account of some obscure stomach trouble that ailed him. It appears that he has tried every known remedy, from hot water bottles to linseed poultices, to banish his pains. After much experimentation, he has found that mild and bitter 'do ease 'em best.' I parted with largesse for conversion into his pet anodyne and sauntered back to 'The Old Walnut Tree.'"

Chapter Nine

Punctually at eight o'clock the same evening, Vereker and Ricardo arrived at Old Hall Farm, and were shown into John Thurlow's study, where Eileen Thurlow sat reading. She rose and greeted her visitors, and, a few minutes later, all three were talking with the ease that comes of sympathy and understanding. Eileen Thurlow at once broached the subject of police investigations into the tragedy of her uncle's death. It was a subject that Vereker had wished particularly to avoid in order to spare his hostess's feelings, but intuitively guessing the reason for his compunction, she had at once assured him that death, to one of her faith, was merely a passing over from one soul state to another without complete severance of communication. She declared that such a conviction was an intense solace to the grief attendant on the loss of a dear relative. Under this encouragement, Vereker briefly narrated all that had so far been discovered, which was a bald précis of Inspector Heather's investigation. Of his own secret work, he said nothing.

Turning to Ricardo, Miss Thurlow then led the talk on to spiritualism, and soon she and Manuel were involved in an eager exchange of their experiences. Under the warmth of a common enthusiasm, they quickly threw off that reserve which accompanies the meeting of strangers, and were soon laughing and chatting like old friends. Vereker, now silent but observant, sat listening to them with a sensation of being a spectator, unable wholly to share their understanding. He noticed, too, that they spoke of the various manifestations incidental to spiritualistic stances with the complete acceptance of belief. He, himself, could never approach the subject without the introduction of the word "evidential," a clear admission of the existence in his mind of doubts that required stilling, of questions that demanded answers. The spectacle of these two disciples discussing their common belief set him musing. He was soon mentally remote from their conversation, lost in a maze of wonder at the psychological aspects of belief. What gave rise to this static pose in the process of thought, this complete satisfaction that the mind has found truth? He asked himself the question. His mind reverted to the subject of early teaching, of instruction given with complete assurance, and thence wandered away to Dr. Pavlov and his experiments on dogs. Stimuli and reflexes!

The light of the summer evening faded and shadows stole into the dark, wainscoted room.

"I think we ought to try out our little experiment now, don't you, Mr. Vereker?" suddenly came the question from Miss Thurlow.

"Yes, certainly. I'm quite ready," replied Vereker, almost with a start, so abrupt had been the arrest of his wandering wits.

"You were miles away, Mr. Vereker," commented Miss Thurlow, and turning to Ricardo, added: "I don't pose as a fully fledged medium, Mr. Ricardo, so don't be surprised if we fail to get results. I think I'm what is generally called a sensitive, and I hope to improve my gift with practice and experience. I'm convinced, however, that my uncle and I had a spirit manifestation in this room on the night of his disappearance, and I'm sure Mr. Vereker's a bit sceptical about it. I hope it'll happen again just to remove his doubts. I really believe this old house is visited by its past owners."

"The manifestation was a musical one, I believe," remarked Ricardo with such gravity that Vereker had some difficulty in suppressing a smile.

"Yes, we both heard an organ playing very faintly but quite distinctly, and my uncle stepped out into the garden to make sure that it was not the church organ we could hear. We have no wireless and no gramophone in the house. To make doubly sure,

I asked the organist next day if he had been practising and found that he had not been near the church."

"And there's not another house within a mile of Old Hall Farm," concluded Vereker.

"Now I propose we just sit as we are, and I'll try to go off into a trance state. I managed it perfectly on the last occasion and think I'll be successful to-night," said Miss Thurlow, and asked: "Are you both ready?"

Vereker and Ricardo assented, and Miss Thurlow, lying back in her chair, composed herself as if about to sleep. For about a quarter of an hour there was absolute stillness in the room, except for the soft ticking of a clock on the mantelpiece. Gradually the light outside waned and the room was filled with mysterious shadows. Ricardo sat calm and expectant: for him, a séance was not a new experience, and he accepted it in the matter-of-fact frame of mind which is usual with confirmed spiritualists at a sitting. To Vereker however, the whole occasion was fraught with an irritating sense of the abnormal. Something in his mental make-up suggested that, on his part, any participation in a séance arose from sheer curiosity, the desire to witness a wonder, rather than from any eagerness to come in touch with that mystery to which human death is the portal. And always there hung in his mind a vague mist of doubt which he had so far found impossible altogether to dispel.

All at once his attention was attracted by Miss Thurlow's distressed breathing. Even in the dusk, he saw her frame quiver with sharp muscular paroxysms, and then her breathing became deep and loud. She had evidently passed into a state of trance.

"I feel a cool breeze blowing through the room," remarked Ricardo, breaking the oppressive silence.

Vereker almost immediately thought he experienced the same sensation and glanced at the windows and doors. They were all closed.

"So do I," he replied. "What does it signify, Ricky?"

"It's a common occurrence at séances, and has been taken as a sign that the other side is trying to get in touch with us."

Vereker said no more, but immediately began to wonder whether he had accepted Ricardo's suggestion of that cool breeze as a fact. He was lost in thought about the vagaries of the human mind under the power of suggestion, when a small table in the centre of the room and close to Miss Thurlow, creaked as if subjected to some strong lateral pressure. Almost immediately afterwards, it gave out the sound of a sharp rap and this rap was followed by definite loud raps from various parts of the wainscoted walls.

"Amazing!" exclaimed Vereker, impressed in spite of himself by this strange but indisputable occurrence.

"An excellent beginning," agreed Ricardo quietly, and he had hardly uttered the words, when the small table near Miss Thurlow moved and then toppled over with a crash.

"Good lord!" exclaimed Vereker. "What's happened?"

"It's all right, don't move, Algernon. The medium is gathering power," adjured Ricardo.

Vereker relapsed into silence, and for the next ten minutes neither spoke. He was now experiencing a feeling of awe and could have affirmed emphatically that something soft and smooth touched his cheek and then the back of his right hand. No further manifestation occurred, however, and as they sat patiently waiting, they heard Miss Thurlow's heavy breathing slowly grow lighter and lighter till it returned to normal. At length, with a sigh, she raised herself to an upright sitting posture in her chair and was awake.

"Did you hear the music?" she asked immediately.

"No," replied Ricardo, "but there was an excellent beginning of spirit rapping. With practice you'd be able to secure messages by the alphabetical method. In any case, you mustn't be disheartened at this early stage, Miss Thurlow. You're undoubtedly a psychic and must persevere. Of course, you were quite unconscious of what was happening?"

"Utterly unconscious," replied Miss Thurlow, and reaching out her hand, switched on the electric light.

Rising from his chair, Vereker crossed the room and lifting up the occasional table that had fallen with a crash, set it upright on its feet. His inquisitive eye swept the floor in the vicinity of that table, and his hands swiftly passed over its polished surface in uneasy exploration. At the back of his thoughts hovered a disturbing scepticism.

"Good job there was no valuable china on it, Miss Thurlow," he said as if to cover his bewilderment, "or you would have had to put in a claim for damages against your spirit control."

"I didn't know the table had been upset," said Miss Thurlow with genuine surprise. "This is certainly a definite beginning!"

The words were spoken with a rising inflection of delight, and Vereker, his eyes riveted on her face, saw that she spoke with utter sincerity or complete self- deception. He was more disturbed than he would have cared to admit and felt that here he was possibly on the borderland of some new and strange world; that he had touched the fringe of some natural fact or occult human power, hitherto undreamt of by him.

An eager discussion of the incidents of the séance followed and gradually exhausted itself. Miss Thurlow once more expressed her regret that the strange music she herself had heard on former occasions had not recurred and proposed that, when she returned from her visit to London, they should make further experiments to recapture the phenomenon. To this, Ricardo and Vereker willingly agreed.

"When do you propose to leave Yarham, Miss Thurlow?" asked Vereker.

"To-morrow afternoon, and I hope you've not forgotten your promise to come and stay here while I'm away."

"No. I shall move in to-morrow, if it's convenient."

"And I hope you'll come with your friend," she added, turning to Manuel Ricardo.

"I'd love to, Miss Thurlow," agreed Ricardo, and added gravely, "but I must make one proviso."

"And what's that?" asked Miss Thurlow with surprise.

"That you leave the key of the wine cellar in my charge."

"Ah, I'm glad you reminded me," replied Miss Thurlow with a laugh. "There are some beautiful wines in that cellar. My uncle was a great connoisseur, though on the whole very abstemious. I'll leave the key with you, Mr. Ricardo, and I hope you'll see that Mr. Vereker doesn't take too much of a good thing."

"That would be impossible in my company," replied Ricardo. "He'll have to be clever to get his fair share."

After making further arrangements to take up their residence at Old Hall Farm during Miss Thurlow's absence and thanking her for her hospitality, Vereker and Ricardo bade their hostess goodnight and set out for the inn.

For some minutes they paced in step along the road without speaking.

"Well, Algernon, what do you think of it?" asked Ricardo at length.

"Frankly, I don't know what to think, Ricky," said Vereker, and asked: "Do you honestly believe that Miss Thurlow didn't knock over that occasional table?"

"My dear Algernon, this is almost blasphemous! Cynic, pagan, unbeliever! How dare you talk like that about an angel? If we were armed with swords, I should ask you to draw and defend yourself. Even if she'd deliberately kicked it over, I'd never admit it. Remember that she's stunningly beautiful and is going to leave the wine cellar key in my charge!"

"You're burking the question, Ricky. Be serious."

"Well, Algernon, who can say? I didn't see her kick it over," replied Ricardo. "She was certainly near it, but if she'd touched it, we'd both have been fairly certain about it."

"Then how do you explain the thing?"

"Well, some mediums have the power to move objects at a distance from them. The power is called telekinesis. At least, that's an attempt at a rational explanation, but don't expect any bright expositions from me. I can't give them. I've seen things that are apparently beyond rational explanation—or rather, they left me guessing feebly."

"Ah well, to-morrow I'm going to have a jolly good look at that occasional table and I'm going to explore Old Hall Farm thoroughly while we're there. I'm disappointed that we missed an organ recital by some departed musician, aren't you?"

"Rotten luck, I call it. I've heard zithers and banjos twanged, and a few accordion notes played, but never an organ. It would be stupendous, and I'm certain Miss Thurlow didn't imagine it."

"In your instances the musical instruments were present in the room, weren't they?" asked Vereker sharply.

"Certainly," replied Ricardo.

"But there's no organ within a mile of Old Hall Farm. This requires some explanation other than telekinesis."

"I hadn't thought of that," remarked Ricardo, "but then it's somewhat on a par with the production of three or more different voices in the séance chamber by what is called a direct voice medium."

"That organ gets my goat!" suddenly exclaimed Vereker.

"I'm glad I don't keep a goat," said Ricardo gaily, as he lit a cigarette. "But why should an organ worry you? Would it upset you to hear a spirit yiddle on a fiddle?"

"I wouldn't object to Paganini or Spohr, but that's beside the question," mused Vereker in a calmer tone. "I'm afraid we've wasted an evening, Ricky, definitely wasted it."

"You're impatient, Algernon. You've just put your money on the horse: he may come in. All this spiritualism doesn't seem to be in the line of your investigation so far, but you never know. As for wasting the evening, thank God we've wasted it so pleasantly. I could waste the rest of my days with Miss Eileen Thurlow!"

Chapter Ten

On retiring to his bed that night, Vereker found that sleep was impossible. A hundred fugitive and distracting thoughts swarmed through his mind, and he felt convinced that from this welter, by some psychological trick, a tangible theory would sub-consciously take shape. He had experienced this mental phenomenon on many previous occasions. It seemed as if in the hidden chambers of the brain disparate observations began to sort themselves out, a mysterious relationship began to assert itself, and like, by some strange magic, flew to like. Finally the irrelevant was precipitated and a bright intuition sprang forth with arresting power.

"Yes, that seems tentative but it points clearly; it gives direction!" he suddenly exclaimed with a note of exultation and began to wish that another day was born.

He rose, lit the lamp on his table, slipped on a dressing-gown, and produced his notebook and pencil. For the next hour he was busy jotting down all his observations and the inferences he had drawn from them. This process seemed to clarify his thoughts, and when he had finished, he thrust the notebook into his pocket, flung off his dressing-gown, blew out the lamp, and with a sigh of contentment and weariness sank once more into his comfortable bed.

"By jove, I think I'm on the trail at last!" he exclaimed, and a few minutes later was sound asleep.

Next morning at breakfast, Ricardo, after a swift glance at his friend, remarked: "You're simply bristling this morning, Algernon. You've picked up some strong scent and look as if you'd suddenly give tongue. Yoicks! Say, guy, you've gotta put me wise!

"We've got to move into Old Hall Farm to-day, but there's a lot to do before we go, Ricky. In the first place, I'm going to call on the Rev. William Sturgeon, and I'd like you, on some pretext, to interview Miss Dawn Garford, if she's still in the village."

"Not my Dawn of yesterday?" asked Ricardo with surprise.

"Must be the same, Ricky; your butterfly among the tombs. A Painted Lady for choice, family *nymphalidae*."

"From her conversation, I'd put her among the moths— Drinker, or Heart and Dart. But how do you know her name?"

"She's a mysterious figure in this Yarham murder mystery. Martin was supposed to be frenziedly in love with her. Thurlow, too, was infatuated. Hence the first idea that the rivals fought and slew each other. She's a young widow and her married name is Mrs. Button, but as she had only been wed a year when her husband, an aviator, met with a fatal accident, she's known to the villagers as Miss Dawn Garford. Being eligible for further experiments in matrimony, she probably prefers to be called by her maiden name."

"I don't blame her. Dawn Button's impossible and suggests a mushroom," commented Ricardo, and asked: "But what's the big idea?"

"There are several big ideas. You must find out as much as you can about her in your inimitable way."

"Right-ho!" exclaimed Ricardo with gusto. "I shall be the special correspondent of the *Daily Report*, or rather, his assistant. I shall take up the line of the interviewer cringing at the feet of a theatrical star. What does she think of the modern girl? Does she chew gum or knit socks? What does she think of the Church's attitude to divorce?"

"Take up any line you like, Ricky, but you needn't ask her what she thinks of the London policeman. I don't think you'll learn much about her relations with Martin or Thurlow, but you can find out her plans for the future. I may want you to shadow her. She runs about in a small car, and you can buy, hire, or steal one from the nearest garage and keep in touch with her immediately she leaves Yarham. I've been told she's very thick with Mr. Orton of Church

Farm. Probe into that if she'll let you. I think it's most important. You've got a stiff job, Ricky; it'll put you on your mettle."

"To pun shockingly, I'm afraid it'll be my mettle but your money, Algernon. First-class shadowing's very costly. From the lady's habits, I should say she frequents exclusive haunts, and that will suit me down to your allowance for expenses. Is she well-off?"

"No; as far as I can gather, she has enough to live on quietly in the country. Yet she gets about a lot and that requires money. You must find out how she manages to perform this miracle. I'm inclined to think she's a smart business woman. The business is a mystery. I want you to get to know the nature of that business."

"Find out a woman's business! A tough proposition, Algernon! You remind me of old Donne and his:

'Go and catch a falling star,
Get with child a mandrake root,
Tell me where all past years are,
Or who cleft the devil's foot.'"

"Don't funk it, Ricky! In any case, you've been trying to catch a star of the first magnitude for some time, so you're in practice, so to speak. Perhaps you'd prefer to interview the Rev. Bill Sturgeon?"

"No. I come from a clerical family, and they're not very entertaining. Their lives are pretty pictures in heavy gilt frames. I'd rather play Phoebus and chase the Dawn in my chariot. But you'd better leave it all to me, Algernon. Where does the lady hang out?"

"She lives with her aunt in one of those modern houses on the road leading out of the north end of the village. You'll spot it without difficulty. It has rather a large garden and is the only one that boasts a garage."

"Right. I'll crank up after another cup of coffee. It's much too early to flood the carburetter with whisky."

"I'll see you at lunch, Ricky," said Vereker.

"You certainly shall, Algernon. I'm not in the mood to miss lunch even for the society of a pretty woman. By the way, do you think I should wear a bowler hat? What do interviewers usually wear to kill?"

"Anything you like, my dear Ricky. You've got a weakness for bowlers and they suit you. Au revoir."

On arrival at the rectory, Vereker was at once shown into the Rev. William Sturgeon's study. He found him poring over a battered copy of an old pamphlet, called "The Legend of Yarham."

"Good morning, Vereker," said the rector.

"I hope I'm not interrupting you over cooking up your sermon, Padre," said Vereker.

"No, no. Sermons never give me any trouble. I'm a born preacher. I can choose my texts on Sunday morning and hold forth at desired length without difficulty at both services. My only fault is that on Sunday night I've completely forgotten what I've preached about during the day," explained the rector, and gave vent to one of his bursts of hearty laughter. On recovering from his mirth, he continued: "I've just been reading up a pamphlet written and printed by a former rector of Yarham. He was an enthusiastic archaeologist, and I have a similar kink, but not to such a pronounced degree as my predecessor."

"I hear you've been working on an old crypt in the church," remarked Vereker.

"Yes, I'm getting quite excited about it. I've often wondered why that stone staircase in the church ended in a brick wall, and shortly after my induction to Yarham, I decided to explore it. But my time was taken up by my parochial duties and I let the thing slip. Then, some time back, I read an account of the quest for an altar of gold in the village of Rodbourne Cheney, near Swindon, in Wiltshire. The church of St. Mary in Rodbourne Cheney dates back to the twelfth century, as does our church in Yarham, and the account I refer to said that a stone staircase, leading to a tunnel, had been bricked up owing to the issue of foul gases from underground."

"It looks as if the same thing had happened at Yarham."

"Exactly. Now, at Rodbourne Cheney they have found that four vaulted passages lead from St. Mary's to various points, Blunsdon Abbey being one. The abbey is three miles from the church, so you can see they were first-class tunnelers in those days."

"But what were those tunnels for?" asked Vereker, deeply interested in the rector's account.

"They were doubtless places for hiding in, or for escaping by, in troublous times. The monks, it is thought, used them later on for concealing the church valuables during the Reformation."

"And do you expect to find hidden treasure in your underground passage?" asked Vereker with an incredulous air.

"One never knows," replied the rector, eagerly rubbing his hands at the thought. "Our church needs a lot of restoration, and a few loads of valuables would come in very useful."

"Is there any legend of hidden treasure?"

"I have asked the oldest inhabitant, and he says he never heard anything about treasure but a lot about ghosts. A ghost is not a negotiable instrument, even if I capture one. But my predecessor, a copy of whose pamphlet I have managed to get hold of, says that, according to an old village legend, King John's jewels, which were supposed to be lost in the Wash, were left at Yarham. How this legend arose, it would be difficult to say, and the writer throws no light on the subject. A similar story is current that King John's treasure is hidden in a subterranean passage between the church at Rockingham in Northamptonshire and Rockingham Castle. Yarham, you must remember, was in close touch with the great abbey of Bury St. Edmunds, and one of its abbots was lord of the manor here. At the high altar of Bury Abbey, the barons swore to recover the lost privileges granted by Henry the First's charter, which was deposited for safety at the Abbey. Afterwards, King John signed that charter at Runnymede."

"Have you any idea where the tunnel from Yarham church leads to?" asked Vereker eagerly.

"One of them, according to my predecessor's pamphlet, runs to Riswell Manor, which is about two miles distant. He says he explored this for the greater part of its length, but found no royal treasure. 'Instead of treasure,' he naively puts it, 'we found an army of rats and were nearly suffocated by the foul air.'"

"Then there are other unexplored tunnels?"

"I'm working on that presumption. In his account, the writer doesn't definitely say so, but he leaves the reader to infer that there are. On this point, I again referred to Chinnery, our oldest inhabitant. He is ninety-three, by the way. He says that his great grandfather told him there were three tunnels. His great grandfather, I must add, was the workman who bricked up the entrance to these vaulted passages at the foot of the stone staircase in the church."

On the rector's invitation, Vereker then accompanied him to the church and inspected the brick wall, through the top of which he had already driven a large hole.

"I keep it covered with that heavy curtain to prevent the musty air from the tunnel entering the church too freely. When I've knocked down the wall, I'm going to buy a gas mask before I venture in. I daresay those vaulted passages are decidedly foul and may be actually dangerous."

"When did you start to knock the wall down, Padre?" asked Vereker.

"The thirty-first of May, the only decent summer's day we've had this year," replied the rector.

After admiring the painted roof of the church and the quaintly carved poppy heads of the oak benches, Vereker thanked the rector for a most interesting morning and left him, hammer and chisel in hand, about to resume his attack on the partly demolished wall.

Returning to the village, he called on Mr. and Mrs. Martin, the parents of Mr. Clarry Martin. On explaining that he was a pressman and had nothing to do with the police, the Martins received him cordially and were eager to supply him with any information he might desire. Vereker found them simple, straightforward, country folk and soon made himself at home in their company. Deftly leading them from one topic to another, he elicited some important facts about Clarry Martin. Mrs. Martin, inclined to be more talkative than her husband, explained that Clarry had been one of the best of sons till he went up to London. Even then he had always been thoughtful of his parents, but a great change had come over him. He had been apprenticed as a youth to a copper-smith, but had forsaken that work for the flash and more exciting motor trade. He had learned to make money, and success had seemingly turned his head. He began to consider the village of Yarham a dull place, and its inhabitants a set of stupid yokels. He had got into a pleasure-loving set and become a boon companion of certain lost souls who danced, drank cocktails, and frequented picture houses. London had a terrible lot of sins to answer for. This had led to a neglect of his flourishing business, and latterly he had at times been short of money. To hasten his downward career, he had fallen in love with that impudent baggage, Mrs. Button, who called herself Miss Dawn Garford, as if she were ashamed of her dead husband. No good could come of being ashamed of the dead. Mrs. Martin could say with truth that Mrs. Button was no better than she ought to be. While leading on poor Clarry for her own selfish amusement, she was cunningly laying her snares for Mr. John Thurlow, in order to get her quick, greedy fingers on his money. Not content with this two-faced conduct, the shameless hussy had also become too intimate with Mr. Orton, the farmer. He, too, possessed considerable means, which clearly showed that Mrs. Button was nothing more nor less than a wretched little gold-digger.

Thence the conversation drifted to the police interrogation that had followed the discovery of Martin's dead body at Cobbler's Corner, and, during a pause, Vereker seized the opportunity of asking a question that had been in his mind during the whole interview.

"Was your son interested in spiritualism, Mrs. Martin?" he queried.

"Never heard him mention the subject in his life, replied Mrs. Martin. "He wasn't interested in anything of that sort. Of that I'm certain."

Vereker recalled to their memory the fragment of a note found in Clarry's pocket, a note in which spirit rapping had clearly been referred to, but neither Mr. nor Mrs. Martin could shed any light on that mysterious point.

Well satisfied with his morning's work, Vereker made his way back to "The Walnut Tree," and just before lunch was served, Ricardo returned.

"Well, Ricky, you look flushed with victory," remarked Vereker as they sat down to their meal.

"Mistaken, Algernon. I merely hurried back to lunch. This East Anglian air gives one a ravenous hunger."

"Did you see Mrs. Button?"

"No, she left for London this morning. I interviewed her aunt, a middle-aged but well-preserved woman. To make her communicative, I treated her as if she were young enough for romance. It was a bad gambit, for she became kittenish. A mature woman who is kittenish ought to have a brutal relative to save her from the derision of strangers and the pity of her friends."

"Your interview was a failure, I take it."

"By no means, Algernon. When you suggested that I should see Miss Dawn Garford, I questioned the wisdom of it. You see, if it were necessary that I should subsequently shadow her, it would be fatal. She'd tumble to the game. I saw her face yesterday and her photograph this morning. I never forget a pretty face and that's sufficient."

"Have you got her London address?"

"No, but her aunt told me that Dawn would be at Barstow in Surrey, next Monday. There's a famous road-house there, and she's going to stay there for a day or two. I, too, shall be there if you can run to the hire of a decent car."

"Certainly; see about one at once."

"I've done so to save time. The local garage has a monster of speed which will suit me admirably."

"Splendid! Your forte is shadowing, Ricky, and you've had quite a lot of experience."

"Yes, Algernon, but the wisdom one acquires from experience is relative to the attendant circumstances. Nothing in life happens just the same way twice."

"I hope you're not making excuses for some prospective escapade with this charmer," remarked Vereker nervously.

"Certainly not. No man is proof against falling in love. Give me my due; I never indulge in escapades. Passion without love is eating without hunger; it's the worst depravity of your finest appetite."

"Ricky, you're pyrotechnic this morning. What's happened?"

"I drank a bottle of Chambertin before lunch. As for my last epigram, I coined it about a month ago, and this was my first chance of trying it out. Sounds a bit laboured, but it'll sparkle O.K. in stodgy company."

"Did you learn anything of the relations between Dawn Garford and Clarry Martin?"

"Dawn liked him because he was such a simple fellow."

"We all like simple people; they haven't the intelligence to do us any harm," remarked Vereker.

"Look here, Algernon, if you're going to compete against me, I shall stop talking like an unsuccessful dramatist. Let's stick to business now. I fished tor information about Dawn's friendliness with Orton, but auntie wasn't having any. Dawn seems to scatter her favours rather generously."

"One of these moderns without any fixed morality," remarked Vereker.

"A fixed morality's the expression of a conscience that's dead, Algernon, and has nothing to do with modernity. After seeing Orton, I should say that there's nothing more exciting than business relations between the two. The burning question is, what's the business?"

"Just so, Ricky, and when you've finished your coffee, I think we'll make our way up to Old Hall Farm. We must see Miss Thurlow before she leaves."

An hour later, Vereker and Ricardo arrived at Old Hall Farm and found Miss Thurlow eagerly awaiting them. She was leaning over the entrance gate to the drive and seemed unduly excited.

"I'm so glad you've come," she said as she greeted them. "A most extraordinary thing happened last night, and I wanted to tell you all about it before I left for London. I was lying awake long after midnight, when I thought I heard the sound of footsteps in my uncle's study, which is just beneath my bedroom. I wondered who it could be and putting on a dressing- gown, I ran downstairs."

"Very plucky of you, Miss Thurlow!" said Ricardo with admiration.

"I don't know so much about that. I did it without thinking. In any case, I went straight into the study and switched on the light. There was nobody there, but the chairs, ornaments, clock, and the little table had all been moved into different positions in the room. As I had been the last person in the room I was thunderstruck! Then I thought I heard footsteps in the wine cellar beneath the study. As I was now too scared to investigate myself and didn't wish to let the servants know what had happened, I locked up the study and went back to bed. I lay awake listening for another hour, but nothing further happened. Eventually I fell asleep, tired out. This morning I told Raymer, the maid, that I had locked up the study and that she needn't bother to tidy it up until I came back. I then went down to the wine cellar, but found it locked as usual. It has a Yale lock, and I at once looked in a drawer in uncle's bureau where he always kept a duplicate key, but the key was missing. I used the key myself the other day and have mislaid it. I've hunted high and low for that key but without finding it, so, Mr. Ricardo, if you want to sample uncle's special vintages, you'll have to burgle the wine cellar."

"This is most exciting!" exclaimed Vereker with an eager light in his eyes. "Were any of the doors and windows of the house open?"

"No. I summoned up all my courage before going back to bed and tried every window and door. They were all securely fastened."

"Amazing!" exclaimed Manuel. "It must have been a poltergeist."

"Exactly what I thought but didn't like to say so. I'm so glad you've suggested it, Mr. Ricardo. I've found a champion at last."

"Yours to command, is the right phrase, I think, Miss Thurlow," replied Ricardo, bowing with exaggerated courtesy. "I shall try and prove a worthy knight. The very thought of a poltergeist sharing the wine cellar with me fires my blood to the point of murder."

"No one has been in the study since you locked it up, Miss Thurlow?" asked Vereker seriously.

"No. I thought I'd like you to see things as they were left. If it was a human being and not a poltergeist, he has probably left some clues."

With these words Miss Thurlow entered the house and, followed by Vereker and Ricardo, led the way to the study. When she had unlocked the door, Vereker suggested that she and Ricardo stayed outside the room while he made a close examination of everything that might yield a clue to the mysterious intruder of the night before.

"All right," agreed Miss Thurlow and added with a smile, "you'll find me and my champion in the drawing-room when you've finished your job, Mr. Vereker. Mr. Ricardo and I think you're wasting your time, because we're convinced that a poltergeist leaves no clues."

"All I hope is that a poltergeist doesn't carry a corkscrew," added Ricardo and accompanied Miss Thurlow into the drawing-room.

Left to himself, Vereker at once dropped to his hands and knees and began a systematic examination of the carpet with his magnifying glass. He had not proceeded far with his examination, when he suddenly rose, left the study, and entered the drawing-room. There he found Miss Thurlow and Ricardo looking at an album of photographs showing "spirit extras" on them.

"Can you let me see the shoes you wore last night, Miss Thurlow? Also the slippers or shoes you wore when you came downstairs to the study after you'd heard the—the—poltergeist?" he asked.

"I wore a pair of patent leather court shoes on both occasions," replied Miss Thurlow and ran upstairs to fetch them. On returning, she handed a dainty pair of shoes to Vereker, who, after a cursory glance at the soles, handed them back to her.

"You're a lightning sleuth," remarked Miss Thurlow. "I thought you were going to put them under a microscope or something of that sort. What have you found out, Mr. Vereker?"

"That there's no sign of chalk on the soles, and that the poltergeist has a remarkably small foot. You take size fives, and the poltergeist can squeeze her feet into threes. Does one of your servants wear size three in shoes?"

"No. Raymer has colossal feet. Payne wears my shoes when I'm tired of them. Cook is a monstrosity; she isn't comfortable in anything smaller than skis."

"Thanks, this is getting quite interesting," replied Vereker and returned once more to the study. After a further examination of the carpet, he picked up from the mantelpiece a cut-glass ornament which Miss Thurlow said had been moved. On this he blew some chalk and mercury powder, a process which clearly revealed the impression of a thumb and two finger prints. A white china vase responded in a similar manner to treatment with graphite. Going back again to the drawing-room, he asked Miss Thurlow it she would lead him to the kitchen and pantries. Miss Thurlow, entering into the game of detection with zest, accompanied him. On entering the kitchen, Vereker asked the cook if he might have a clean tumbler on a tray. To assuage that genial woman's roused curiosity, he remarked that the tumbler was rather large to conjure with but he'd make it do. Raymer was then asked to bring a soup plate, and Payne, a silver cream jug. Raymer was allowed to place the soup plate on the tray, but when Payne was about to do the same, Vereker suddenly remarked:

"I'll take the cream jug. As it's solid silver, I'll make it vanish first."

Returning to the drawing-room with the tray, Vereker at once set it aside and asked Miss Thurlow to press her finger tips on his silver cigarette case. When she had done this, he placed the cigarette case on the tray beside the tumbler, soup plate, and cream jug and having obtained a clean tea-cloth, carefully laid it over the tray.

"What's the next step in the programme?" asked Miss Thurlow, as Vereker leisurely took a seat.

"I've finished work for the present," he replied.

"What a disappointment! I was waiting for you to say, 'Hey, presto, begone!' and lift the tea-cloth to show that everything on the tray had vanished."

"I'm not a spiritualist, Miss Thurlow," laughed Vereker. "I'm only going to make a study of finger prints to see that the poltergeist has fingers as well as feet."

"I half guessed that was your conjuring trick," replied Miss Thurlow, "but why did you prevent Payne from putting the jug on the tray?"

"Because she was holding the jug by its very small handle. When she gave it to me, she naturally clasped the bowl of the jug and turned the handle to me. I wanted a full impression of some of her fingers."

"I'm now certain that all detectives are tricksters!" said Miss Thurlow with a smile, and after a glance at the clock, added: "I must get ready to start. Cornish will be round with the car in half-an- hour, so I'll leave you two gentlemen to entertain yourselves."

With these words she left the room to dress for her journey, and before she entered her car to go to the station, reminded Vereker that he could ransack the whole house, if he thought it necessary for his investigation into the Yarham mystery. She also asked him if he would kindly see Mr. Arthur Orton of Church Farm on her behalf and tell him to get the repairs to his barns, which he had mentioned at their last interview, done by Cawston, the builder. Apologizing for this request, and with a final injunction that they were to make themselves at home, she bade Ricardo and Vereker good-bye, and a minute later her car had vanished out of the drive.

"You've made a very favourable impression, Ricky," said Vereker jokingly, on Miss Thurlow's departure.

"So has she!" replied Ricardo with a sigh.

"What about Gertie Wentworth now?"

"Faded out considerably. That's the worst of an amorist; his heart's a painful palimpsest and not an ordinary blood-pumping gadget."

"Sigh no more, Ricky. Go and fix up definitely about that car at the local garage. Tell 'em you'll buy it if necessary. You must be ready to start after Miss Dawn Garford in a couple of days' time. I'm going to run down to 'The Walnut Tree' for my special camera and enlarging apparatus. We'll have tea here at five and dinner at eight."

"Sounds rather regal. For some months now, I've been on a bread and cheese lunch and a Cambridge sausage tea. A month or two at Old Hall Farm would put me in fettle for writing another domestic serial with strong love interest."

Chapter Eleven

As he was entering the inn, Vereker was overtaken by Inspector Heather, who seemed considerably more cheerful than he had appeared of late.

"What has happened about the inquest?" asked Vereker.

"The inquest has been adjourned indefinitely. That gives us time to get on with our job, which is going to be a tough one," replied the inspector.

"There's a sanguine note in your voice, Heather. You've struck a hopeful trail?"

"I've struck a trail and that's something to go on with," replied Heather.

"And suspicion points to?" suggested Vereker.

"Several people, but Mr. Ephraim Noy is first on the list."

"You've been digging into his past?" asked Vereker.

"We have and we've managed to trace his activities back to Chicago. He was for some time an active member of a Chicago booze racket."

"Well I'm damned!" exclaimed Vereker with such vehemence that the inspector looked up sharply at him. "You're on his track, too, Mr. Vereker?" he asked

"No, Heather, no. I was merely astonished, that's all. Go on with your yarn."

"After a period of being mixed up with a gang of hoodlums, as they call them across the water, Ephraim turned police informer or 'stool-pigeon.' Then things became too hot for him and he skipped it back to England."

"How does John Thurlow or Clarry Martin come into the story, Heather?" asked Vereker.

"On his arrival in England, Noy made it his duty to hunt up Mr. Thurlow. Many years ago, in India, they had business relations together, but the exact nature of those transactions we can't find out. We've an idea that Thurlow helped him with money on his return to England from America, but of this we're not certain."

"His settling down at Yarham, close to John Thurlow, seems a bit mysterious," suggested Vereker.

"Yes, and we're busy on that line. There was probably blackmail or something like it hiding behind the scenes. I'm going to give Mr. Ephraim Noy a bad half-hour when I see him."

"I don't like the look of the man, Heather, but that's neither here nor there. Anything more of Runnacles?"

"Nothing much. He told us that on the Tuesday night, that is the night after Thurlow's disappearance, he was at home all evening with his wife. This was a lie. He didn't get home till early in the morning. The same happened on Monday night, the night of Thurlow's disappearance."

"A Mr. Barney Deeks told you so, Heather," said Vereker with a smile.

"How do you know Mr. Barney Deeks?" asked the inspector with a start of surprise.

"Met him casually in the tap-room of this inn. He told me that he knew Runnacles was out past Cobbler's Corner on Tuesday night. He had passed him on the road between ten and eleven o'clock, which to my mind implicates Deeks as much as Runnacles."

"You suspect Deeks's honesty?" asked the inspector.

"No. I think he was telling the truth, but the man's stupid and a bit of a braggart. He's an old-time poacher and proud of it. Likes publicity in his old age and hopes to be paid in beer for a good news story. He bears Runnacles some grudge. It's a little poaching vendetta, if you ask me, and arises out of professional jealousy. To return to more important things, Heather; have your pundits at Hendon, 'The Brain Box' I think you called it, let you know the nature of the substance that was on the sleeve of Martin's jacket?"

"It was yeast!" replied Heather with a laugh. "On the night of his disappearance, if you remember, he was seen with Mobbs, the baker. We've questioned Mobbs, and he admits that Martin had been chatting with him in the bakery before they crossed to 'The Walnut Tree' for the evening. That afternoon Martin must have put his elbow into the yeast while he was in the bakehouse."

"Sounds conclusive, Heather. And the strands of rope found on Martin's coat, what about them?"

"Only strands of sisal fibre from which some ropes are made. They seem to lead nowhere. Might be more important if we could find the rope itself."

"Of course. Also Martin's attaché case and Thurlow's cap. That reminds me, were any keys found in Thurlow's pockets?"

"Yes, I have them here. I'm going to return them to Miss Thurlow. There are a few papers and a notebook, which will be handed over later. You might tell her."

"Is there a key to a Yale lock on the bunch?"

"Yes; anything important about it?"

"Most important, Heather. Miss Thurlow has asked me to stay up at Old Hall Farm during her absence in town, and that's the key of the wine cellar."

"You can have the bunch on one condition, Mr. Vereker; that I may call on you every evening. But what are you going to do at Old Hall Farm? I thought you were busy on the Yarham murders?"

"I'm going to ghost hunt in my spare time. It's getting so exciting that it's keeping me off the main job. To be serious, I've got permission to go through John Thurlow's private papers, and the key of the bureau is probably on the bunch."

"Now you're talking sense. I expect you to tell me if you find anything important."

"Most assuredly, Heather. We travelled along the same lines in 'The Ginger Cat Mystery,' as I like to call our last case, but this time we seem to be on totally different tracks."

"Perhaps it's better," laughed Heather. "If you recollect, we made rather a hash of that affair and were both wrong in our final deductions."

"In spite of my harping all the time on the one important clue. I was led astray by my homage to your experience, Heather."

"That be damned for a tale! We were both led astray by our own confounded conceit. This time I'm going to put it across you good and hearty."

"I'll congratulate you if you do and stand you a barrel of the best beer you can drink."

"Thanks, and I'll put down my usual stake on the contest. If you score, it's another packet of 'Players' for you."

For some moments Vereker was silent and then remarked: "There's one thing that intrigues me mightily about this case, Heather, and that's the planting of those bodies at Cobbler's Corner."

"It struck me as a bit theatrical, and I haven't got quite used to the idea yet," remarked the inspector.

"There are a hundred places where they could have been dumped that would have been safer for the dumper. Say, in one of the numerous coverts about here. In that case they mightn't have been found for some weeks, perhaps months. What do you make of it?"

"Want of time was the principal factor, I should say," replied Heather. "Perhaps it was the murderer's intention to dump them in the big covert above Noy's bungalow. He was possibly on the way and somehow got the wind up at the last moment and decided to get rid of the cargo. I'm presuming that the bodies were taken to the spot in a car, or some other vehicle."

"That's how I worked it out. I'd like to know what Runnacles and Deeks were doing on that road at eleven o'clock on Tuesday night."

"I'll tell you if it'll help you, Mr. Vereker. Runnacles had been to Sudbury and missed the last bus home. He walked back the ten miles, but took the shortest cut by that road. Deeks made no bones about his purpose. He was going up to the covert to see what had happened to some rabbit snares he had laid the night before."

"Seems all above board, Heather," commented Vereker.

"You never know. Neither Runnacles nor Deeks is any relation of George Washington's, if you ask me. Then there's another important point I must give you. One of my men has been to Martin's London digs. On his dressing-table was an empty envelope which had been through the post. The address was in block capitals like those in the fragment of the note we found in Martin's pocket."

"By jingo, that's important, Heather! Where was it posted and when?"

"It was posted in Yarham two days before Martin left London for this village."

"I suppose it's impossible to find out who posted that letter?" asked Vereker casually.

"We did our best. You see, in a small village like Yarham, the postmistress can see everyone who drops a letter into the post-box, and as she isn't overburdened with mails, I thought there was just a chance she might remember. I asked her. She remembered taking the letter out of the box and noticing that the address was in block capitals as she cancelled the stamp. She couldn't be sure who posted it, but she has a vague idea it was Miss Dawn Garford, or Mrs. Button, to give her her proper name."

"And was it?" asked Vereker eagerly.

"Apparently not. We asked Mrs. Button when she was in Yarham the other day, and she denied it. She said that the postmistress must have imagined that it was she, because Clarry Martin was supposed to be her lover. She said she had not written to Martin for months, and, in any case, never used block capitals when writing a billet-doux."

"A smart defence, suggesting that the postmistress was led into error by an association of ideas," commented Vereker.

"She went one better than that," added Heather. "I asked her if she'd mind writing out 'soap box broken' in block capitals for me. She thought this a huge joke and assented readily. Her block capitals were nothing like those on the scrap of paper in my possession."

"She may have disguised her block capitals," suggested Vereker.

"I'm not such a bonehead as all that, Mr. Vereker. After talking to her for a while, I asked her if she'd repeat the experiment. She did, and I compared the two attempts. They were exactly similar. When a person fakes handwriting, he can never fake it exactly the same way twice unless making a copy with a specimen of the first before him."

"Then it's obvious that she didn't write that note."

"As certain as it's possible to be," concluded Heather.

"But it doesn't prove that she didn't post it," added Vereker.

"We've only got the lady's word for it, and she seemed to be speaking the truth. But there's another thing that's troubling me sorely, Mr. Vereker, and that's your barleycorn. Did you find out anything special about it?

"Yes; the barleycorn was malted. You know the process of putting barley on a heated metal floor and keeping it moist till it begins to grow. When the corn throws out little roots, it's ready. This increases its sugar content, and after drying it's called malt."

"I don't see much in your discovery. What has it got to do with Martin's murder?"

"Possibly nothing at all, but where did he pick it up?"

"There are several maltsters within a few miles of Yarham, and their motor vans run through the village nearly every day. No, that bit of investigation leads us nowhere."

"It seems useless, Heather, but so is half the work done in any complicated case," agreed Vereker and, glancing at his watch, added: "I must get back to Old Hall Farm for tea. Shall we see you to-night?"

"No; I shall be too busy. When you've discovered the best wine in the cellar, let me know, and I'll make a point of calling."

"I won't forget, but before I leave you there's one point I've remembered. Has your pathologist, Sir Donald Macpherson, given any definite opinion on how Martin met his death?"

"Being rather uncertain, he has given a very guarded opinion. Experts are mighty cautious. Only the general practitioner feels he has to be certain. The bullet wound, if received during life, could hardly have proved fatal. He was almost certain it was inflicted after death. There were no signs of poison in the stomach. On the other hand, there was considerable cerebral congestion, which points to apoplexy, but this symptom might be the result of some obscure narcotic poisoning. He inclines to the latter suggestion. The venous system was filled with dark coloured blood. There were no signs of a struggle, beyond the bruises left by his attempt to free himself from the cords which undoubtedly bound his hands and feet prior to death. Make what you like of that, Mr. Vereker. To me it's simply Greek."

"I'm not a medical man, and it doesn't tell me much, but I'll bear the narcotic poisoning in mind. By the way, I'm going to look through some of Thurlow's private papers to-night. If there's anything important among them, I'll let you know. So long Heather."

Leaving the inspector, Vereker walked leisurely back to Old Hall Farm. As it was now four o'clock and Ricardo had not returned from his visit to the local garage, Vereker found that he had an hour on his hands before tea would be ready. Taking the bunch of keys which Heather had handed over to him, he went into the study and after a few trials, found the master key which opened all the drawers of Thurlow's bureau. Glancing through the contents of one of the drawers that had been unlocked, he came upon an odd Yale key which had evidently been thrust hastily among the papers.

"Probably a key to the wine cellar," he mused and, taking it out, compared it with the single Yale key on the bunch in his possession. They were exactly similar, and without further examination of the drawers, he promptly made his way down to the wine cellar. He tried the loose key and found that his surmise was correct. Opening the door, he glanced at the Yale lock and observed that the door could be opened from the cellar side by turning a coin-shaped knob with a milled edge. The lock was exactly similar to thousands fitted to the front doors of ordinary suburban houses. Switching on the electric light, he glanced round the cellar with its neatly stocked bins. Small cards were fixed to the woodwork of these bins and bore the names, dates, etc., of the special wines they contained. At the moment, however, Vereker was not interested in wines, and taking from his pocket a powerful electric torch, for the cellar installation consisted of one lamp of low power, he made a swift examination of the four walls. In one of these walls was a door-shaped opening into a further cellar. Passing into this adjunct, which was considerably larger than its neighbour, he discovered that it was empty, except for a pile of wooden boxes and a heap of the straw jackets in which wine bottles are encased for transit. After a brief scrutiny of the walls of this musty and cobweb-festooned chamber, he was making his way back to the cellar containing the bins, when, flashing the ray of his torch along the floor, he noticed a white streak between two of the large paving stones. At once he halted and examined this streak.

"Chalk, by jove," he exclaimed and after a careful inspection, stood erect and began to whistle an air from an old Viennese opera that he loved. It was a sure sign that he was suppressing considerable excitement. Seemingly fired by this discovery, he made a close survey of the whole of the floor, except that portion covered by the heap of empty wooden cases and straw bottle-jackets. He then pursued his task into the adjoining cellar until he reached the door leading up to the ground floor of the house. Evidently thoroughly satisfied with his investigation, he closed the door, which automatically locked itself.

In the study once more, he sat for some time at John Thurlow's bureau, his hands thrust in his trousers pockets, his eyes gazing unfocussed at the wainscoting in front of him. Then, pulling himself together with an effort, he resumed his task of going through the contents of the drawers.

As he rapidly turned over a mass of papers of no importance to his quest, he suddenly came across a book of printed receipts and, running through the counterfoils, his eye was arrested by the counterpart of a receipt issued to Arthur Orton for the half-yearly rent of Church Farm. This incident at once reminded him of Miss Thurlow's request that he should tell Orton to proceed with the repairs to his barns. He glanced at his watch. It was nearly six o'clock, but there would be sufficient time to fulfil his promise to Miss Thurlow and be back at Old Hall Farm for dinner at eight. Locking up the drawers of the bureau, he left the study and shortly afterwards was pacing briskly along the main road to the village. Before reaching the drift which ran from this road up to Church Farm, he decided, from his knowledge of the district, that by crossing several meadows he could cut off an angle and shorten his journey by half a mile. Vaulting a gate leading into a meadow, he began his tramp across the rising pasture land towards his destination. In the distance, above the timber-clad hill, he could see the small factory chimney of Orton's steam corn mill.

Half an hour later, he found that by his plan of avoiding the drift he was unable to approach the farm by its main entrance, and to reach the dwelling-house he was obliged to pick his way through the miry yard and cattle sheds lying behind it. As he was skirting a pond to reach the farm-yard, he noticed that a motor lorry standing in the yard was being loaded with sacks of grain. Two farm labourers were busy on this operation, and as Vereker watched with admiration the ease with which the burlier of the two men lifted the sacks on to the lorry while his companion arranged the load, a third man suddenly joined them. He was, by his dress and manner, evidently Arthur Orton, the master, and in his hands he was carrying two two-gallon cans of petrol. These cans he, in turn, handed to the labourer in the lorry, who carefully secreted them under a sack of grain. At this moment Orton happened to glance in Vereker's direction and almost started on seeing him. Recovering from his surprise, he gave some order to the two men and came slowly forward to meet his unexpected visitor.

"Well, sir," he said as he glanced suspiciously at Vereker: "Did you want to see me?"

"If you're Mr. Arthur Orton," replied Vereker amiably, "I certainly do."

"My name's Orton, but if you're a traveller for cattle foods and such like, I warn you that you'll be wasting your time. I don't want anything in that line at present."

"No, I'm not going to try salesmanship on you, Mr. Orton," continued Vereker smiling. "I merely came to deliver a message. I'm staying at Old Hall Farm during Miss Thurlow's absence in London, and she asked me to tell you to go ahead with the repairs to your barns which you spoke about when you saw her last. Cawston was the name of the builder she suggested, if I remember rightly."

"Oh, thank you. I'll write to Cawston to-night. You're a stranger to Yarham, aren't you?"

"No, not quite; I've been here nearly two months now. My name's Vereker."

"Ah yes, I've heard the rector speak about you. You were at college with young James Sturgeon."

"Yes, we've been friends for many years now."

"I didn't know that Miss Thurlow was going to London," remarked Orton thoughtfully. "When did she leave?"

"This afternoon. She wished to apologize for not having let you know about the barn repairs herself. The matter slipped her memory."

"In the circumstances, she oughtn't to have troubled about those repairs at all. She has been through a rather terrible experience. Do you know when she's coming back?"

"Not definitely, but she's only going to be away a few days."

"Gone to her solicitors, I reckon. She comes into a nice little fortune by her uncle's death, I hear."

"I couldn't say," replied Vereker cautiously.

"May I offer you a drink now you're here, Mr. Vereker? From the way you came, I should say you cut across country. It's a rough journey and you'll be feeling you need a refresher."

"Thanks, if I'm not putting you to any trouble," replied Vereker.

"No trouble at all; it'll be a pleasure," replied Orton and turned towards the farm-house.

The front door of the farm-house opened on to a spacious hall, beautifully furnished with a few genuine antique pieces, showing that its tenant was a man of taste as well as of ample means. Opening a door on the left of this hall, he led Vereker into a dining-room in the centre of which was an old oak refectory table, surrounded by high-backed carved oak chairs. The whole furnishing of the room was in keeping with its oak beams and plain distempered walls and struck a note of old-world dignity and charm. Noticing Vereker's air of appreciation, Orton smiled with undisguised satisfaction.

"You like my dining-room?" he asked.

"I certainly do," replied Vereker sincerely.

"It's a nice room. I'm very fond of it. These old houses have a way with them that's hard to resist. They get under your skin. Shall I bring you whisky, or would you prefer wine?"

"Whisky, thanks."

"Good. I can offer you something very special in whisky," replied Orton and left the room.

During his absence, Vereker took the opportunity of looking round the room, and on a small oak table in a corner, he noticed a pile of uniformly bound books. Books give such an insight into the tastes of their owners, that Vereker could not resist looking more closely at these. To his astonishment, they were bound volumes of music, and on their backs were the names of the composers, Handel, Haydn, Beethoven, Mozart, etc. At once Vereker remembered that Miss Thurlow had said that Orton was fond of music, and he was pondering on this bent, rather an unusual one in a farmer, when Orton returned with a tray in his hands. On the tray were glasses, a greybeard, a siphon of soda, and a jug of water.

"My housekeeper has gone to Sudbury for the afternoon, so I've got to look after things myself," he explained.

Orton picked up the greybeard, poured out whisky into one of the glasses to Vereker's nod, and told him to help himself to the "dilution." During this operation Vereker seized the chance of more closely observing his host. He was a man of about forty years of age, lithe and strong, with a hard, clean-cut face, and a glance like a hawk. The face was unequivocally handsome, but there was a cynical, almost distrustful cast about it, which seemed to say that he knew his fellow- men and harboured no illusions about their shortcomings. After a stiff glass of spirit the outlines of his face softened genially, and he spoke with greater freedom and frankness. Choosing the subject of painting, he probed Vereker as to his aims in that art, and showed a surprising knowledge and appreciation of its technique, past and present. Then noticing that his guest had glanced at the grandfather clock in a corner of the room, he remarked:

"I see you're eager to get back to Old Hall. If you dine at eight, you'll be there in nice time. But I should keep to the drift; the going's easier and just as quick in the long run. When you've got an hour or so to spare, look me up again. I've thoroughly enjoyed our chat."

Secretly glad of the invitation and promising to return, Vereker rose to go. As they made their way to the front door, Orton suddenly halted in the hall, as if arrested by the recollection of something important that he had forgotten.

"I don't know whether Miss Thurlow has told you anything about her future plans, but I'd like to know whether she's going to stay on at Old Hall Farm, Mr. Vereker."

"She told me very definitely that she was going to stay, and I don't think I'm abusing her confidence in repeating it."

"Ah, so she's going to stay. I had an idea she'd get away from the place after what has happened. Between ourselves, I'd like to buy up the property, including this farm. I mentioned the matter to my old friend Thurlow, but he didn't want to sell. Perhaps Miss Thurlow will change her mind later. She is young, and Yarham's no place for a young woman like her to bury herself in. She ought to get about and see a bit of the world. Money won't be any hindrance to her now."

On stepping out from the front door, Orton summoned one of the two men who were still busy with the motor lorry in the yard, and on his coming up, turned to Vereker:

"Battrum will show you the way round to the drift, Mr, Vereker," he said, and then addressing Battrum, added: "When you've done that, Joe, see and get that lorry away. It's high time it was on the road."

Escorted by Battrum, who led the way without speaking a word, Vereker passed through the white entrance of the farm into the drift. Anxious not to be late for dinner, he quickened his pace immediately and had nearly reached the main road, when he met the Rev. William Sturgeon.

"Good evening, Vereker. I see you've been up at Church Farm. Is that man Orton at home?"

"I've just left him, Padre. You seem ruffled. What's the matter?"

"Ruffled? I should say I was ruffled. It's enough to make a saint shy his halo about with intent to do grievous bodily harm. Thank your stars you aren't a parson with a parish like Throston-cum-Yarham. It's a life of strife, I tell you, and that fellow, Orton, is at the bottom of all the trouble."

"What's the trouble?" asked Vereker, suppressing with difficulty a desire to laugh.

"My congregation have sent me in a petition asking me to brick up the wall which I've spent hours in knocking down. They complain that the foul smell issuing from the tunnel is making attendance at services impossible. As if a farmer wasn't used to a wide assortment of stinks! It's all a put-up job, and Orton is the ringleader of the obstructionists. They've not got one atom of historical curiosity in their thick heads. After all the work I've done too! I tell you it's no joke chiselling through a four foot brick wall; and yesterday, to make things more unpleasant, I hit my thumb with the hammer. However, I must catch Orton while he's at home. I'm going to give him a jolly stern lecture. A member of the church council, too!"

With this threat, the Rev. William Sturgeon pulled out his handkerchief, mopped his perspiring brow, and hurried on to battle like a Christian soldier.

On returning to Old Hall Farm, Vereker found a two-seater sports car standing on the gravel approach in front of the house. The bonnet of the car was lying across the leather-cushioned seats, and an oily and begrimed Ricardo was bending over the engine with a box-spanner in his hands.

"I suppose you've been trying her out, Ricky. I expected to see you at five o'clock," said Vereker.

"Yes, I wanted to see how she behaved. Not a bad old bus. She was a bit difficult to start up. Her plugs were none too good, so I've fitted some new ones. Now if you just look sternly at her, she flaps her wings."

"Was she expensive?"

"Dirt cheap, Algernon. If you don't want to keep her as a pet, you can sell her later on and get most of your money back. Or you can let me have her on the hire-purchase system."

"The latter alternative meaning that I'll get damned little of my money back," added Vereker.

"You horrid, cruel man! I felt that retort coming along like a steam-roller. Unlike the car, my reimbursements would be slow but sure. But look at the advantages you gain. You'll have added a

miniature flying squad to your detective bureau. And think of it—
the car's yours till the last farthing has been paid by me!"

"I'll think over your proposition, Ricky," replied Vereker
dubiously. "In the meantime, let's go in and get ready for dinner."

Chapter Twelve

After dinner Vereker returned to the study and continued his task
of looking through the papers in John Thurlow's bureau. Ricardo,
reclining in an easy chair, was reading a battered old volume
which he had found in one of the well-stocked book-shelves that
ranged along two sides of the room. It was a history of Yarham,
published in the early part of the nineteenth century.

Pausing for a few moments in his work, Vereker glanced at
Ricardo and saw that he was engrossed in his book.

"Got hold of something interesting, Ricky?" he asked.

"A history of Yarham."

"Anything about the church in it?

"That'll come later on. The writer jumps off with a heavy wad
of the early history of East Anglia in general. I'm now learning
all about an immigration of Flemish weavers to Yarham in the
twelfth century. Mind-bleaching stuff! It's so dry that I think I'll go
and explore the wine cellar. As I pointed out to you at dinner, no
connoisseur would spoil a good wine by drinking it with a meal.
Now's the hour to savour a really heroic vintage!"

"By jove, this is tremendous!" interrupted Vereker with
startling vehemence.

"What's tremendous?" asked Ricardo, turning round sharply.

"A letter from Ephraim Noy among Thurlow's papers. It's—it's
of cardinal importance!"

"Who the devil's Ephraim Noy?" asked Ricardo with
bewilderment.

"Heaven above, don't you remember? The man who discovered
the bodies of Martin and Thurlow at Cobbler's Corner."

"Ah yes, now I recollect. What's his letter about?"

For some minutes Vereker did not reply, for he was reading the letter with eager concentration and undisguised excitement. Then he laid the double sheet flat on the bureau and turned towards his friend.

"Looks like blackmail, Ricky. After upbraiding Thurlow for refusing to see him on his arrival at Yarham, Noy goes on to say that he still remembers a very unpleasant little affair that happened in India many years ago. In that affair, Thurlow played some obscure but important role. Whatever the affair was and whatever Thurlow's part in it, the result was the murder of a man whose wife, Suvrata, was a Nautch dancing girl. Thurlow was in some way mixed up with that dancing girl, because Miss Thurlow has a hazy recollection of her parents discussing the affair when she was in her 'teens. Noy points out that it would be very disagreeable for Thurlow if the details of that bygone episode with Suvrata were made known in Yarham, where he was held in such high esteem. To obviate this, he would be well advised to call at the bungalow any evening and have a quiet chat over the business."

"Isn't that simply diabolical!" exclaimed Ricardo vehemently. "The vermin! He ought to be boiled in oil. Poor Thurlow, as I figure it, arrives in India with all the charming illusions of a young Englishman. He sees a Nautch-girl dancing and falls over head and ears in love with her. Can you blame him? Imagine the atmosphere: Indian moons and mysticism, tom-toms and jasmine blossoms, bangles and brown limbs and—and the shadow of the Taj Mahal, for I can think of nothing else at the moment. Again, the very word Nautch-girl breathes warmly; it makes a susceptible person's knees tremble. I'd be bowled out first over. Then some stray lunatic, probably another frenzied lover, despatches the charmer's husband, and Thurlow's name is dragged into the ghastly business. After the whole affair is decently buried and forgotten, this ghoul rakes it up in the hope of squeezing cash out of poor old Harlequin, who subsequently in a chastened mood offered his prayers to Mammon instead of Venus!"

"Just one minute, Ricky, and we'll make sure," said Vereker, as he glanced at the date of Noy's letter and then ran through the counterfoils of one of a bundle of old cheque books.

"Here's a cheque for five hundred pounds made out to Noy a week after that letter," he exclaimed at length, and added: "Looks almost too accommodating to be true. I say, Ricky, get out that bus of yours and run me down to 'The Walnut Tree.' I'm going to give Heather this tit-bit. He'll be delighted, for he rattles handcuffs whenever the name of Ephraim Noy is mentioned."

"An unpleasant sound for anyone, but what noise annoys a noisy Noy, etc. Why are you going to tell Heather? You ought to keep him in the dark, Algernon."

"The information may have that effect," replied Vereker with a mysterious smile, "so hurry up!"

"Right-ho! We'll think about the wine on our return. I had put 'Gladys' to bye-bye, but I won't be long waking her up again. She'll run us down to 'The Walnut Tree' while you're shutting her door."

Ten minutes later "Gladys" purred into the yard of "The Walnut Tree" Inn, and Vereker stepped out as she came to rest. In the yard, at the time, stood a motor lorry ostensibly laden with sacks of grain. One glance at this lorry informed Vereker that it was the property of Arthur Orton of Church Farm, and he surmised that the driver was snatching a meal before starting on a lengthy night journey. For some moments he stood hesitant and then crossing to the window of the tap-room, peered through into the brightly lit interior. Hastening back to Ricardo, who had just turned the car round in readiness for leaving the yard, he took him by the arm and led him towards the door of the inn.

"While I'm discussing business with Heather, Ricky, wait in the tap-room for me. In there, you'll find the driver of the lorry that's standing beside your car. Engage him in conversation if you can, stand him drinks, do anything to keep him there till I rejoin you."

"Say boy, have you got a gat handy?" asked Ricardo dramatically.

"Don't play the fool, man! I'm deadly serious. Have you a spare can of petrol in the car?"

"You'll find two in the dicky, but I'm not going in there if you're going to fire the place. What d'you want petrol for?"

"I'll tell you later. Now put a jerk into it before it's too late. The lorry-driver's name is Joe Battrum by the way."

Entering the inn, Vereker went up to Benjamin Easy, the landlord, and asked him if Inspector Heather was in his room. Ben Easy wasn't certain, and leaving the bar hurried upstairs to find out. He reappeared a few minutes later to say that Inspector Heather was away and had left word with Mrs. Easy that he wouldn't be back in Yarham till next day.

"Tell him I want to see him some time to-morrow, Ben. It's most important," said Vereker.

"Very good, sir," replied the landlord, and Vereker, returning hurriedly to the yard, peered again through the tap-room window. Seeing Ricardo in earnest conversation with Joe Battrum, he made his way quickly back to the yard of the inn. There he lifted himself up by the tail-board of the motor lorry, and clambered on to the sacks of grain that constituted its load. Thrusting his hand between the sacks in the centre of the load, his fingers came in contact with the handle of a petrol can. With some difficulty he moved a superimposed sack and dragged out the can. Jumping down from the lorry, he crossed to "Gladys," pushed the can into the dicky, and in a few minutes had substituted one of Ricardo's cans of petrol for the one he had abstracted from the lorry. Breathless from exertion, he entered the inn, thrust his head into the tap-room and called out:

"Come along, Ricky, we must get back. There's no time to waste!"

Hurriedly drinking his beer and wishing Joe Battrum good-night, Ricardo joined his friend, and a minute or so later, with a roar from her exhaust, "Gladys" was speeding back to Old Hall Farm.

"What's all the hurry for, Algernon?" asked Ricardo when they were on their way. "Did you see the inspector?"

"No, he's away and won't return till to-morrow. Things are warming up, Ricky, and I'll have to hustle. I feel somehow that Heather has struck the trail, and I want to show him a clean pair of heels."

"Where has he gone?" asked Ricardo.

"Left no word, but I've a shrewd idea."

On arriving at Old Hall Farm, Vereker extracted one of the petrol cans from the dicky of the car.

"I'm going to keep this petrol. I shall need it for several jobs I have on hand. Get another can for yourself at the garage," he said to Ricardo, who was looking at him with questioning eyes.

Taking the can with him, Vereker entered the house and immediately repaired to the study. Later on, Ricardo, having tucked up "Gladys" for the night, sauntered into the room. To his surprise, he found Vereker pouring a little of the contents of the petrol can into a china saucer.

"What's the experiment, Algernon?" he asked. "Reminds me of a demonstration in 'stinks.'"

"In a way, it is," replied Vereker, as he screwed the stopper of the can firmly down and placed the can in a corner of the study. Taking an automatic lighter from his pocket, he applied its flame to the liquid in the saucer. At once that liquid ignited and burned with a clear blue flame.

"Rum kind of petrol!" remarked Ricardo, on at the performance with roused interest. "What have you mixed it with?"

"Brains, Ricky, brains, as Whistler said on a historic occasion," replied Vereker with an eager light in his eyes, as he watched the blue flame flicker and die out in the saucer.

"I didn't think you'd have any to spare for a bally burnt offering," remarked Ricardo, and seeing that Vereker was apparently not disposed to be communicative, he picked up the history of Yarham. Sinking into the depths of a comfortable chair, he lit a cigarette and commenced to read.

Some time elapsed before Vereker, with a note of seriousness in his voice, broke the silence.

"I think you'd better get on the tracks of Miss Dawn Garford to-morrow, Ricky. The sooner you discover what she's up to, the better. It'll fill a big gap in my theory about the Yarham mystery."

"This is Saturday and she won't be in Barstow till Monday," replied Ricardo, looking up from his book.

"I know, but I want you to call at all the roadhouses she mentioned when speaking to Orton in Yarham churchyard. If you pick her up at any point, stick to her like a terrier. Also, you can look up your old friend Poppy Knatchbull at 'The Blue Bottle.' Take a high hand with her and pretend you are acquainted with Dawn Garford's business. If it's above board, she'll soon let you know what it is. Don't be afraid to chuck your money about in order to ingratiate yourself. I'll let you have a substantial cheque, which you can cash at my bank in London."

"To-morrow being the sabbath, I won't be able to fondle the dough till Monday, Algernon," commented Ricardo.

"I'll give you sufficient to tide you over."

For some moments Ricardo looked at his friend with an affectionate but puzzled expression on his face.

"You're a rum old stick, Algernon," he said at length. "On most occasions you're as careful as a French peasant, and then, on some thankless game like this, you're a Jubilee Plunger. I'm not raising any objections to chucking your money about, mind you. I love ingratiating myself in a congenial atmosphere with the right kind of people, but your attitude leaves me guessing. I can't understand a man spending his money through a proxy."

"I'm busting it on my only hobby, Ricky. Thanks to my guv'nor's financial genius, I've been left, as you know, with a very substantial income. My pictures, by an irony of fate, sell well, just because I don't need the money. I live very quietly. I've no use for fine clothes. My flat's not too expensive. I merely keep on old Albert because he's such a trustworthy simpleton and would probably be selling matches if he wasn't looking after me. My only extravagances are a little good wine, this detection, and lending you money which you intend to repay when you've written something bad enough to sell well."

"I must say you're very confiding, Algernon. The kindly way you put it brings a blush to my hardened cheeks. Still, the intention to pay you back's a great driving force in my life. It urges me on to write a story that is a story. Bung full of human interest, sincere love, charm, and wish fulfilment. In the meantime, papa's cheque is due and every time I see his illegible signature, it impresses me with the dignity and nobility of fatherhood. You shall have that cheque. You've been a good friend to me, Algernon, but I'm getting Uncle-Tom's-Cabinish..."

"Among Thurlow's papers, I've come across Miss Dawn's London address—a flat in Clarges Street," said Vereker, interrupting his friend and handing him a card. "Nice address for a young lady of limited means. You might nose round and see what sort of a place she runs."

"By jove, Gertie Wentworth's place is in the same block, Algernon," replied Ricardo excitedly, as he glanced at the card. "Those flats are luxurious!"

"You needn't trouble to call on Gertie Wentworth," said Vereker with a frown.

"She may know something about Miss Dawn Garford," suggested Manuel gravely.

"Not enough to repay me for the loss of my time and your sense of direction," said Vereker, and paused to let the admonishment sink in. He was about to return to his task at Thurlow's bureau, when he suddenly sat bolt upright in his chair.

"D'you hear anything, Ricky?" he asked excitedly.

For some moments Ricardo sat with all his senses alert and then, in a voice from which he could not restrain a note of awe, replied: "I think I hear the sounds of an organ. Do you?"

"That was my impression," replied Vereker. "Let's stop talking and listen."

"Switch off the light, Algernon," said Ricardo in a whisper. "If it's a manifestation, darkness is more suitable."

Vereker, rather to oblige his friend than with any faith in the efficacy of his suggestion, switched off the light and resumed his seat.

Both men now sat listening in the pitch-dark room, and as they strained their ears, there came in faint gusts the unmistakable sound of an organ being played with no mean skill. At times those waves of sound surged up with vibrant strength and then faded away again until they were barely audible. Rising from his chair, Vereker silently crossed the study floor, opened the door leading out on to the lawn, and stepped out into the starlit night. There, he was unable to detect any clue to the origin of the amazing phenomenon that was manifesting itself in the study. Rejoining Ricardo, who sat dumbfounded in the dark, he listened intently for some seconds and then proceeded from the study to the hall outside, closing the door behind him. Again he found that he had passed beyond the range of that weird music. Taking an electric torch from his pocket, he made his way to the steps leading down to the cellar and descended as noiselessly as possible. Opening the door of the cellar silently, he passed in and quickly flashed his torch in all directions. The bright circle of light danced over the walls and floor and flickered in reflection from the bottles stacked in the bins, but revealed nothing that could suggest the agency from which that strange organ recital sprang. With a growing feeling of awe, he passed from the wine cellar into the empty adjunct beyond. Here, everything was as he had seen it on his last visit; and he was about to retrace his steps, when he again heard the faint, far-off strains of an organ. Standing still, and overwhelmed with astonishment, he listened intently.

The sound seemed to him to be trembling in the motionless air with increased volume; whole passages were at intervals clearly audible, and somehow those passages seemed very familiar to him. Passing round the cellar, at every few paces he placed his ear against the walls, but this device disclosed nothing and only left him more bemused than before.

"Amazing!" he soliloquized. "I must have a good look into this to-morrow."

He had hardly uttered the words, when the faint music ceased altogether with disconcerting abruptness. Now an oppressive silence reigned, and the damp, musty air of the cellar seemed to grow chilly and sinister. His mind reverted to the séance in which he had taken part with Ricardo and Miss Thurlow. He remembered the cool wind that had apparently blown through the dark study without any explicable source of origin; he recalled the loud and vibrant tapping that had resounded from the table and the surrounding wainscoting. He called to mind Ricardo's narration of his strange experiences; of seeing actual materialization; of hearing several loud voices speaking together; of witnessing the movements of objects beyond the possible reach of the medium. His scepticism was badly shaken, and with a faint but undeniable inrush of dread, he hastened from the empty adjunct into the wine cellar proper and reached the outer door. He was about to pass out and close the door, when, regaining control of his feelings, he experienced a sharp spasm of annoyance that he had allowed himself to be overcome by an unreasoning fear of the unknown. With an air of resolution, he quickly retraced his steps and, glancing along the tickets affixed to the woodwork of the bins, drew out a bottle of choice claret. Thrusting it in his pocket, he left the cellar, quietly closed the door, and ascended to the study. There he found that Ricardo, having switched on the light, had calmly resumed his reading of the history of Yarham.

"Well, Ricky, what do you make of the elfin music?" he asked.

"I don't know what to make of it, Algernon. I'm almost certain it has nothing to do with departed spirits."

"Oh, this is surprising from you. I expected to find you entranced when I opened the study door. What's your objection to the theory that it's a linking up with something beyond the veil, or with some musician in Summerland, as they call it?"

"In the first place, there's no medium present, which is unusual to say the least of it. Again, neither you nor I are psychic. Somehow I feel certain there's a natural explanation of the business if we could only tree it."

"The music seems rather familiar to me. Did you recognize it?"

"Yes, I did. The invisible organist was playing snatches from Haydn's 'Four Seasons.' I twigged it when he tried over the bass song, 'From out the Fold the Shepherd Drives.' My musical memory's none too bright, but I'd put my only dress shirt on that. He must be a Victorian spook."

"Ah yes, now I recollect. This is excellent. Haydn, yes, Haydn, now I've got it!" said Vereker with a certain note of jubilation. "I think that's worth a good bottle of claret between us. Will you go down into the cellar and fetch one?"

"Not to-night, Algernon, not to-night! I don't mind seeing wonders with solid human beings to right! and left of me, but I jib at saying, 'How d'you do' to a grisly horror in the gloom of a wine cellar."

"You're not scared, Ricky?" asked Vereker, glancing at him with some surprise.

"Scared be hanged!" exclaimed Ricardo, jumping to his feet with a laugh. "I was just seeing if you'd volunteer. You looked rather green about the gills when you returned to the room. Name your tipple and I'll go and fetch it. I'd wrest a bottle of the worst Lisbon wine from the hands of a matricide's ghost!"

"You won't need to. I've brought a delightful claret back from the cellar with me. Go and get a couple of glasses."

Flinging aside his book, Ricardo disappeared. A few minutes later he returned with the glasses and a corkscrew and laid them on the study table.

"Now let's enjoy ourselves quietly, Algernon," he said. "The subject of spectres is taboo from now onwards. It's very nearly bedtime. I'm not easily scared, but I simply can't sleep with my head under the bedclothes!"

Chapter Thirteen

Next morning, after breakfast, Ricardo brought out his car from the garage, fixed his suit-case firmly in the dicky and stepped into his seat at the wheel.

"Now remember, Ricky, strictly business is the order of the day. When you've got the information I want, and any other knowledge you can pick up, return as quickly as possible. Speed is paramount," said Vereker.

"I get you, Algernon. Built-up areas and mandatory regulations cease to be. I refuse to apply my brakes till I hear the windscreen splinter. Au revoir," replied Ricardo, and with a sustained blast from his horn, disappeared down the drive.

An hour later, Vereker entered the village and crossing the green, called at the Yarham cobbler's tiny shop. The cobbler, sitting at his last, was driving nails with monotonous rhythm into the sole of a shoe, using a heavy file as a hammer. On Vereker's entry he looked up, extracted half a dozen nails from his mouth, and rose from his seat.

"Yes, sir," he said inquiringly.

"I wonder if you can give me some information, Clarke," said Vereker. "Among your customers, is there a lady who wears size three in shoes?"

Simeon Clarke scratched his head vigorously, as if to rouse a sluggish memory, and replied: "I can only remember one at the moment and that's Miss Garford, sir. She has a wonderful small foot for a lady of her build."

"No one else?" asked Vereker.

"Not as I can recollect at the moment, but my memory is getting shocking bad." Turning round to his assistant, he asked: "D'you know any of our lady customers as wears size three in shoes, Jasper?"

Jasper, in turn, tried to recollect with an air of complete vacancy. "No," he replied, "can't just think of no one. There's Crazy Ann takes fours. You don't mean she by any chance?"

Jasper was told rather brusquely that the question didn't refer to size fours and therefore not to Crazy Ann.

"Who's Crazy Ann?" asked Vereker, amused.

"She be one of the maids at the rectory," explained the cobbler, and there the matter ended.

With a puzzled air, Vereker left the cobbler's shop and called on the church organist. The latter denied having practised on the church organ the previous night and didn't know of anyone who had. Satisfied with this information, Vereker returned to Old Hall Farm, He spent the greater part of the day photographing, developing, and enlarging finger prints, and at the conclusion of his task, began a careful comparison of the prints. It was not long before a satisfied smile crossed his features, and he exclaimed with some excitement:

"The poltergeist was certainly not Miss Thurlow or any of the servants in the house. That's something definite at last!"

He had barely made this startling discovery, when a maid announced that Inspector Heather had called and would like to see him.

"Well, Heather, how's the hunt proceeding?" asked Vereker on entering the drawing-room.

"Damned slowly, Mr. Vereker. Very little headway since I saw you last, and I don't want any more verdicts about some person or persons unknown. Have you had any luck rummaging among Mr. Thurlow's papers?"

"Came across something that'll interest you. It concerns your friend Ephraim Noy. Here I have a peculiar letter from Noy to Thurlow. Read it and tell me what you think of it."

Vereker passed the letter to the inspector and watched his face while he read it. But Heather was not a man to disclose his feelings readily, and when he had finished his perusal, he handed the letter back to Vereker.

"Looks as if Noy was trying to twist the old boy's tail. I wonder if the dodge proved successful."

"I can't say definitely, but it looks like it, Heather. A week after the date of that letter, Thurlow drew a cheque for five hundred in favour of Ephraim Noy."

"That's interesting, Mr. Vereker. It looks suspicious, but you never know. Thurlow was a generous man and might simply have been helping an old business pal over a big stile. You see, it was years ago since they had any business connections with one another, and Thurlow probably knew nothing of Noy's racketeering exploits in America. We've got further information from the American police, and find that Noy participated in bumping off several members of a rival gang in the booze racket. He managed to keep out of the clutches of the law on that count, but it shows he's a man who doesn't stop at murder. I've been trying to tighten the net round him, but so far without success. What have you been doing yourself?"

"I've been mighty busy on a ghost hunt, Heather. The night before Miss Thurlow left for London, a woman got access to this house after everyone had gone to bed. She moved all the ornaments and a lot of the furniture into other positions in Thurlow's study, and got away again without being seen."

"How did she get in?"

"I don't know yet. Miss Thurlow, thinking she heard noises during the night, came down to investigate. She tried all the doors and windows herself and found every window closed and all the doors locked. She put the rearrangement of the study furniture down to a poltergeist!"

"Bless my soul, and what's that!"

"A mischievous spirit, Heather," replied Vereker with a laugh.

"In this year of grace, too! Do you believe that rot, Mr. Vereker?" asked Heather impatiently.

"No, I don't. This ghostly visitor, I must tell you, left the print of a woman's shoe in chalk on the study carpet. Also I've got her finger prints on some of the ornaments. She was a bit too material for a poltergeist."

"Was it one of the servants or Miss Thurlow herself?" asked the inspector.

"No; that's the mysterious part about it. The finger prints are not those of anyone in the house. The size of the shoe is a three, and that doesn't correspond with the shoe of any of the ladies here."

"Then there must be some method of getting in and out of this house other than by doors or windows," declared Heather emphatically.

"I agree, Inspector, but I haven't discovered the method yet. I must admit that I haven't made a thorough search for that secret trap-door. I've been so busy in other directions that I haven't had time. Another remarkable thing happened last night which comforted me considerably."

"I wish something would comfort me. What was it?"

"Ricardo and I heard the mysterious music which Miss Thurlow spoke about. We couldn't find out how the magic was worked. I questioned the church organist this morning and found that he wasn't playing the church organ last night."

"But this has nothing to do with our case; it's all so irrelevant, I simply don't know what you're driving at, Mr. Vereker."

"I feel certain it's going to have something to do with our case. Otherwise, I wouldn't trouble myself any more about it. What pleased me about hearing the music was that it proves that such a phenomenon did occur on the night of Thurlow's disappearance. I was half afraid that Miss Thurlow's story was pure moonshine, a figment of her lively imagination. To return to the poltergeist business in the study, I'm convinced that a human being played that trick. But what was her motive? I don't think for a moment that it was merely a practical joke."

"The ghost business has often been played to scare a person out of a house," remarked the inspector casually.

"So I believe," said Vereker, and at that moment the muscles of his cheek hardened, because Heather had shrewdly hit on one of his own secret convictions.

"Anybody want to buy the property?" asked Heather, lighting his pipe.

"Yes, Orton of Church Farm wants to buy. He frankly told me so himself, but he's not a woman with a size three foot."

"Why don't you pump the village cobbler? It's an unusual size, and he might be able to tell you right away."

"I did, Heather. The only woman that he could name was Miss Dawn Garford, or rather Mrs. Button, and she wasn't in Yarham that night as far as I could ascertain."

"There have been faked footprints, I believe, in criminal history," continued Heather, "but I've never come across an actual case and don't know anyone who has. They really belong to the world of the detective story writer. I know this Miss Dawn Garford benefits under Thurlow's will, but I can't connect her up with his murder in any way."

"Heather, that's just where my methods score. From my observations in this Yarham case, I've slowly pieced together a very amazing story. There are some nasty gaps still waiting to be filled in, but they won't wait long. Mere facts lead to the ordinary process of deduction, but unless you can make a big intuitional jump, those deductions frequently get you nowhere. You've made fun of my barleycorn, you've pooh-poohed the spirit music, the poltergeist and so forth, but I've fitted them into a complicated scheme of things. You may as well own up that I've got you whacked to the wide, and hand me over my packet of 'Players.'"

"Not if I know it," replied Heather with well- assumed truculence. "We're just beginning and I'm going to put up a stiff fight. I've got my eye fixed on a barrel of beer and that adds weight to my punch."

"Have you cut Runnacles completely out of your list, Heather?" asked Vereker after a pause.

"No, he's still running, but he has fallen behind. I tackled him about being on the road near Cobbler's Corner on that Tuesday night, and he gave me a fairly reasonable explanation."

"Why did he lie about it and say he was at home all evening? Even his wife backed him up in the yarn," asked Vereker.

"He's a bit of a simpleton in some ways. Having come up against the law and served a sentence before, he thought he'd be connected up with this case by a vindictive police force. He knew he was on the road either before or after those bodies were planted, and got the wind up. When I cornered him with Deeks's statement, he owned up and told me why he had lied. He then promptly split on Deeks and his poaching. Deeks, however, is a much shrewder man. He at once owned up to poaching, knowing it would serve to clear him from any connection with the major crime."

"Did either of these men pass or see the car which Ephraim Noy has spoken about?" asked Vereker.

"Deeks says no. Runnacles says a motor lorry passed him. He was a bit blinded by its headlights, but thought it was one of Orton's lorries from Church Farm."

"Was it?" asked Vereker.

"I questioned Joe Battrum and he didn't think it could be. If it was, he wasn't the driver, for he was in bed at that hour on Tuesday night."

That was somewhere about eleven o'clock?" asked Vereker quickly.

"Yes."

"And you have asked Orton if one of his lorries was on the road at that hour?"

"I did. He said that Runnacles must be mistaken, because both lorries were in the yard long before dusk on the Tuesday evening."

"What do you make of it, Heather?"

"Can't make head or tail of it. There's a liar among them, I should say. I promptly pumped Joe Battrum's missus before he could get back and coach her. She said that her husband didn't get home till midnight on that Tuesday. On being pressed, however, she began to wobble and said it might be Wednesday. She couldn't be sure. Sandy Gow, another of Orton's men who drives a lorry, said he thought Joe had one of the lorries out late on Tuesday. Again, he wouldn't be dead certain."

"It's all so damned inconclusive, Heather," agreed Vereker, and asked: "When did you see Orton?"

"This afternoon. I ran up to Church Farm after lunch."

"What do you think of him?"

"Seems a decent sort. Very generous with his liquor. Rather a superior type from what I could gather. While he was out of the room for a minute, I had a look at what he was busy on, for there were papers and books lying on his table. He was copying out music. I was surprised, because it's a rum sort of hobby for a farmer."

"Did you notice the name of the composer of the music?" asked Vereker casually.

"No, I'm blessed if I did, and in any case I'd have forgotten it if I had," replied Heather.

"Did you see Orton's housekeeper during your visit?"

"Yes, Mr. Vereker, I did. She brought in the whisky and what not for Orton and a jug of ale for me. Best beer I've tasted in Suffolk, and that's saying a lot."

"Did you notice anything peculiar about the housekeeper?"

"Can't say that I did. She was good looking in rather a hard way, and seemed to treat her boss rather familiarly."

"That's a prerogative of housekeepers, Heather. Was she tall, short, stout, or thin?"

"Medium height, well-built; not slim and yet not stodgy; sort of comfortable like. I can't describe her better than that. One thing I did notice particularly. She had very small and finely shaped hands. But why are you so interested in the lady, Mr. Vereker?"

"I'd heard some village gossip about her and Orton, and I was naturally curious. You see, she has a rival in Miss Eileen Thurlow, and I was thinking that the latter, being an heiress, might put the housekeeper's nose out of joint."

"That's quite possible," replied Heather, rising and stretching himself. "There's an old saying, 'He who has the money laughs,' and there's a lot in those old sayings. Well, I must be going. It's getting late and I've a lot to do. When you've spotted the culprit in the Yarham murders, let me know and I'll come along and put the darbies on him."

With these words, Heather took his departure, and Vereker strolled out into the beautifully kept gardens for a breath of fresh air, for he had been busy indoors all the afternoon. As he wandered round, lost in thought, he suddenly met Runnacles, the gardener who was putting away his barrow and tools prior to leaving off work.

"Oh, Runnacles, I've just had a visit from the Scotland Yard inspector," said Vereker. "He was telling me that you thought you had passed a motor lorry from Church Farm, near Cobbler's Corner, on the night after Mr. Thurlow disappeared."

"That's right, sir, but it was a good bit this side of Cobbler's Corner," replied Runnacles.

"What made you think it was one of Orton's lorries?"

"General look of the thing, just as you can tell a man at night even though you can't see him too clearly. Besides, I thought I heard Joe Battrum give a cough as he swung past me. There's no mistaking old Joe's cough; you can hear it a mile off."

"Thanks, Runnacles," said Vereker, and was about to let the gardener depart, when the latter stood hesitant, as if eager to unburden himself.

"If it's a fair question, sir," he finally stammered, "can you tell me why the inspector is so anxious about my comings and goings on that Tuesday night? I've told him fair I had nothing to do with the master being knocked on the head, and yet he comes asking me the same questions again and again."

"I shouldn't get worried about it, Runnacles, replied Vereker amiably. "You're not the only person to be questioned in this affair, and the inspector naturally asks you the same questions over and over again to see that you don't contradict yourself. You mustn't blame the inspector for trying to get at the truth; it's his job."

Appearing considerably consoled by these words, Runnacles thanked Vereker and, picking up his barrow, proceeded on his way. A few minutes later, Raymer, the maid, came running into the garden to tell Vereker that he was wanted on the telephone. He hastened into the house, wondering who the caller might be. It was Manuel Ricardo.

"That you, Algernon?" he asked, and on Vereker's reply, added: "I've picked up the trail already. Also I've an idea about the nature of the lady's mysterious business. I'll be able to get confirmation of it from Poppy Knatchbull. After a good skirmish round, I'll return to Yarham. How do you like being all alone in a haunted house?"

"It's rather depressing, Ricky, and I'm looking forward to your return. I'm dining alone to-night, which is anything but exhilarating, and I shall turn in early. Cheerio."

"Same to you, old horse. When does Miss Thurlow return to Yarham?"

"I can't say definitely."

"Didn't she give you any idea?"

"Only roughly. But why?"

"Oh nothing, but isn't she simply lovely? I can't get her face out of my mind. Good-bye."

After dinner Vereker went into Thurlow's study and, looking about for something to read, found the history of Yarham which Ricardo had left lying on the table. He picked it up and drawing an easy chair close to one of the windows, for it was still possible to read by the evening light, sat down and opened the book. Becoming interested, he read on till the falling dusk made it impossible to continue. Closing the book, he laid it aside and, being tired and somewhat depressed, closed his eyes and let his mind wander. In spite of himself, his thoughts took on a grey and cheerless hue, and an acute feeling of loneliness slowly gained possession of him. He opened his eyes and glanced round the room. Its sombre tones, which he had at first thought so restful, now by an association of them with the tragedy which had so recently overtaken Thurlow, took on a sinister and funereal significance. He closed his eyes once more, as if to shut out an unkindly and uncongenial world, and gradually his thoughts became more and more fugitive and incoherent till he fell sound asleep.

He was awakened, he afterwards concluded, by a dim consciousness that a light had passed swiftly over his features. When he opened his eyes, however, they encountered an almost impenetrable darkness, and he guessed that he had slept soundly for some hours. He stretched himself lazily and was about to rise from his chair when, by some obscure process of his senses, he became aware of a human presence in the room. Without moving, he peered anxiously into the surrounding wall of blackness, in an effort to locate that strangely felt presence. Gradually, as his eyes became accustomed to the gloom, various articles of furniture in the room fixed themselves dimly on his vision. Then, all at once, a human form took shape and was faintly silhouetted against the dark wainscoting. At first Vereker thought he must be mistaken, that this apparition was some extraordinary illusion springing out of a sharply roused mental expectancy. He closed his eyes and looked again. The figure was still visible, statuesquely motionless.

A sharp sensation of fear assailed him. All his life he had been sceptical of anything in the nature of an apparition. In spite of all the "authentic" ghost stories he had read, notwithstanding the actual experiences related to him by several of his friends, he had always felt certain that such a phenomenon would never be seen by him. Had this, the incredible, come to pass? Was he at last to fall in line with all those who firmly believed in the supernatural, with all those who in past ages had gone in fear and dread of a world of spirits, good or evil, puckish or malignant? His scepticism was struggling desperately for mastery over a reluctant acquiescence in what he had always considered ignorant superstition, when his quick ear caught the faint creaking of a floor-board in the vicinity of the spectre. In a flash his dread of the dead gave place to the quick alarm roused by the possibly malicious intention of the living. Keeping his eyes fixed on that greyish white shape across the room, he suddenly realized that it bore some resemblance to the general carriage of Eileen Thurlow. This unaccountable assumption gave rise to another, and he thought he could recognize in the air of the room a faint trace of the scent which he knew she used. He was filled with a sense of utter amazement, but keeping control of his feelings, tried to rise very quietly from his chair. That chair was of wicker and creaked noisily as he moved, and at the same moment he discerned a quick movement on the part of the figure. Instinctively he thrust his hand into his pocket in search of an electric torch, but remembered to his dismay that he had left the torch on the hall table. The switch of the electric light was on the other side of the study by the door, close to which the figure stood. He decided at once to reach that switch and unmask the mysterious intruder. With a sudden bound he was on his feet and across the study floor, but before he had reached his objective, the figure had apparently dissolved and was gone.

He stood in the now brilliantly lit room, listening intently. Faint sounds were audible in the passage beyond. He stepped quickly outside and listened once more. He thought he heard the sound of distant footsteps, and it appeared to him that those sounds came from the cellars below. Without a moment's further hesitation he ran down the passage, descended the steps to the wine cellar, and entered. Switching on the light, he made a hurried search of the whole underground storage, but discovered nothing. The ill-lit cellars were apparently as he had found them on his last incursion into them. Greatly astonished, but now with a grave suspicion that the "manifestation" he had witnessed was a material one, he ascended once more to the ground floor.

His amazing experience had given birth to a new idea, and he decided that in the morning he would pursue a line of investigation indicated by that conception. He glanced at his watch and found that it was half-past eleven. It was earlier than he had thought, but he felt that as he could do nothing further till daylight, he would go to bed. He had just entered the study once more when, to his surprise, he heard the sound of a car outside, and a few minutes later the front door bell rang. As the servants had retired, he answered the summons himself, thinking that some sudden impulse had driven Ricardo back to Yarham. The visitor, however, was Doctor Cornard.

"I saw a light in the study as I was passing, Vereker, and thought I'd call. I'm not unwelcome, I hope," said the doctor.

"I'm jolly glad to see you, Doctor," replied Vereker, and asked him to make himself comfortable. "Did you want to see me specially?"

"No; just thought I'd drop in for a chat before going home. I'm a late bird and hope you're one too. There's absolutely nothing to do in this dismal hole of an evening, and I'm not a sleep hog."

"I'm very glad of your company, Cornard. I wanted someone to talk to. I've just had a most amazing experience."

"Oh, and what was it?" asked the doctor, settling himself in his chair and lighting his pipe.

"I've seen a ghost!" said Vereker with a smile.

"That's a common experience in Yarham. The place is simply steeped in a belief in the occult. We live in the middle ages here. What can you expect?"

Vereker then quietly narrated what had occurred, much to the doctor's amusement and incredulity.

"Your nerves are out of order, Vereker. I'd give this detection game a long rest," he suggested at the conclusion of the story.

"I don't think my nerves had anything to do with it, Doctor," argued Vereker and then, after a pause, suddenly asked: "Do you know Miss Thurlow at all well?"

"Fairly well. She has been to me occasionally for small complaints. Nothing more serious than a bad cold or a touch of 'flu. Why do you ask?"

"I wondered if you knew her general disposition and mentality," remarked Vereker.

"I think so. Strictly between ourselves, I think she suffers from a kind of dual personality. There's the sweet, common-sense girl who takes life quietly and rationally and enjoys herself in an ordinary way. Then there's the hysterical creature who messes about with the occult, with stances and spooks and all that damned nonsense. I've had a suspicion for some time that she's an epileptic and does all sorts of things without afterwards being aware that she has done them."

"Good heavens! Do you think she's sincere in her belief in spiritualism?"

"Oh, most certainly! That's the dangerous feature about it. And what's more, once people get imbued with this belief, they'll go to all sorts of extremes to convince other people of its truth. I'm perfectly certain that they'll descend to trickery to gain their ends. Their mental attitude is paradoxical, for even in fraud they're convinced they're honest. I said 'paradoxical'; it would be nearer the mark to say psychopathic."

"Would you say that my seeing a spook to-night was due to a psychopathic state of mind?" asked Vereker.

"It looks damned like it, Vereker, unless someone was having a lark with you and playing a silly kind of practical joke."

"I'm certain that my ghost was living flesh and blood, Doctor. I heard the floor-boards creak beneath the movement of her weight; I fancied I smelt the scent she used; and I don't think I'm quite cracked."

"I'd certainly hesitate to certify you, Vereker," said the doctor with a laugh, and asked seriously, "But tell me, what's the idea behind this ghost game?"

"I haven't the vaguest notion at present, Cornard, but I'm going to get to the bottom of it. It's not the meaningless foolery that it appears on the surface."

"I don't know so much about that," argued the doctor. "No one but a born idiot would play such monkey tricks. If I caught the lady at it, I'd guarantee she wouldn't do it again. But I'm keeping you out of bed and must get home. Keep me posted about further psychic experiences. Whatever they are, they're exciting, and any kind of excitement is welcome in Yarham. Good-night."

A few minutes later the doctor had gone, and Vereker, switching off the light in the study, went upstairs to bed. He was in a very disturbed state of mind, but gradually he gained control of his thoughts, subsided into equanimity, and fell into sound and refreshing sleep.

Chapter Fourteen

The whole of next morning Vereker spent in a fruitless search for some trap-door, or means of entering and leaving Old Hall Farm, that was unknown to its occupants. The thickness of the wall on the south side of the entrance hall intrigued him, but after a careful investigation, he left the riddle unsolved and decided to pursue his inquiries into the Yarham mystery further afield. He passed through the village and continued his way northwards till he arrived at Ephraim Noy's bungalow. The owner was rather surprised to see him, but invited him in.

"In search of further sensational rubbish for your rag of a paper?" he asked when Vereker had seated himself.

"No. I came to see you on a matter concerning yourself, Mr. Noy," replied Vereker seriously.

"How d'you mean?" asked Noy with a swift, anxious glance at his visitor.

"While Miss Thurlow's away from home, I'm staying at Old Hall Farm. Before leaving, she asked me to go through her uncle's papers and diaries for her, and among those papers I found a letter from you to Thurlow. In that letter you refer to some affair in India in which he got mixed up many years ago. You appear to know all about that episode."

"* Well, what the devil has it got to do with you?" asked Noy with sudden truculence.

"Nothing whatever. I'm not interested in it personally, but as it may have some bearing on Thurlow's murder, I naturally mentioned it to the police."

"You're nothing but a damned busybody! What have my private relations with Thurlow to do with his murder?" asked Noy with rising anger.

"I hope for your sake they've nothing to do with Thurlow's murder. Now, Mr. Noy, there's no need to lose your wool. Doesn't it strike you that this dancing girl business may have some connection with it? It's possible that someone who was wronged at the time may have at last taken his revenge."

"Rot! The affair is past and done with. This revenge idea is sheer moonshine. People don't take revenges in real life unless they're bughouse."

"I think you're right, but of course, there's just a chance that a lunatic killed Thurlow."

"Bunk, sir, bunk!" replied Mr. Noy emphatically.

"Well, Mr. Noy, your opinion on that episode is worth having," said Vereker diplomatically.

"Take it from me, Mr. Vereker," continued Noy, considerably mollified, "that that Indian affair has nothing to do with the present case, nothing at all."

"Do you know all the details of the Indian business?" asked Vereker.

"I certainly do. I was instrumental in clearing Thurlow's character when he was under suspicion of being mixed up with the murder of the woman's husband. I tell you, it was a narrow squeak for old John. He was very grateful to me for my help."

"You were a good friend," suggested Vereker pertinently.

"I certainly was. I told you when you last saw me that I knew nothing of Thurlow. I did so to safeguard myself, because I didn't want to be dragged into any police inquiry into his murder. My own record is none too good, and once you've been in trouble, the police are biased against you. I've had enough trouble in my life without getting into any more."

"You had a rough time in the States, I believe," remarked Vereker.

"My God!" exclaimed Noy with a groan. "Is that all going to be raked up again. I suppose this Scotland Yard man has been poking his long snout into my past history."

"You might have expected that, Mr. Noy, and the best thing is to be quite frank with the police. If you try to beat them off with falsehoods, they'll only suspect you of implication in this Yarham affair."

"But how do you know all about this?" asked Noy, after a pause.

"I'm not at liberty to answer that question," replied Vereker.

"Ah, I see! As I said before, you pressmen are always hand in glove with the police. Well, you can tell the inspector from me that I've got a clean sheet on this count. I admit I got mixed up in a booze racket in Chicago some years ago, and our gang bumped off some of the rival guys. Over here you think that's just ordinary murder. It isn't. It's only a kind of warfare on a small scale. A gangster is nothing more nor less than a hired soldier. You stand to be shot at and you shoot first if you can. Then one of our men, Gumshoe Jim, got into serious trouble. He was always too ready to flash a gat, that is draw a gun, and he knocked off a harness bull."

"What on earth's a harness bull?" asked Vereker.

"When I get excited I fall back into American slang," remarked Noy apologetically. "A harness bull's a policeman in uniform. That was more than I could stand, so I chucked the racket. I managed to make a getaway and returned home to England. I thought I was safe here but bless my soul..." Ephraim Noy left the sentence unfinished and ran his fingers wearily through his unkempt hair. "Have they got a line on the man who did this Yarham job?" he asked after a pause.

"That I can't say; I'm not in the know. Have you any idea of what lies behind it?" asked Vereker.

"No, but only a year or so ago, Thurlow did some sharp work through agents on the American stock market. I only have that on hearsay, but there may be some truth in it. Somebody's probably got his own back."

"You never quarrelled with him yourself?" asked Vereker.

"Never in my life. Thurlow was very good to me. When I came and settled down here, I found out he was living in Old Hall Farm. I went to look him up, but he didn't want to renew our old friendship. I was rather sore about the way he did it. Simply turned me away from the door. He might have been more tactful. In the heat of temper I wrote and reminded him of that Indian affair, and told him I could make the place pretty hot for him. Not that I meant it. Later on I met him and apologized. He found out that I was in rather low water, and gave me a cheque for five hundred to set me on my feet. He was a generous man when he liked. That was the last time I ever spoke to him. If I knew anything about this dirty business of his murder I'd put the police wise right away." '

"Has the inspector been to see you?" asked Vereker.

"No. Did he say he was coming?" queried Noy anxiously.

"I'm almost certain he'll question you about the Indian affair," replied Vereker guardedly, "but as far as I can see, you've nothing to fear on that score. I should also be perfectly frank with him if he probes you on your activities in America, because he's sure to know all about them."

"I guess he does. In any case, he can do nothing to me about that now," replied Noy, but his tone lacked conviction.

For a few minutes he sat lost in his own thoughts. From the expression on his face it was evident to Vereker that there was something on his mind that was troubling him.

"There's a question I'd like to ask you, Mr. Vereker," he said at length, "but you needn't answer it unless you like."

"Put the question, Mr. Noy, and I'll soon let you know," replied Vereker eagerly.

"Did the inspector mention my name in connection with some trouble at Doncaster some time ago?" queried Noy and looked at Vereker with anxious eyes.

"No, he didn't, but don't persuade yourself that he's ignorant of it because he didn't mention it to me. What was the nature of the trouble?"

"If you don't know, I'm not the man to tell you. I daresay the police ferreted that out when they were going into my past history in America," replied Noy, and by turning the conversation on to the well that he was having sunk behind his bungalow, indicated that his secret was not going to be wrested from him.

A little later, on Noy's invitation, Vereker accompanied him to the well shaft and inspected the progress that had been made in that operation. Feeling that no more information was to be gained by prolonging his visit, he bade Noy good-morning and took his departure.

On returning to Old Hall Farm, he learned from one of the maids that Ricardo had rung him up on the telephone during his absence. Ricardo had given no message, but said he would ring up again about lunch-time. The maid had hardly left Vereker when the telephone bell rang again, and he answered it himself.

"That you, Algernon?" came the query.

"Yes, Ricky, anything important? Where are you?"

"London. I've made thumping good progress and am returning to Yarham to-morrow."

"Seen Miss Garford?"

"Not yet, but when I do I'll put her through a mild form of third degree. I'll tell you all about that when I see you."

"D'you think she has any connection with this Yarham case?"

"At present I see no connection myself, but when you bring your amazing powers to bear on the matter, perhaps you'll spot the connection."

"Good. I want you to do another job for me at once, Ricky. Go along to the British Museum Reading Room and get permission to hunt through the newspaper files. Go back two or three years. Our friend Ephraim Noy got into some trouble at Doncaster some time back, and it may have been reported in the London Press. If it was at all valuable from a news point of view, you're almost certain to run across it. Copy it out and bring it along with you. So long. I'll see you to-morrow."

"Right-ho!" came Ricardo's reply. "I'll get on with the job right away. I'll just have time to finish it and take Gertie Wentworth out to Crawley for tea. She thinks my car's quite a dandy projectile. Good-bye!"

Vereker had hardly laid down the receiver when the front door bell rang, and a few minutes later the Rev. William Sturgeon was ushered in.

"I thought I'd call and see how you were getting on, Vereker," he said. "Solved the Yarham mystery yet?"

"Not quite, but I've made a little progress. It's about lunch-time. Will you stay and lunch with me?"

"My dear boy, that's what I came for. Timed it beautifully," replied the rector with his boyish laugh. "Old Hall Farm always puts up an attractive meal, and on the quiet, I'm a bit of a gourmet. Heard from Miss Thurlow?"

"No; have you?"

"She never writes to me. When is she coming back?"

"I'm not quite certain. By the way, Rector, do you know the lady very well?"

"Yes, I think I can say I do. I knew her parents, too. Why do you ask?"

"Is there any mental trouble in the family?"

"Nothing very serious. Her mother, you know, suffered from minor epilepsy. That's bad enough, but it didn't affect her general health to any degree. She was all right as long as she took care of herself and lived quietly. I think they call the trouble *petit mal*."

"Has Miss Eileen any tendency that way?" asked Vereker anxiously.

"Never shown any to my knowledge. Old Cornard thinks it may develop. That's why I've tried to get her to discontinue this cult of spiritualism. It will do her no good. But she's rather a strong willed young lady, and in some things it's useless to advise her. She goes her own way in spite of everyone."

For some minutes Vereker was lost in thought. His mind had reverted to the strange apparition of the night before and its general resemblance to the height and build of Miss Eileen Thurlow. He had, of course, only seen that figure in the gloom of an unlighted room, and yet the resemblance had struck him forcibly. But he could not, by any stretch of imagination, see why Eileen Thurlow should carry out this ridiculous deception. Against his theory that it might be she, was the incontrovertible evidence afforded by the finger prints he had discovered on certain ornaments and articles of furniture, after a previous visit of what Eileen Thurlow had called a "poltergeist." Those finger prints were certainly not hers and could hardly have been faked. Faked finger prints were in the same category as faked footprints, a very remote possibility.

"Hello, what have you got here?" suddenly asked the rector, his exclamation rousing Vereker rudely from his reverie.

"Oh, that book; it's a history of the village. My friend Ricardo, while he was here, picked it out when looking over the books in Thurlow's library."

"And I've been on the track of this volume for ages. It's long since out of print and has no value, but it gives a very full history of the village, especially of my church. Are you reading it?"

"When I had nothing else to do, I dipped casually into it, but it'll be of more interest to you than me."

"I'll borrow it if I may. Miss Thurlow wouldn't mind, and I'll let her have it back when I've finished with it."

The rector relapsed into silence as he pored over the pages of his discovery. After a few minutes he began to fidget excitedly in his chair and then, unable to contain himself any longer, remarked: "So that's the truth about the tunnels leading from the church!"

The exclamation at once roused Vereker to attention. The history of those tunnels had intrigued him considerably for some time, but for reasons quite different from the rector's.

"What does it say?" he asked eagerly.

"That there are three tunnels leading from the crypt at the foot of the stone steps. The writer explored two of them; the one leading to the right and the one leading directly ahead from the central vault. The central one leads to Riswell Manor. This I knew. The one to the right to Old Yarham Hall. The third tunnel was not explored."

"Where is Old Yarham Hall?" asked Vereker.

"This house is the old hall or manor. When the Honington family died out, it became a farm and then got its present name, 'Old Hall Farm.' Subsequently its fortunes went up in the world and it reverted to a country house, which it has been ever since."

"By jove, that's most interesting!" exclaimed Vereker in undisguised excitement.

"It is, and to think that that man Orton has put an end to my idea of exploring those underground passages. He's an obstructionist of the worst type."

"Why? What has happened?

"He organized the villagers into petitioning me to have restored the brick wall that I was demolishing. I kicked against it at first, but when they threatened to take the matter further afield, I reluctantly agreed to have it rebuilt. There's a man on the job now."

"Pity!" agreed Vereker, "but I don't think you'd have discovered King John's treasure there. You've not lost much, Rector. You've got the history complete except for one tunnel."

"Yes, but that blessed tunnel will worry me for the rest of my life. It'll keep me awake at night thinking of what it may conceal. Apart from royal treasure, there may be priceless church plate hidden away in it."

"Why don't you suggest that the wall be demolished and a stout wooden door put in its place. That would serve the purpose of plugging the entrance almost as well as a wall," suggested Vereker.

"Now I hadn't thought of that. A splendid ideal But, alas, where are the funds to come from? I can't afford to have the wall replaced by a stout door," complained the rector with a hopeless air.

"Look here, Padre, if you're going to spend sleepless nights for the rest of your life over that tunnel, I'll foot the bill, provided you can get the consent of the authorities and the goodwill of the parishioners. It'll be my contribution to your next Easter offering."

"This is most generous of you, Vereker, most generous, and I'm very grateful," said the rector beaming with pleasure. "I hope you didn't think I was cadging for assistance when I referred to the operation being beyond my means."

"Not at all," replied Vereker. "I'm interested in that blessed tunnel myself."

"Because I'm so used to cadging that I do it unconsciously now," added the rector with a broad grin. At this moment the gong sounded for lunch, and rising to his feet with alacrity he exclaimed, "I've been waiting for that. Not one moment too soon. Hungry as a hunter, too. This is one of my lucky days. Everything going along merrily in the right direction. It's really good to be alive!"

After lunch the Rev. Sturgeon, taking the history of Yarham with him, set out for Church Farm to interview Mr. Arthur Orton and suggest the erection of a stout wooden door to serve the purpose of the brick wall in the crypt. Vereker, after a brief rest, called at "The Walnut Tree" in the hope of finding Heather. In this he was unsuccessful, for Heather had just left the inn to meet the local inspector. As he stood talking to Benjamin Easy at the bar, the burly figure of Joe Battrum lurched unsteadily in and demanded a pint of mild and bitter.

"No, Joe, can't be done. You've had enough and that's saying a mighty lot," replied Ben firmly.

"Can't be done?" stuttered Joe, staring with wild, bloodshot eyes at the landlord.

"No. Can't be done. You take my advice Joe and get along home. Best place for you."

"Go to hell!" exclaimed Joe, and without further argument, turned round and staggered out of the inn.

"Battrum has caught the brewer early in the day," remarked Vereker.

"Yes, and he'll be back again before long. Either he's as obstinate as a pig or he forgets I've refused to serve him. Not often Joe has one over the eight, but when he does he's a confounded nuisance."

"Gets pugnacious, I suppose," remarked Vereker.

"Yes, and he seems half mad. This morning he was sitting alone in the tap-room, talking to himself about seeing ghosts at Church Farm. I don't think he's very strong in the head. Said something about going to chuck up his job, but I dessay he'll think better of it in the mornin'. They allus do."

Shortly after this incident, Vereker left the inn. As he paced back along the road, his thoughts reverted to the rector's discovery in "The History of Yarham" that one of the tunnels from the church led to Old Hall Farm. At the moment he had at once guessed that that tunnel, if the historian's statement were correct, would probably account for the mysterious organ music which had been ascribed by Miss Thurlow to spirit manifestation. To add force to this theory, that music had begun to manifest itself, according to Miss Thurlow's statement, towards the end of May of that year, and this date corresponded with that of the piercing of the brick wall by the Rev. Sturgeon in his archaeological activities. The sole argument against this theory was the organist's denial of having played the organ on the nights of the manifestation. Vereker decided to make further and stricter inquiries on this detail, now that a rational explanation of the phenomenon had presented itself. The existence of such a tunnel, too, would elucidate the mystery of the secret entry and exit used by some person as yet unknown in playing, first the poltergeist and later, a ghostly apparition. The pressing problem now was to discover where in Old Hall Farm the entrance to that tunnel lay. Once discovered, it might yield some definite information as to how John Thurlow disappeared prior to his murder. As he pondered on this point, it flashed on him with sudden illumination that Thurlow must have discovered that entrance to the tunnel when seeking a material explanation of the mysterious organ music.

"By jove, things are beginning to take shape at last!" he exclaimed and resolved to spend the remainder of the afternoon in a very careful exploration of Old Hall Farm.

On his return to the house he set to work, starting with the servants' wing which he had not yet thoroughly searched. When the dinner hour arrived, he had completed this portion of his task without any discovery. After dinner, though tired, he was about to resume his task when Inspector Heather called to see him. The inspector, in spite of his effort to suppress any sign of it, was unmistakably excited.

"Come along, Heather, cough it up. I can see by the sprightly tread and the upward twist of your moustaches that you're bursting to tell me something. Help yourself to a whisky and let it rip!"

"Things are beginning to happen, Mr. Vereker," replied Heather. "What do you think's the latest?"

"Don't keep me in suspense, Heather. I'm trembling to hear the latest."

"Well, I thought I'd run up to the bungalow this evening and put Mr. Ephraim Noy through a few mental jerks. I was going to give him a strenuous half-hour about his past life in America."

"Before you go any further, Inspector, can you tell me if Noy got into any trouble up at Doncaster in Yorkshire some time back?"

"Yes, he did, but it wasn't anything very serious, that is, serious in comparison with the crime of murder. He was collared by the excise authorities for being in possession of illicit spirits. On searching his rooms they found a small spirit still and a barrel of wash. The Government chemist analysed a sample and reported it to be crude stuff, real fire water. Noy was fined heavily, and paid the fine in lieu of going to prison for six months. You see, he had gone back to his American tricks. It had become a bad habit with him."

"Does that sort of distillation pay?" asked Vereker.

"You bet it does. Spirits made in such a way cost only half a crown a gallon at the most. The workers in an industrial area like whisky, but can't afford to buy it at present prices. The illicit distiller can manage to get a return of a pound for every bob he spends. The game is so profitable that it is increasing at an alarming rate. In 1934 the Customs and Excise made a big haul in Edmonton, another up at Skipton in Yorkshire and another at Hampstead. In 1936 at Liverpool and at Sheffield."

"Thanks, this is most interesting information, but what about our friend Noy? Have you caught him at the liquor game again?"

"No. I went up to the bungalow with malice prepense. To my surprise the front door of the shack was wide open. I knocked but got no answer. Then I strolled round the garden to make sure that Ephraim wasn't among the gooseberry bushes. Returning to the bungalow, I took the liberty of walking right in. Not a soul about the place. I entered the living-room and found it in a state of terrible disorder. Chairs upset, table knocked over, broken crockery all over the floor and splashes of blood on the floor and wallpaper.

"And did you find Noy's dead body?" asked Vereker, unable to restrain his impatience.

"No, not a sign of Noy. Whatever had happened, he had vanished. There had evidently been a terrible struggle and serious wounds inflicted, judging from the quantity of blood about."

"I saw and spoke to him this morning," explained Vereker. "He was all right then, though rather disturbed at the idea of a further police interrogatory. He was frank enough with me about his doings in America and hinted that you probably knew all about his exploits at Doncaster. It's a rum business. What do you think has happened, Heather?"

"God knows," replied Heather.

"Do you think someone has done him in and removed the body?" asked Vereker.

"That explanation struck me as probable. Again, there may only have been a desperate fight, and Noy has made himself scarce. It probably has some connection with this Yarham business. I've always thought that Noy was implicated in it. I didn't quite like the man's story of his discovery of the bodies of Thurlow and Martin. Godbold, the local constable, was of the same opinion, and he's a shrewd chap is Godbold. No frills or fancies about him. Godbold's line is hard facts!"

"He'd appeal to you, Heather," remarked Vereker with a smile. "Relying on my stupidly unorthodox methods, I can't at present connect up Noy with the Yarham murders. Tell me just how you arrived at your theory that he had a finger in the pie."

"I think I've got a little clue to his connection," replied Heather complacently. "You'd call it an evidentiary item. Evidentiary was always one of your favourite words. It used to annoy me till I got used to your funny habits."

With this remark, Heather produced from his pocket a sheet of note-paper and handed it to Vereker.

"Have a squint at that and tell me what you think of it," he added.

Vereker read the note, which ran: "Situation getting worse. Advise you to clear out."

"By jove, Heather, I apologize. This has some indirect bearing on our case. It's written in exactly the same block capitals as the note found on Clarry Martin's body. What are you going to do about it?"

"I've sent out a message to all stations round to keep a look out for Noy. I've given them a description of the man, and he's such a striking figure that you could spot him in a Derby crowd. Once we lay hands on Uncle Sam, as you called him, things'll begin to hum."

"Possibly, and possibly not," commented Vereker quietly, "but I wish you luck, Heather. By the way, when we made our usual bet, I didn't stipulate the size of the cask of beer that I was prepared to pay for. I now make it nine gallons."

"Nine gallons be hanged! Nothing less than thirty-six will liquidate your debt, Mr. Vereker."

"I'll risk it, Heather. Make it thirty-six, but you must make your packet of 'Players' into a fifty box."

"Agreed," replied Heather. "You seem confident of winning, Mr. Vereker. Made any new discoveries?"

"Several important ones. I believe I've discovered the explanation of the spirit music heard by Thurlow and his niece on the night of Thurlow's disappearance. I'm not quite certain, but I think I've spotted the mysterious musician. I've an inkling as to how Thurlow vanished from the house without the trouble of dematerializing. Then there's the poltergeist to be explained away, and since I spoke to you last I've seen a ghost."

"Great Scott!" exclaimed Heather. "I see you're going to make a thorough ass of yourself in this case, Mr. Vereker. What with a poulterer's ghost, spirit music, and seeing spooks, I don't know what's come over you. You used to be quite sensible, too, in some things. By the way, if you'd like to have a look at the mess in Noy's bungalow, you'd better do so now. I can let you have the key to the place. I locked up everything and brought the keys with me. You might pick up a few hints that would put you on the right track, instead of wasting your time on spooks. Might I ask when and where you saw your last spectre?"

"In this very study, Heather. I had fallen asleep and was wakened by a flash of light on my face. I wasn't particularly anxious to see a ghost, but when I opened my eyes and got used to the darkness, I spotted her. It was certainly a woman. I reckoned that the lady was going to run through the poltergeist programme once more, and having flashed a small electric torch round the room, was surprised to see me asleep in this easy wicker chair. She must have heard me move, and it must have disclosed to her that I had wakened and was taking notice. She, therefore, stood deadly still for a few moments, probably stiff with fright at the thought of being discovered. I put my hand in my pocket for my electric torch, but remembered I'd left it on the hall table earlier in the evening. There was nothing for it but to try and reach the electric light switch on the other side of the room. I was sitting by the window, you see. I made a desperate bound to get to that switch, but she was gone like a flash. I didn't see her go, because I was intent on getting at the electric light switch without crashing into any of the furniture. I'm pretty certain, however, that she slipped through the half-open door. I stepped into the dark passage outside immediately and was quite certain that I heard the sound of scurrying footsteps below. I jumped to the conclusion that she had made her way into the wine cellar, and I scuttled down after her as fast as I could. I was either too late or had taken the wrong turning, for she wasn't in the cellarage."

"So you knocked the neck off a bottle to get over your disappointment, I suppose," commented Heather airily.

"I felt like it, I can assure you. Anyhow, I'd made a thorough botch of my job, and what's more I haven't got to the bottom of the mystery yet."

"It must have been a real ghost after all, Mr. Vereker," said the inspector with mock gravity. "But about this key to Noy's bungalow. Are you going to take it and have a look around the place?"

"No, Heather, I'm not. I'm not very much interested in Ephraim Noy's exploits at the moment, though I may be more so, later. I'd only be poaching on your preserves. We've taken absolutely different lines in this case, and I don't think they are going to converge as they've done on some former occasions. But there goes the gong for dinner. You'd better stay and share it with me. There's always enough and to spare."

"Thanks, I will. Anything good to drink?"

"What would you like?"

"Anything but lime-juice and its nasty relations. About this woman in white you saw. What was she like? Did she resemble any of the servants or any woman in the village?"

"It was too dark to see her features. It's strange that you should have asked me that question, Heather, because I've been very much troubled by the cut of the intruder. I can't explain why, but it struck me that she bore a strong resemblance to Miss Thurlow. She was about the same height, and the pose was rather characteristic. Then I thought I smelt a faint trace of scent in the air, and that scent was certainly the same as Miss Thurlow's favourite brand. Mind you, this may be pure fancy on my part, and as for the scent, that's easily explained when you remember that Miss Thurlow uses this room a great deal."

"Oh yes, I spotted that scent on coming into the room this very evening. You can't make much out of that. And now I'm going to give you a helping hand. I hate to see a pupil floundering about on the wrong lines. To ease your mind, I can tell you that Miss Thurlow is in London. I had my suspicions about her sudden departure from Yarham, so I've had her kept under observation."

"Well I'm jolly thankful for the information, Heather. I'm rather favourably impressed by Miss Eileen Thurlow, and I'd hate to think she had any hand in this ghost business."

"Then that's satisfactorily settled, but don't let your favourable impressions get any stronger. You've been in the danger zone before, rather too frequently in my opinion, and it would never do for an amateur detective to fall in love. It's against all the rules of the game, even in detective yarns."

"I don't read them, so I don't profess to know. Now I think we'll go into the dining-room."

"And discuss the right kind of spirits over our grub," concluded Heather as he gave an extra twirl to his pointed moustaches.

Chapter Fifteen

Next day, about noon, Ricardo arrived in his car at Old Hall Farm. He looked tired from his recent activities and the strain of the journey, but greeted Vereker with his usual perky cheerfulness.

"You're looking excited about something, Algernon. I'm not conceited enough to think it's at my return," he remarked as he glanced at Vereker, who was standing at the entrance to Old Hall Farm with a measuring tape in his hand.

"I've made a momentous discovery, Ricky," replied Vereker with a preoccupied air.

"That's a habit with me. I make several every day. This morning when I was shaving, I found that my ears weren't in alignment. 'Manuel,' I exclaimed, 'you're a monstrosity,' and the thought depressed me till breakfast time. I forgot all about it after my second egg, which was bad, but it'll recur every time I look in a mirror. I hardly dare brush my hair now."

"Never mind your ears, Ricky. Come into the study and see my discovery for yourself," said Vereker, and led the way to that room.

There, taking his tape measure, he measured the floor from the eastern and inner wall to the western outer wall.

"Twenty-four feet, six inches, Ricky!" he exclaimed.

"Frightfully interesting, Algernon. Now, I'd have sworn it was only twenty-four feet, five and a half inches. It just shows you how easily you can be mistaken."

"The joke's rather moth-eaten, Ricky. The length of the room is twenty-four foot six, but if you measure the wall outside, from the junction of the inner dividing wall to the gable of the house, it's twenty-nine feet. What do you make of it?"

"The calculation's abstruse, but there's a difference of four feet six inches. I was always dux when it came to what was called mental arithmetic."

"It means that there's a space of four feet, six inches between the wainscoting and the facing bricks outside. In my opinion that wall cannot be solid."

"Well, don't get upset about it. What does it matter? It's not your wall anyway, Algernon."

"There's a secret passage in that wall, Ricky, and I'm going to find the entrance to it."

"A secret passage? Where on earth will it lead to?"

"The church, I think."

"But no one would want to go to church by a secret passage. Church-goers must be seen. It's the outward and visible sign of the inward and spiritual grace, especially in rough weather. That's why I never go when it's fine..."

"To change the subject, I believe you've got some important news for me," interrupted Vereker.

"Stunning news, Algernon. You can't guess what's happened."

What?" asked Vereker, looking up with a shade of anxiety on his face.

"I'm engaged."

"What, again? Who's the victim this time?"

"I am, of course. I proposed to Gertie Wentworth and she has accepted me."

"But, Ricky, surely you haven't wasted your time..."

"Algernon, how can you be so stupid! She's fabulously rich and she's simply crazy about me."

"She's simply crazy, you mean. Haven't you done the job I asked you to?"

"Of course! I took that in my stride, so to speak. Firstly, about that business of Noy's. I copied out the police court proceedings from the *Daily Report.*"

"You needn't trouble about that now. I've found out all about it from Heather. Anything about Dawn Garford?"

"Amazing news of that young woman. Let me tell you the story without interrupting me peevishly. I was waffling along very pleasantly and had nearly reached Braintree, when I felt thirsty for the first time. I stopped at a roadside inn, and on entering the saloon bar, there was Miss Dawn. She was just coming out, figuratively wiping her mouth on the back of her hand. I simply necked my beer, and as she got away in her car, I stepped into 'Gladys.' Dawn took the road running west to Dunmow, and keeping well in her rear, I followed her as far as Chipping Ongar."

"Splendid!" ejaculated Vereker.

"That splendid's a bit premature. At Chipping Ongar she stopped once more, at a tea-shop this time. I didn't tittup after her in case she spotted me. Besides, I didn't want tea. I hied me to the nearest pub, where I got into an animated argument with a very pretty barmaid. We debated whether a pretty woman should use face powder. The subject is whiskered, but it somehow appeared dewy fresh at the time. She said powder was a necessity, and I suggested that in using it she was merely powdering the lily. It wasn't anything cataclysmic in the way of a compliment, but she blushed so coyly that I ordered another drink. From this pub s window I could see the tea-shop that Dawn had patronized. I ought to have kept my eyes glued on that shop instead of talking poppycock to Hebe. After another spot of lubricant, I glanced across at the tea-shop and found that Dawn's car had gone. I didn't see her again..."

"I might have expected that," interrupted Vereker dismally.

"Let me finish my sentence, Algernon. I didn't see her again till I reached London. Having lost track of her, I dismissed the subject from my mind, and late that night, I looked in at the Blue Bottle Club. To my unbounded delight, she was among the crowd of dancers. It was just my astonishing luck. I immediately put on my pair of dark spectacles as an impenetrable disguise. By the way, I must really carry a false beard on future occasions. A blond beard, I think. However, Dawn spotted me and, doubtless thinking it funny that the gent she had met near Braintree should reappear at the Blue Bottle, hurriedly left. But not before I'd pointed her out to Poppy Knatchbull. 'You don't mean to say you know her?' asked Poppy. 'She's Mrs. Button, alias Miss Dawn Garford,' I replied. Then Poppy waxed confidential. 'Ricky, have nothing to do with her; she's a dangerous lot,' she warned me. Poppy, by the way, thinks I'm a nice, ingenuous boy and always tries to play the guardian angel to me. I like to be mothered and encourage her propensity. I told her I was rather infatuated with this Miss Garford. She warned me again, but wouldn't give me any reason why I should be so cruel. To get the secret from her, I became heroic and said I was determined to marry the lady or perish in the attempt. I tried to look like a sheep and got a most effective bleat into my voice. This wrung her heart, and at last she told me that Miss Garford was a tout for 'hooch.' 'Hooch,' I believe, is Americanese for illicit drink, stuff that has escaped paying excise duty. You can imagine my astonishment, but I had to continue the role of boob, and said I couldn't and wouldn't believe it. As a last resource, Poppy took me into her office and, after swearing me to secrecy, she corroborated her story by producing a little sample of hooch that Miss Garford had left for her consumption. We necked it together."

"That's most satisfactory, Ricky. Sorry I was impatient with you," said Vereker, his eyes beaming with excitement.

"Next day I blew in at Gertie Wentworth's flat in Clarges Street. As I told you before, it's in the same block as Miss Garford's, in fact, the flat below hers. They're palatial flats, and the rent of one would keep me in dissipation for a year. So now you can see how Miss Garford pays her way. I don't know whether this discovery is vital to your work, but it's interesting per se."

"Has this Poppy Knatchbull bought any of the stuff from her?" asked Vereker.

"Not on your life, Algernon. Poppy's much too eelish to run her pretty neck into that noose. She says that it's only a matter of time till the game's found out, and she's not going to have the 'Blue Bottle' struck off the register for the sake of a little extra profit. It wouldn't pay her. She keeps strictly to the letter of the law. All her members are respectable people with reputations to lose, apart from their money. I'm one myself, without the money. It was now my turn to play the guardian angel, and I solemnly warned her to have nothing to do with such a risky enterprise. In fact, I said I was going to make a scoop of it by blowing the gaff to the Press. I went further. To ease her conscience, I confessed I'd known the secret all the time, and if she'd been ignorant of it I was going to warn her. Elated with my success, I proposed to Gertie Wentworth next day. That's the worst of success; it breeds success. I'm rather regretting it now. It's rather humiliating for a man of my principles to marry money. But there, our moral judgments are invariably on a higher plane than our lives!"

"Don't worry about it. You've never got further than an engagement before, and history ought to repeat itself if it's a friend of yours."

"History has always been kind to me, but chiefly in the matter of making dates. Now I've got that off my chest, what's this obsession of yours about a secret passage, Algernon?"

"That reminds me, the rector has borrowed the book you were reading on the history of Yarham. A chapter on the village church in that book says that one of three secret passages runs from the crypt to Yarham Old Hall, this house. If you consider it for a moment you'll see that it goes a long way to explain the strange organ music we've heard. The tunnel evidently broadcasts the sound. Get me?"

"By jingo, Algernon, I thought I was right when I expressed the opinion that it had nothing to do with spiritual manifestation. Now you mention it, a similar thing happens somewhere else in England."

"Is it at Rodbourne Cheney in Wiltshire?" asked Vereker.

"That's the place. I read an account of it some time ago. What made you think of Rodbourne Cheney?"

"The rector mentioned it when speaking of these underground tunnels. Another fact which strengthens my belief in the origin of that music is that the 'manifestation' first occurred to Miss Thurlow at the end of May, at the very time that the rector pierced the wall sealing the entrance to the secret passage. Now we've got to find the outlet at this end."

"It may be sealed like the other end," suggested Ricardo.

"No, I don't think so. In fact, I'm certain it isn't."

"What makes you so sure?"

"While you've been away, I've had a ghostly visitor," explained Vereker and narrated to the wide-eyed Ricardo the details of that fantastic occurrence.

"You're sure it was a woman?" asked Ricardo.

"No doubt about it, Ricky."

"But how amusing! Sounds like a mediaeval intrigue between ye blacksmith's daughter and ye knight's son. What a pity you didn't catch her. I'd give something to collar a ghost. Look at the Christmas story it'd make! Let's get busy and find the entrance to that passage, Algernon."

"We'll start after lunch, if you're game," replied Vereker.

"Certainly. 'No sooner a word than a blow' is my motto. You've no idea who this woman is?"

"No; that's the most puzzling part of the whole affair. And why did she want to come here? If we could only hit on a motive, it might give us a pointer, but I see no motive."

"Poor girl, she probably thought I was still in residence! But let's get that grub. I only had a snatch breakfast this morning and I'm ravenous."

After lunch the two men returned to the study and rested for a while before commencing their search for the entrance to the secret passage. It was not long before Ricardo, after stifling several yawns, fell sound asleep in his chair. Vereker, without waking him, rose and once more began a very careful examination of the wainscoting along the western wall. The panels close to the study door especially engaged his attention, for it was at this point the "spectre" had stood before she had suddenly vanished. As his keen eye wandered over the old dark oak, it was arrested by a small disc-like insertion in the woodwork. That disc was about the size of a shilling and so neatly fitted that it was scarcely perceptible. Even the grain of its wood had been made to conform with the general grain of the panel's surface, rendering its detection almost impossible to anyone not searching for it. Filled with sudden excitement at this discovery, Vereker pressed the disc with his forefinger. To his amazement the whole panel into which that disc had been inserted, immediately moved away from him and left a double entrance, one on each side of it, into a narrow, dark passage beyond. Overwhelmed with astonishment, he called out loudly to Ricardo, still asleep in his chair:

"Ricky, wake up and come and look at this!"

"Hello, where the deuce am I?" asked Ricardo, opening his eyes and looking round with sleepy bewilderment.

"The question's a revelation as to your habits, Ricky," said Vereker, smiling at his friend's stupefaction. "Come here; I've got the blessed thing at last!"

Ricardo, now wide awake, jumped to his feet and joined Vereker. After looking at the panel for some moments, he asked: "How did you twig it, Algernon?"

"Just a chance in a hundred. I've looked carefully at that panel several times before, but never spotted the push, so discreetly has it been made to match the surface. Now let us see how we bring the panel flush with the rest of the wainscoting again."

"Get on the other side and push, I suppose," suggested Ricardo.

"There'll be some gadget for closing it from this side," remarked Vereker, and fell to examining the adjacent panels. After some trouble, he discovered another disc in the woodwork to the right and pressed it as he had pressed the first. At once the panel that had receded moved forward silently into position again, fitting so beautifully into the wainscoting that both Vereker and Ricardo stood lost in admiration.

"A choice example of the cabinet-maker's art! I think that's the correct description," remarked Ricardo. "What about a spot of exploration beyond, Algernon?"

"Just what I was thinking," replied Vereker.

"It would only be seemly if we both said, 'Open sesame,' when you touch the hidden spring, Algernon. We must work a little atmosphere round this adventure."

"You can do that, Ricky, by going to my investigator's case upstairs and getting a couple of electric torches, the batteries, and all the candles and matches. Also bring my two automatic pistols and some cartridges."

"What on earth do you want with pistols and cartridges?"

"They instil confidence when you're in a tight corner, Ricky."

"You wouldn't say so, if you knew what an erratic shot I was. When cornered, I blaze all round to prevent being taken in the flank or rear. But it'll be your funeral. And why candles when we've got electric torches?"

"You'll see later. Now beat it! We've got a lot of work ahead."

Without further comment, Ricardo vanished and a little later returned with the articles Vereker had specified. Vereker handed his friend one of the torches, a candle and matches, and finally a Colt. 45.

"You thoroughly understand the mechanism of that automatic?" he asked.

"You pull the trigger and it goes off, I presume," replied Ricardo.

"Yes, and you can keep firing till..."

"Algernon, I'll be serious. My flippancy's wasted on you. I know all about automatic pistols. Push the secret spring in the panel and let's get on with our job. I'm itching to know what's beyond."

A minute later both men had entered the gloomy little passage, Vereker leading the way. A few paces to the right led them to a narrow stone staircase which descended spirally for some twenty or thirty feet and brought them to another narrow and vaulted passage which ran straight ahead once more. They had only proceeded a few yards along this passage, when Vereker suddenly halted. At the base of the wall on his right, he had, as he flashed his torch about him, discovered a small rectangular iron grating.

"What's up, Algernon?" asked Ricardo.

"Nothing much. A ventilator," replied Vereker, and sinking on his knees, put his torch to the grating and peered through. "It's on the floor level of the wine cellar and under one of the wine bins. I can see the legs of the bins on the opposite side. A wonder I missed it from the cellar side, but even I'm fallible."

"So am I," agreed Ricardo with facetious heartiness, and added: "That accounts for the organ music being heard in the cellar, Algernon."

"Your first correct deduction in this case, remarked Vereker as he rose to his feet, "but let's get a move on, Ricky," and suiting action to words, began to push forward at a brisk pace.

For half an hour they made their way along the tunnel without encountering anything unusual until Vereker, suddenly feeling the ground soften under his foot, stood still and flashed his torch downwards.

"Getting damp underfoot," he said, and bent down to examine the earth. "Chalk, of course! I ought to have thought of that, and, by jove, the impression of a woman's shoe. Look and tell me what you make of it."

Ricardo, in turn, carefully examined the impression.

"Exceptionally small," he remarked. "I don't like tiny feet on a woman. I've made a profound study of women's feet and have always found that small feet, like small ears, denote spitefulness and envy. It's a right foot and there's the print of a left foot just ahead. The outside edge of each impression is deeper than the inside. Correct deduction number two; the fair spectre's slightly bandy-legged! There's also the impression of a man's foot, Algernon."

"Yes, I think that must be John Thurlow's. You're getting quite professional, Ricky. Anything else?"

"The lady wears high-heeled shoes. They disclose an amorous disposition. Flat feet for saints and simpletons. By the way, I don't dismiss slightly bandy legs as altogether unattractive. Their curvilinear grace has the charm of the unusual and appeals strongly to connoisseurs. By the right, quick march! The air here isn't conducive to bright generalizations."

At this point, Vereker produced from his pocket a compass and glanced at its dial.

"We're making for the church all right," he remarked, and turning round to Ricardo, added: "You might light one of your candles, Ricky. Attach it to this wire and keep it about two feet from the ground."

"What's the idea, Algernon?"

"Watch the flame of the candle and let me know if it shows any sign of guttering out. These underground tunnels sometimes contain gas, carbon dioxide. The candle's not a perfect test, but it'll do. A candle won't burn in choke-damp, as miners call it. Being heavier than air, it collects along the ground in greater density."

"Is it explosive?" asked Ricardo with some alarm.

"No, it's a narcotic poison and pretty deadly."

"Ah, well, that's not so bad. I'd rather be narcotized than blown up," remarked Ricardo in a calmer tone, and attaching the candle to the wire, he lit it and lowered it to the height that Vereker had specified.

After this operation, they trudged forward again at a slower pace till they reached a spot where a smaller tunnel diverged at right angles from the one they were traversing.

"This is getting interesting," remarked Vereker, and he had hardly uttered the words, when both men stood stock still with astonishment, for clearly audible somewhere ahead of them in the dark, was the sound of knocking and then the sharp ring of metal on some hard surface.

"Put out your torch and candle and listen," whispered Vereker.

For some minutes both stood with ears strained to catch the sounds they had just heard. After a brief period of intense silence the knocking was resumed.

"What do you make of it?" asked Ricardo at length.

"That's the sound of someone at work on the wall sealing the entrance to these tunnels from the crypt of the church. It definitely proves how the sound or the organ is carried along to Old Hall Farm. I'm glad we've settled that point," replied Vereker with a note of satisfaction.

"Great Scott! What the blazes is that?" suddenly asked Ricardo with alarm.

"What do you see?" asked Vereker calmly.

"See? Nothing, but something brushed against my feet!"

"I felt it too, Ricky, but don't get the wind up. It was only a large rat. I've seen several as we came along."

"Then let's get a move on. I bar rats polishing my shoes."

"I think we can light up again now," remarked Vereker, and added: "Let me see, looking from the crypt of the church, the tunnel we're in is on the right. This alley must be a connecting subway to the central tunnel. The question is, shall we go on or turn to the right? What do you think?"

"The scenery is so interesting that it's hard to choose. Where does the central tunnel lead?"

"Supposed to lead to Riswell Manor."

"Well, I've seen the church, so let's take a toddle to Riswell Manor."

"It's three miles away and they won't be expecting us," replied Vereker with a smile. "In the meantime, I'd like to explore this connecting passage, so we'll try it out."

After a spell of marching in single file, they eventually came upon another and larger tunnel into which the connecting passage debouched at right angles.

"Just as I thought," said Vereker, "the subway we're traversing cuts across the Riswell Manor tunnel and proceeds, I reckon, to tunnel number three."

"What's the terminus of number three?" asked Ricardo.

"It hasn't been explored in recent times. Even the writer of your history of Yarham throws no light on the subject."

"Then I vote for clearing up the mystery. It may not prove exciting, but it suggests a saleable magazine article to me. I'm a firm believer in money and money's worth. Go ahead!"

Crossing the major tunnel, they pushed steadily on for another quarter of an hour without speaking, and finally reached the third and ostensibly the last tunnel. Without halting Vereker turned to the right and pushed forward, with Ricardo following close on his heels.

"This adventure has cleared my mind on one thorny topic, Algernon," said Manuel at length.

"Then it has been worth while," remarked Vereker.

"Well worth while. It has absolutely settled for me the controversial subject of miners' wages. I'd give 'em a rise of five bob a shift from to-morrow onwards."

He had hardly spoken the words, when coming to a sudden halt, he exclaimed: "I say, Algernon, the candle seems a bit querulous. What's your opinion?"

"Must be some carbon dioxide about, but I'm going to push on. We're clearly nearing the end of the journey and I think we ought to risk it. Besides, I've come across the impression of that lady's shoe again, and where she ventured, we can go."

"Oh, definitely, Algernon, definitely! I'd forgotten her, but the recollection revives my interest. A woman is always charmingly mysterious, but a mysterious woman is simply irresistible."

Another hundred yards brought Vereker to a standstill.

"We've arrived at last!" he exclaimed with a note of excitement, and as the tunnel at this point opened out into a fairly large chamber, Ricardo came abreast of him.

"Decidedly whiffy, Algernon, and the candle has gone out," he remarked.

"So I see. We mustn't linger too long in case we're overcome, but we must make a rapid inspection."

"Strange smell about the place. What is it, and what on earth is that large wooden tub?" asked Ricardo.

"Just what I expected," said Vereker, as if speaking to himself. "The strange odour comes from that tub. That tub is used for fermenting wort or wash, and is technically called a wash back."

He had hardly spoken the words, when he stumbled over something and nearly fell. Recovering his balance he quickly flashed his torch on the floor and discovered that the object over which he had tripped was a heavy baulk of timber very much decayed at one end. Swiftly examining it, he noticed that it had recently been broken off at the rotten extremity. A further search disclosed a stump, sunk into the chalk floor of the chamber, and, judging from its fractured end, obviously a portion of the balk. He was on the point of crossing the chamber to the wooden vat, when he uttered an exclamation of jubilant surprise and stooped to pick up some objects from the floor.

"What's the treasure, Algernon?" asked Ricardo eagerly.

"A cap and some pieces of rope. This is stupendous! Shove the cap into your pocket and take charge of these strands of rope. Don't lose them for heaven's sake; they're priceless clues," replied Vereker as he handed his finds to his companion.

"That vat intrigues me, Algernon. What's in it?" asked Ricardo.

"Probably empty, but have a look while I examine the wall of this chamber. Don't make any noise and talk in a whisper or we may be heard and discovered."

Ricardo crossed to the vat and noticing a small ladder leaning against it, made a cautious ascent. He flashed his torch into the vessel only to find that it was empty. When he had satisfied his curiosity, he descended once more to discover that Vereker, with a jack knife in his hand, was cutting away lumps of chalk from the wall of the chamber.

"What the devil are you up to, Algernon?" he asked.

"Got it!" replied Vereker mysteriously as he extracted some object from the hole he had excavated and thrust it quickly into his pocket. "Now, come on, Ricky; this place isn't healthy. Let's go into the still room," he added, and swiftly passed through a narrow and rising passage into a further chamber, with his companion close behind.

"What in the name of Smith..." began Ricardo excitedly, when Vereker cautioned him to speak in a whisper, and added:

"You'd better take the safety catch off your automatic and be ready to shout, 'Stick 'em up,' to any intruder. If we can make an examination and get away without being interrupted, so much the better."

"I prefer "Hands up' to 'Stick 'em up,' Algernon; it's shorter and more dignified," whispered Ricardo, "but for heaven's sake tell me what those pear-shaped grotesques are."

"They're stills for distillation. One's a wash still and the other a spirit still. They were probably erected ages ago, but they're still in working order. Now, stand-to with that automatic while I have a look at 'em."

With these words Vereker clambered on to the brick furnace of the wash still and closely examined a piece of mechanism fixed near the apex of the pear-shaped vessel.

"Ricky," he whispered with unmistakable glee, "I've found that the soap box is broken!" Jumping once more to the ground, he turned his attention to a small glass tank near the spirit still. After a brief inspection of this receptacle, he added, "And that the spirit taps need new washers."

For a few seconds he stood still, his electric torch flashing hither and thither in front of him. Then, darting forward, he seized a square object in his hand, and bringing it across to Ricardo, remarked: "Just the very thing we need. A small attaché case. There are some copper-smith's tools in it, but you can squeeze in the cap and strands of rope. Get a move on, old boy."

Ricardo, producing the articles mentioned, hurriedly thrust them into the attaché case and closed it.

"Now let's beat it, Ricky," said Vereker with a swift final glance round the chamber.

"Anything to oblige, I'm sure," replied Ricardo and following the excited Vereker, dashed back into the adjoining chamber.

Thence they rapidly made their way into the tunnel from which they had emerged, and keeping up a brisk walking pace, returned without further adventure to Old Hall Farm. On entering the study once more and closing the secret panel behind him, Vereker, breathless with excitement, sank lazily into an easy chair. Ricardo, even more breathless, wearily dropped the attaché case he was carrying on the floor, and flung himself full length on a divan.

"Something attempted, something done," he muttered, "has usually earned me a sleepless night wondering whether an editor would reject it, but I hope you're satisfied with our little exploit of this afternoon, Algernon."

"My work on the Yarham murders is nearly complete. One or two more moves of the pieces and I think I'll be able to say, 'Checkmate,'" replied Vereker, who was sitting with his eyes fixed in an unfocussed stare, as if deep in thought.

"I know you're very grateful and so forth, Algernon, but don't trouble to thank me. It's all in a day's work, so to speak. It gives me great pleasure to have achieved this result so easily," said Ricardo airily.

At this moment the maid entered and asked Vereker if he would like tea.

"Please, Raymer, and we'll just have it in here, if it's no trouble."

"No trouble at all, sir," replied the maid and disappeared. On her return, she said that Inspector Heather had arrived and would like to see Mr. Vereker.

"Show him in, Raymer, and bring another cup and saucer. The inspector will have tea with us."

A minute later, Heather had entered the room.

"Well, Heather, how goes it? Got your man, Ephraim Noy, yet?" asked Vereker cheerily, for the inspector's face was graver than usual.

"Not a trace of him so far. It looks as if one of his old confederates has bumped him off and disposed of the body," replied Heather.

"That's possible. Anything might happen to a man like Noy. I'm sorry he has vanished. We shall certainly want him later."

"Have you heard the latest Yarham news, Mr. Vereker?" asked Heather with a note of eagerness.

"No; I haven't been in the village. Ricardo and I have been very busy together in another direction. What's the news?"

"You've heard of a man called Joe Battrum?"

"Yes; one of Orton's men. What has he been up to?"

"His body was found in the pond behind his cottage, early this morning. He has been drinking very heavily of late. I've seen his wife, and she said he hadn't been sober for two days. Last night, after threatening to do her in, and muttering all the time that he was being haunted by ghosts, he left the house. She thought he'd gone across to the pub for more liquor, but Easy says he didn't call at 'The Walnut Tree.' He failed to return home, and early this morning, a neighbour going to the pond, found his body. His feet and legs were on the bank and his head in less than a foot of water. It might have been an accident, but to me it looks more like suicide."

"Very strange, but I'm not surprised," remarked Vereker. "His suicide, for I feel pretty certain it was suicide, may have some connection with our case."

"I don't see how you make that out," remarked the inspector, looking up with sharply roused curiosity.

"It's only surmise on my part, Heather—another of my intuitions. Now I've got some very startling news for you. I hope you've got a pair of handcuffs ready and also a box of fifty cigarettes," said Vereker quietly.

"They'll be ready in due course," replied the inspector, "but don't keep the news too long to yourself, or it'll get stale."

"It's a long story all about the Yarham case, so make yourself comfortable. Bit by bit, I've pieced the fragments of the case together, and this afternoon I approached the climax."

"Anything to do with spooks?" asked Heather with an attempt at ridicule.

"Yes; spooks and spirits come largely into the yarn. After we had begun our work on this affair, the first thing that set me thinking seriously was Miss Thurlow's story of the mysterious music she and Thurlow had heard on the night of the latter's disappearance. In good faith, Miss Thurlow ascribed it to spirit manifestation. Though I'm interested in spiritualism, I couldn't quite swallow that theory. All along I've been seeking a material explanation of the mystery. To-day, thanks to my scepticism, we've solved it. You'll remember that after Thurlow left this house for good, next morning the maid found all the doors of the house locked and only the window of this room open?"

"That was the maid's yarn," said Heather. "To explain it away Miss Thurlow had some fanciful idea about her uncle being able to decompose. Was that the word?"

"Dematerialize was her word. Neither you nor I thought much of the dematerialization idea, and yet neither of us could see why he should have left by the window. Personally, I felt certain he hadn't left the house by the window, and if all the doors were locked next morning, there was only one conclusion possible. He must have departed by some secret exit."

"We have no proof that he was good enough for translation," remarked Ricardo, shaking his head gravely.

"Once I had conceived that idea," continued Vereker, after telling Ricardo to "shut up," "there came along a possible confirmation that it was correct. In the district it's well known that there are underground tunnels radiating from the church to various points around. The rector was aware of this and was bent on exploring them. When I learned of their existence, I was convinced that therein lay a possible explanation of the organ music which Miss Thurlow and her uncle had heard, and which Ricardo and I were to hear subsequently. Now, in a book on the history of Yarham in Thurlow's library, the rector found that the legend of three tunnels running from the crypt in the church was correct. One led to Riswell Manor; the second to Yarham Old Hall, in other words, this house; and the third had not been explored by the writer of the book. When I knew that this house was connected by a tunnel with the church, all doubt about the origin of the organ music disappeared. I was quite certain that the tunnel carried the sound. The reason why that music has only manifested itself within the last three months can now be given. The rector only pierced the wall sealing the entrance towards the end of May. This corresponds with the date given us by Miss Thurlow of the first 'manifestation' heard by her. This spirit music and tunnel, however, seem minor factors in our case. Their significance can only be appreciated if you remember that through them Thurlow's mysterious disappearance can be accounted for rationally."

"I thought you'd found out that the organist hadn't practised on the nights when the music was heard," interrupted Heather.

"That's true, but if the organist didn't practise on those nights, someone else must have done so. This was a question I could easily have answered by exhaustive inquiry. For the time being it was irrelevant to me who had played the organ, and the discovery would have taken up too much precious time. You see, the mysterious organ music was only an indirect factor in the whole business. The cardinal factor was the tunnel by which Thurlow disappeared. If I could find that tunnel, I argued, I might find out where he went to after disappearing. My mind was very much preoccupied with the idea of that tunnel, when visitations by a poltergeist and a spectre, confirmed the fact that there was a secret entrance to it in this house. The spectre left finger-prints and footprints which put her beyond the region of the supernatural. You follow me clearly, Heather?"

Quite clearly," replied Heather, now deeply interested.

You've omitted to tell Heather of my brilliant deductions that the spectre was bandy-legged, wore high-heeled shoes, and had tiny feet," said Ricardo.

"You've supplied the omission, Ricky, and I can add that her shoes were size three. But now I must go back a little. On Martin's body was found a note, referring to a soap box being broken and also mentioning spirit taps. For a while, I accepted that note as being connected in some obscure way with the spiritualistic business on which Thurlow was engaged prior to his disappearance. From Martin's parents, I learned that Clarry Martin had never mentioned the subject of spiritualism to them. It was not a subject in which he was interested at all. This gave me my first shock. Then, when I was discussing the subject with Ricardo, he referred to spirit rapping, and assured me that spirit raps were a common feature of a séance. I noted that he did not call them 'taps,' and it at once suggested to me that spiritualism might not be the subject referred to in the note. From ethereal spirits to material spirits seemed at first a big jump. I was averse to taking it; it seemed too far fetched. Still, I bore it in mind. At this point, Heather, you will remember my discovery of a malted barleycorn embedded in the soft chalky clay adhering to Martin's boot."

"I certainly do. I christened it 'John.' I wondered at the time why you were so interested in that seemingly useless item. Now I gather that it bore some relation to your thoughts."

"Not at first, Heather. It fell into place subsequently. However, it gave me a sort of distant signal and I'm glad I didn't altogether disregard it. To return to the subject: having got an alternative translation of the word, 'spirits,' I kept my eyes open in that direction. I knew, and you confirmed it, that illicit distillation was becoming rife because it offered such large profits to the distillers. In spite of keen excise supervision, it's a most difficult kind of revenue leakage to discover. The process of distillation is childishly simple. It can be done on a fairly large scale in one room. Even a large kettle can be transformed into a spirit still without difficulty. In addition to all this, a sparsely inhabited county like Suffolk is, when you come to think of it, an ideal setting for such a business. Complete supervision over such an area is well-nigh impossible. The prime difficulty in illicit liquor traffic, however, is the distribution. I began to concentrate on the whole subject and wondered if I could find any trace of such traffic. At this time, too, the words 'soap box' suddenly jumped into my mind with a new meaning of cardinal significance. Some years ago, when I was painting in the Loch Lomond district, I visited a small distillery. It was what is called a pot-still distillery, to distinguish it from a patent or Coffey's still distillery. The latter is a much more scientific affair, though connoisseurs profess that the spirits produced by it lack flavour, owing to the absence of certain essential oils which are not eliminated by the older and simpler process. Now, in the old process there are two stills, one called a wash still, and the other, a spirit still. On one of the stills is a contraption called a soap box. This gadget was pointed out to me and I've never forgotten it."

"What's the nature of this bally soap box?" asked Heather.

"It's only a rectangular metal box into which a bar of ordinary castile soap is pushed. The hot liquid in the still melts the soap, and it forms a film of a fatty nature over the liquor in the still. The oily film prevents impurities in the wash being driven off in the spirit vapour. It's merely a clever filter and the soap, of course, never permeates the final spirit."

"What a memory, Algernon!" exclaimed Ricardo. "I always thank heaven that one of my greatest talents is a faculty for forgetting. I now see why you're a confirmed bachelor and a most miserable creditor."

"Having accounted for the soap box in that note, the words 'spirit taps' at once took on their correct interpretation," continued Vereker, ignoring Ricardo's interruption.

"It looks very simple now," remarked Heather, "but it has been Greek to me ever since the note fell into my hands."

"Having definitely reached the conclusion that illicit distillation had some bearing on our case, I began to keep my eyes well skinned. Then a gorgeous bit of luck came my way. Miss Thurlow had asked me to give a message to Arthur Orton of Church Farm. I called one afternoon as they were loading a motor lorry with sacks of barley. For a few minutes I watched Joe Battrum flinging up the sacks on to the lorry, while Sandy Gow, his mate, put them into position. Suddenly Orton came out of the house with a couple of two-gallon petrol cans and handed them up to Gow who stowed them carefully under a sack. This operation was carried out with such an air of concealment, that my suspicions were immediately roused. I decided to bear the fact in mind and wait my chance. That chance came sooner than I expected. Before setting out on his journey with that lorry, Battrum called, the same night, at 'The Walnut Tree' and had a meal and a pint. I got Ricardo to keep Battrum busy while I had a lock at the load on the lorry. Ricky did his job well, and during that time, I substituted a two-gallon can of petrol from our car for one of those hidden under the sacks of barley. I have it here and will let you see it later, Heather. When we got back, I poured a little of the contents of that can into a saucer and set fire to it. It burned with a clear blue flame. It was not petrol, but spirit!"

"Well I'm hanged!" exclaimed Heather. "But go on with your yarn, Mr. Vereker."

"After reaching this point in my investigation, my thoughts reverted to those tunnels, and here came in the clue of the chalk on Thurlow's dress shoes. As the soil of this district is loam, with a subsoil of clay over-lying the chalk some twenty feet below, Thurlow must have gone down some distance to reach that chalk. What more reasonable than that he had been through that long sought tunnel. Chalk, you must remember, is a perfect medium for a tunnel. I've spent many hours trying to find the entrance from this house to that underground subway, and this afternoon, I hit upon it. The spectre which I had seen in this room, Heather, vanished mysteriously from a point near that study door, and I centred my search on the wainscoting near the door. Success attended my efforts at last, and I discovered the spring that works the panel masking the entrance to the tunnel. Before showing you that panel, Heather, I must here give my friend Ricardo his due for some work well done on my behalf. His work put the final corroborative touch to my conclusions."

"I like that corroborative touch, Inspector," interrupted Ricardo. "With my usual skill I absolutely put the tin hat on the whole business. In short, I reduced Algernon's vague fumblings after truth into something like Scotland Yard certainty. I know you'll understand me, so I won't say any more. Or shall I continue the thrilling story, Algernon?"

"Go ahead, Ricky, it'll give me a rest."

"You see, Heather, while Vereker was steeped in a study of spooks, I at once connected up with Miss Dawn Garford. I have an uncanny flair for getting hold of the right end of the stick, instanter. No shillyshallying, but one stark leap *in medias res*. Metaphors a bit mixed but they'll have to do. Miss Garford was so good looking that I suggested shadowing her to see what her little game was. Algernon concurred, probably to get me out of his way. After untold hardships and some very delicate and skilful work, I picked up the lady's car travelling south. At this point I knew that she had discovered that the relentless Ricardo was after her. She doubled on her tracks to throw me off the scent. I doubled on them too. We doubled and redoubled till it suggested to me a vital clue—whisky! Then, just to make the game more exciting, I let her go. This, of course, was pure subtlety on my part. It lulled her into the belief that she had given me the slip. You can imagine her consternation when I reappeared in immaculate evening dress before her eyes at a night club in London, the same evening. It must have given her a ghastly shock, but there, I like to dramatize life."

"What was the name of the night club, Mr Ricardo?" asked Heather.

"Seeing that its character is unimpeachable, I can tell you, Inspector; 'The Blue Bottle.'"

"I know it. Respectable so far," commented Heather.

"Therefore, so far, so good! Knowing the proprietress of this club, I immediately got into confidential conversation with her. To cut a long story short—I know you'll be disappointed, but I can't possibly reveal my methods to a professional rival—I elicited the fact that Miss Garford was touting illicit spirit to various clubs and road houses round London. This information was priceless to Algernon. It put mortar into the hands of a bricklayer who was standing gaping beside a pile of silly bricks. Immediately I divulged the secret to him, the air of frustration vanished from his face. He began to look like a human being with an aim in life. Sequel: after a little fiddling about with the wainscoting of this room, he discovered the entrance to the elusive tunnel. Resume Algernon, I'm dying for a cigarette after that sustained bit of narrative."

"Immediately we discovered the entrance, Ricardo and I promptly began our exploration."

"Not quite correct, Algernon. We lunched first. Accuracy is the handmaiden of truth and the fickle mistress of the liar. That's why I'm always beautifully vague," interrupted Ricardo.

"We tramped about a mile along the subway, which was leading us in the direction of the church," continued Vereker. "Then we came upon an inter-secting passage which connected it with the central tunnel to Riswell Manor, and finally to the tunnel which had never been explored. This last tunnel was the one I was eager to investigate. It finally brought us to the object of my whole quest, namely, the spot which Thurlow eventually reached after he had disappeared from Old Hall Farm. At this spot the tunnel opened out into two large chambers. The first, on lower ground, contained a large wash back for brewing the wort or liquor made from barley. This was an exciting discovery, but more was to follow. After tripping over a heavy timber baulk lying on the floor, I flashed my lamp about and came across a cap and some short strands of rope."

"Was it Thurlow's cap?" asked the inspector eagerly.

"I think we can definitely say it was. The strands of rope, one of which was still attached to the balk of timber, were probably the strands that bound Clarry Martin's wrists and ankles before he died."

"But the question is, what killed him?" remarked Heather.

"On this point I'm not certain, but I infer that he died from carbon dioxide poisoning. The gas still pervaded the chamber when we visited it, but it would have been in much greater density when the wort was brewing in the vat. When yeast is added to wort, it converts the sugar content into alcohol and throws off carbonic acid gas in the process. I have an idea Martin was tied to that heavy post, and in his struggles the post snapped off at the base and he fell with it. Carbonic acid gas being heavier than air naturally collects along the floor, and Martin, lying prostrate and unable to free himself from his ligatures, would soon succumb to its effects. Carbon dioxide, being a narcotic poison, would produce the symptoms discovered by your pathologist, namely cerebral congestion and apoplexy. Cases, however, are extremely rare, and that would account for the guarded nature of the doctor's report."

"That's sound enough. We can almost take it for granted that that's how Martin met his end," commented Heather.

"We then proceeded into the adjoining chamber which contained the stills. Here I discovered that my inferences about the note found on Martin were correct. The soap box was broken, and the spirit taps on the worm of the spirit still evidently needed new washers."

"What was the worm, Algernon?" asked Ricardo.

"The worm is a spiral lead pipe which runs from the apex of the spirit still through a tank of cold water. This process condenses the spirit vapour into liquor. One of the taps opened on to a small glass testing tank filled with clear water. If the spirit is sufficiently refined, it drips into the tank of water and makes no visible impression. If it's not pure enough, it turns the water milky. These details, however, are unnecessary. Just as we were about to leave, I caught sight of a case lying on the brick furnace of the spirit still. It contained tools, and I think I'm right in saying the attaché case belonged to Martin. He was carrying one on the night of his disappearance. And if you remember, Heather, Martin was apprenticed to a copper-smith before he took to the motor trade. Copper stills naturally come in the copper-smith's line of business."

"Splendid, Mr. Vereker, and now we come to the main point! Martin, on that night, was, so he said, going to see Mr. Arthur Orton about some repairs to a motor lorry which he had sold him. Orton confirmed this. I take it that was camouflage, and that the distillery is below Church Farm. Martin was going to mend the stills."

"That's fairly certain, Heather. When I saw the brick furnaces under the stills, I wondered where the smoke from them would issue when they were alight. Then I remembered that Orton was also a miller and ground his corn by steam. I guess the flues from those furnaces run into the small factory chimney which is such a landmark in the rural scenery of Yarham."

"Now we come to the crux of the business, Mr. Vereker. Why was Martin bound hand and foot? Who smashed Thurlow's skull, and why did Thurlow shoot Martin when he was evidently a corpse?"

"We've still got a lot of work ahead, Heather, and here I shall have to hand over the reins to you. But this is how I've figured things out. Martin, as you know, was not doing very well in the motor business. His finances were getting low. I suggest, of course, it's only a guess, that he tried to twist money out of Orton. Orton resented this attempt at extortion on the part of Martin, whose knowledge of the distillery put him in a commanding position to indulge in a little blackmail. Martin, who was probably drunk at the time, was bound hand and foot and kept a prisoner in the chamber containing the wash back, till he sobered up and thought better of it. He struggled to get free and met his death as I've already described. As for Thurlow, after leaving Old Hall Farm, he made his way along the tunnel and by some mischance took the way we deliberately chose to-day. I reckon that, after solving the riddle of the spirit music, he explored the third and unexplored tunnel. He knew of the existence of these tunnels from reading his book on the history of Yarham. He arrived at length at the secret distillery and tripping, as I did, over the baulk of timber, fell. He was carrying his loaded revolver in his hand, in case of emergency, and as he fell it was discharged, and the bullet passed through Martin's shoulder."

"Did you hunt for the bullet?" asked Heather.

"Naturally. Taking a line from the lie of the timber post, I searched the wall of the chamber. This wall is of primeval chalk and has no brick facing. As you know, chalk walls support themselves. In it I found a hole, and following up this hole, I finally dug out the bullet with a jack knife. I have it here, Heather, and hand it over to you for examination under a comparison microscope. I think you'll find that it was fired from Thurlow's revolver."

Taking the bullet from his pocket, Vereker gave it to Heather, who, placing it in a matchbox, carefully stowed it away.

"But the question is, who killed Thurlow?" asked Vereker.

"I said the sparrow!" murmured Ricardo sleepily from his chair.

"Arthur Orton, undoubtedly!" chimed in Heather. "Thurlow's revolver shot brought him at once into the chamber and, seeing a stranger there, armed with a revolver, he tackled him. Thurlow evidently turned tail and was going to make a run for it, when Orton picked up the fold-drift and hit him over the head with it. I'm afraid I've lost the game to you this time, Mr. Vereker, and may as well buy those fags for you."

"Somehow, I can't think of Arthur Orton as a murderer," remarked Vereker, shaking his head. "From what I saw of the man—and here again I rely on intuition and my knowledge of psychology—he's not the type. Although he resorted to this distillation business to make money, he was probably led into it by the presence of the plant under his farm. Any kind of smuggling has, apart from commercial gain, an extraordinary appeal to the mind that's a bit romantic and loves to take a risk. Orton's that type, I'm sure. He probably began the game for home consumption, and when he found it profitable, his business instincts took command, and he put the whole thing on a commercial basis. Miss Dawn Garford, with whom he was friendly, was let into the secret. Knowing her habits and her love of money, he chose an excellent agent for distribution. As for his murdering Thurlow to keep himself out of the hands of the law, I simply can't swallow it. He would know that discovery would at the worst mean a very heavy fine, and he is doubtless well enough off to pay the damages. No, Heather, I don't think you've spotted the murderer yet."

"Let me put you all right," interrupted Ricardo, rising to a sitting posture on the divan. "As you all know, Joe Battrum, Orton's man, must have been in the know with his boss. In fact, he carried out the delivery of orders taken by the charming Miss Garford. He was probably in the secret when Thurlow came on the scene. He was a thorough yokel and had a firm belief in the supernatural. Taking Thurlow for a ghost, he laid him out. From Runnacles, the gardener's story Joe Battrum was with his lorry at Cobbler's Corner, the night previous to the discovery of the bodies. Therefore, I deduce that Battrum planted the bodies of Thurlow whom he killed, and of Martin who clearly met his death by a kind of misadventure. This killing of Thurlow preyed on the poor fellow's mind. He began to think he was haunted by the dead man's ghost, and finally, clean off his chump, committed suicide."

"Excellent, Mr. Ricardo! Not a bad theory, but as Battrum's dead, he's not of much use to me. I want to arrest somebody. I'm itching to do so, and it'll have to be Orton for being an accessory, if not the actual murderer. I'll stick to my guns, however, and put him down as the killer."

"Now that you've definitely placed your man, Heather, I'm going to make my suggestion. I have an idea that when Ephraim Noy came to Yarham, he came with a definite purpose. He had been in the liquor traffic in America; he resorted to it again on his return to England, and was caught and fined at Doncaster. Leaving Doncaster, he probably returned to London and tried the game again there. While engaged in it, he came across the Yarham firm of distillers. A man of his habits would be almost certain to meet some of Miss Garford's customers. Seeing that it was a flourishing concern, he promptly traced its origin to this village. After the manner of the American gangster, he 'muscled in.' From the note found in his bungalow, we may take it that he succeeded. That note, like the fragment found on Martin, was evidently written by Orton. Now, Noy, as you know, Heather, was a man who had not hesitated to take human life in his previous career. This is a definite and very strong pointer in his direction. He was probably assisting in operations in the distilling chamber when Thurlow entered and fell and accidentally discharged his revolver. Picking up the fold-drift, Noy promptly ran into the adjoining chamber, where he was confronted by Thurlow. We are fairly certain he bore Thurlow a grudge. The men had known one another years ago, and when Noy turned up at Yarham, Thurlow definitely refused to have anything to do with him. This snub doubtless rankled bitterly and Noy wrote to Thurlow. Seeing that Thurlow paid Noy five hundred pounds shortly after receiving that letter, we won't be far wrong in putting that transaction down as the result of blackmail. Face to face once more with Thurlow, and knowing that Thurlow was armed, Noy waited his chance and when his enemy had turned away from him, he struck the fatal blow. Heather, you'll have to arrest Ephraim Noy, and if you've got sufficient evidence, charge him with Thurlow s murder."

"So that's your solution, Mr. Vereker! I can't agree with you. And how do you account for the recent row in Noy's bungalow, the smashed furniture, and the blood spatters? Doesn't it strike you that after Orton had written to him, advising him to quit, that Noy refused to budge. Say, Noy threatened to blow the gaff. There would be a fight. Orton doubtless came armed, killed his man, and has since disposed of the body, possibly in one of those secret tunnels. Now that I come to think of it, the letter was probably written after the row, to make it look as if Noy had taken the tip and cleared out. In support of my theory that Noy is not the murderer, there's his story to us of seeing a motor car down at Cobbler's Corner on the night previous to the discovery of the bodies. If he were the murderer, he wouldn't be such a fool as to put us on to his own tracks like that."

"You're now working purely on surmise, Heather. That's my amateur method. It's not like you and I think you're a bit rattled because you know you're whacked," argued Vereker, smiling at the inspector. "Against your theory that Orton came to Noy's bungalow and killed him to prevent him informing, it's hardly likely that he'd have done so in broad daylight. I saw Noy in the morning. You visited the bungalow in the afternoon and came and told me a little later. Your theoretical murder must have occurred in the interval. Of course, it's possible, but it's hardly likely. I think Noy felt that we were on his tracks when he found me nosing round his shanty. His story about the motor car at Cobbler's Corner was a ruse to fling us off the scent, for we knew that he had no motor car. He probably thought his story of that motor car would be corroborated by some other chance witness, and the fact would certainly tend to deflect suspicion away from himself. I feel sure Noy is very much alive, and it's your job to find him. As for the smashing of his furniture and the blood stains about the room, it's clear there was a fight. When you spoke to Battrum, did you mention that car lights had been seen on the road near Cobbler's Corner?"

"I did. Orton and he had told me, just after I took up this case, that they had seen Thurlow step into a car at the corner of Yarham green, on the night of his disappearance. When I learned that Noy had seen a car on the road at Cobbler's Corner, I questioned Orton and Battrum again in the hope of getting some information about the appearance of the car and its number. I told them Noy had confirmed the presence of a strange car in the mystery."

"As you know, Heather, Runnacles said that he was sure that it was a motor lorry, and that Joe Battrum was driving it. Battrum may have taken it into his head that Noy had split on him and was trying to fling suspicion his way. He was drunk for some days before he committed suicide, and I daresay he thought he'd have it out with Noy. They probably quarrelled and came to blows. But all this is highly supposititious."

"Ah, Algernon, you've got the word correct! I once mixed it up with a medical term and have never forgotten it since," interrupted Ricardo, laughing loudly at the recollection.

For some moments there was silence, and then Vereker exclaimed, "I've still to find out the identity of the ghost who visited me in this room, when I was alone. On that point I'm still at sea."

"I can shed some light on that subject, Mr. Vereker," said Heather. "When I first called on Mr Arthur Orton, I was met at the door of Church Farm by a buxom young woman. She is Orton's housekeeper, and from what I can gather, has intentions of making the gentleman her husband. I have seen her again since then, and the first thing I noticed about her was her remarkably small feet. You were on the track of a lady with small feet, and this led me to look at her tootsies. You mentioned that the ghost's feet were capable of wearing size three in shoes. I couldn't say off-hand that Miss Shimpling, for that's her name, wears size three, but it's probable. In the light of your tunnel story, I reckon she's your ghost. What do you think?"

"That's the lady. I've had her in my mind for some time, Heather, but have never had the chance of measuring her for shoes. Also, Clarke the cobbler, mystified me by saying that Miss Garford was the only woman in the village who wore size three in shoes, as far as he knew. The ghost, however, is a side issue, and I haven't troubled myself much about her."

"But what was her motive?" asked Ricardo. "That ghost was the only person in the case that interested me after Miss Thurlow and Dawn Garford."

"I see the motive clearly now," resumed Vereker. "In my first conversation with Miss Thurlow, she told me frankly that Orton admired her. He possibly admired her future wealth at the same time. She, in turn, was attracted by Orton. The housekeeper, if I am a judge of women, would soon tumble to the fact that there was just a chance of Miss Thurlow becoming Mrs. Orton. After Thurlow's murder, the opportunity presented itself of scaring Miss Thurlow out of Old Hall Farm. She knew about the secret passage to this house and worked out her scheme. However, it's not likely that Miss Thurlow will trouble her any more on that score. As for Orton, Heather, what are you going to do about him?"

"I'm going to arrest him right away on suspicion. In any case, I've got him on the illicit distillation business, if not on the major count. Now, gentlemen, I think I'll go and carry out that very pleasant task. It's the first time for a long while that I've snapped the darbies on my man. My car's down at 'The Walnut Tree,' and it's not in first class order. It would take some time before I could get it seen to. You've got a car here, Mr. Ricardo?"

"I have, and she's fighting fit. 'Gladys' will be delighted to carry such a famous 'tec to make an arrest. Shall I get her ready?"

"By all means, and if she'll carry four passengers, she's just the thing."

"You can squeeze yourself and prisoner into the dicky, Heather. You'll probably like to sit on top of your prey, so to speak, so that'll be O.K."

"Come along then, Mr. Vereker. We'll all go together. As you've played the leading part in the case, you ought to be in at the kill."

"No, Heather, I'm not coming. I don't like to be in at the kill on any occasion, and I've a decided aversion to seeing Orton arrested for murder. Though he's doubtless an accessory and wanted for the job of illicit distillation, he has been driven into an awful hole by force of circumstances. He'll have to face the music now, and that'll be what he deserves, but I'm not going to chortle over his discomfiture. By the way, he's fond of music and an admirer of Handel and Haydn. When you've cleared up the history of the Yarham case, I'm sure you'll discover he was the mysterious organist, who first put me on the track of a solution of the whole business. I've got to thank his musical leanings for that first extraordinary clue. If he had thought his organ playing could be heard at Old Hall Farm, he'd have chucked it before he did."

"Perhaps he did guess," remarked Heather. "He seemed to have a strong objection to the Rev. Sturgeon's excavations."

"That arose from his fear that the rector would finally find his way to Church Farm, Heather. It was one of the factors that led me later to suspect that Church Farm was probably the terminus of the unexplored tunnel and the centre of the hooch factory."

"I must say that nothing escapes you, Mr. Vereker. But if I don't hurry, the gentleman may escape me. He may get the wind up at any moment now and make a dash for liberty. Come on, Mr. Ricardo, we must go."

"Au revoir, Heather. Miss Thurlow returns to-morrow, I believe. At least, that was her intention. I shall sleep at 'The Walnut Tree' to-night, pack up, and after bidding the lady good-bye, return to my flat in town. I'll see you both at the inn, later on to-night, I suppose. When you've finally caught the real murderer, Ephraim Noy, I'll expect you to ring me up in London and fix a rendezvous. The bet was fifty cigarettes, Heather, and I'll take the money now."

"Oh no, not yet, Mr. Vereker. I was on Ephraim Noy to start with. Since then I've swapped horses with you, because I'm sure you were on Orton when you began. I've still got a chance of that barrel of beer. I may score my K.O. in the last round. Stamina's my strong suit, and I still hope to administer the sleep wallop, as they call it. So long, for the present."

Chapter Sixteen

About eleven o'clock the same night, Vereker sat in his private sitting-room in "The Walnut Tree." He had packed all his belongings, and his interest in the Yarham murder had fallen almost to zero. To kill time, he was reading an essay of his favourite author, Ralph Waldo Emerson. Neither Ricardo nor Heather had returned, and he was wondering what had happened to them. Knowing his friend's propensity for speed, he was disturbed by the thought that there might have been an accident. As time passed, he grew more and more anxious on that score.

Then, to his relief, he suddenly heard the sound of a door being closed below. There followed the rapid ascent of familiar footsteps and the next moment Ricardo entered the room.

"I'm damned glad to see you back, Ricky! I expected your return long ago. When you didn't turn up, I began to think you'd had a smash. What has kept you?"

"A smash, Algernon, but fortunately Gladys wasn't involved."

"A smash. What do you mean?"

"Let me begin at the beginning, Algernon. Once upon a time there lived in Yarham..."

"Shut up, and get on with the story!"

"Right-ho! After leaving you at Old Hall Farm, the inspector and I made our way straight to Church Farm. We moved somewhat, for Heather was blowing with impatience and rattling his handcuffs in a very irritating manner. He was the incarnation of law and order and you-must-do-what-you're-told! We left the main road and turned up a lane that must have been made by the first barbarous inhabitants of Suffolk. Heather said it was called a drift. I'd like to know who put the 'd' into it. We bumped up this natural chasm at a great pace, and Heather began to cushion off the coach-work in thrilling fashion. It reminded me of a good rally at Wimbledon. Suddenly we saw a car approaching us from the farm. Orton was driving the car at a comfortable pace, but when he spotted the inspector in 'Gladys,' he promptly accelerated. The drift is wide, so I slewed well away from him, in case his intention was to bullock into us. Heather hailed him to stop, but he ignored the summons and fairly whizzed past us. 'He's smelt a rat!' said Heather. 'After him as fast as you possibly can, Mr. Ricardo. We mustn't let him escape.'

"I spun the car round as if it was on a pivot, and after him we went, hell for rubber! Heather's weight tested the springs to the utmost as we progressed like a chamois down the drift once more. When we got on the tarmac road, I felt happier and let 'Gladys' stretch herself. Orton was about a couple of hundred yards ahead of us, and by the way he let his bus rip, we knew our purpose had been discovered. Up went the speedometer, forty, fifty, sixty. I thought we'd overhaul him easily at that speed, but I was mistaken. He began to draw away, and I began to envy him the possession of his car. I had my misgivings about 'Gladys's' ability to sustain the pace, and I think Heather guessed my thoughts.

"'Take her muzzle off!' he said grimly. 'We must overhaul him at all costs.'

"'She's doing seventy now, Heather, but none too sweetly. I don't think she can do much more,' I replied.

"'The blighter's leaving us standing. Take off her muzzle, Mr. Ricardo!'

"'I've taken off everything possible, Heather. She's sprinting in her bloomers,' I replied testily.

"'Bust her if necessary,' advised Heather feverishly, but that, of course, was a counsel of perfection. Still I was doing my best to follow his instructions. It seemed useless. Orton's car began to increase the distance between us. Slowly but surely he was drawing away. It was damnable, Algernon. My excitement began to ebb and give place to a horrible feeling of being licked. You know when you're beaten at boxing and are only waiting for the K.O. It was something like that. I was quite certain when we started in pursuit that 'Gladys' would wheel round her opponent like a bird of prey. Instead, she was being made to look like a penguin after a swallow. Our speedometer trembled up to seventy-five and we hung on to our man somehow. Fortunately the roads were clear of traffic and fairly straight. Corners we skated round on our outside edge. Mile after mile we slugged away after him, and it gradually began to dawn on me that we had got his measure.

"'I think we can manage to keep him in sight, Heather,' I remarked at length with a certain amount of satisfaction, for my spirits were beginning to rise once more. You know the effects of a bottle of Pol Roger at eleven o'clock in the morning. It was like that.

"'Good lord, is that all we can do!' groaned Heather dismally. 'I thought this car was a greyhound. It's more like an overfed Peke. I wish we'd taken my old bus.'

"This rattled me into my habitual flippancy. 'Have you got a revolver, Heather?' I asked. 'What d'you want a revolver for?' he queried. 'I don't want one,' I replied, 'but if you're a good shot, you might puncture his rear tyres neatly. It has often been done—in fiction. If you're a poor marksman, you could keep firing it behind us. The explosions would give us an extra kick.' This reduced him to speechlessness, and he began twisting his moustaches savagely. I had barely got the words out of my mouth, when I noticed that we were beginning to creep up on our adversary. Either he was slowing down, or something had gone wrong with his car.

"'We're pulling up on him, Heather. What do you think has happened?' I asked.

"'A miracle!' replied Heather curtly, but I could see he was getting buoyant once more. 'Take her bloomers off!' he roared hoarsely as he saw we were coming up with Orton at a magnificent rate. But we were soon to discover the reason for Orton's slackening up. The road was getting narrower and twisting about in the usual Suffolk style. Then, all at once, there was a hairpin bend ahead and one of those prehistoric bridges common in these parts. I couldn't see it, but we were to learn the fact a few minutes later. Orton possibly knew that feature of the landscape and was going to play for safety. But he was going too fast and couldn't keep his car under control. He went into a skid, tried to skid out of it, and then there was an almighty crash! His bus bullocked into the old stone wall of the bridge tore it up like blotting paper, and did a somersault sideways. I had just a nice distance to let 'Gladys' come up panting to the scene of disaster. Heather popped out like a frog escaping from a duck, and I joined him with my instinctive, leisurely grace. We just managed to extricate Orton before his bus burst into flames. He was unconscious when we got him out. We both thought he was done for and were going to put him gently on the side of the road, when he opened his eyes and stared rather wildly at us.

"'I agree with Samuel Butler when he says that Handel's music...' he began, but never finished the sentence. He had relapsed once more into unconsciousness.

"'Looks as if he's pegging out, Heather,' I remarked.

"'It does. Perhaps the best thing that could happen,' replied Heather, and the hardened old devil's voice was quite tender with sympathy.

"Heather then carried Orton to the grassy roadside beyond the bridge, took off his own jacket and tucked it under the poor fellow's head. He made him as comfortable as possible, and having lit his pipe, sat down beside him. We waited there a few minutes to see if Orton would revive, but he didn't. Then a big saloon car hove in sight, and Heather signalled the driver to stop. The car had no passengers, so he commandeered it as an ambulance and, putting the unconscious Orton comfortably inside, they drove off to the nearest hospital. Before he left, he gave me a message for you. 'Tell Mr. Vereker, if I don't see him to-morrow morning, I'll ring him up when I return to London.' I then got into my old traction engine and took my time coming home. That's the end of the news summary."

"Do you think Orton's gone west?" asked Vereker after a brief silence.

"Couldn't say, Algernon. He may be severely injured, or he may only be suffering from bad concussion. We'll have to wait for Heather's report."

"Pity it wasn't Ephraim Noy," was Vereker's sole comment, and rising from his chair, he added: "I'm going to turn in. We've had a purple day, Ricky!"

"No use my going to bed yet," replied Ricardo. "I must let the effervescence die down a bit before I can sleep. I think I'll have a cigarette or two and a bottle of 'Guinness.' That'll pull my shattered frame together. Good-night, Algernon, good-night, goodnight!"

*

Next morning Vereker called at Old Hall Farm and found that Miss Thurlow had returned. She was eager to hear all that had happened in her absence, and Vereker told her briefly the whole story of his investigations into the Yarham mystery. She received a painful shock on learning of Arthur Orton's implication in the affair, and was clearly disappointed at the material explanation of the "manifestations" which she had ascribed to spirit agency. She kept, however, a complete mastery of her feelings, and when Vereker, after thanking her for her hospitality, took his departure, she had evidently regained that remarkable serenity and composure which had distinguished her bearing from the beginning of the tragic affair.

One evening, some weeks later, Ricardo and Vereker were sitting in Vereker's studio in Fenton Street, discussing the painter-detective's latest picture.

"But, Algernon, you must admit that it lacks architectural form and significance. You've said clearly what you wanted to say in terms of paint, but you convey no distinct message teleologically!"

The shrill ringing of the door bell put an end to Ricardo's joking at the expense of Art criticism, and Albert, Vereker's batman, announced shortly afterwards that Inspector Heather had called.

"Show him in, Albert, and bring a large jug of beer and glasses," said Vereker.

A few minutes later, Heather entered the studio and was promptly pushed into a small wicker chair by the boisterous Ricardo.

"It's a bit inadequate for your bulk, Heather," he said, "but I've always maintained that a big egg looks most imposing in a small basket."

"Make yourself comfortable in the Minty, Heather. Help yourself to beer and tell us all the news. We've been expecting you now for over a week," said Vereker.

Heather settled himself more comfortably in a larger chair, filled a pewter mug, and lit his rather massive pipe.

"You want to hear the rest of the Yarham murder story, I suppose," he began. "Well, after I left Mr. Ricardo at the end of a most exciting run, I took Orton to the nearest hospital. He was very badly injured about the spine, but eventually regained consciousness and began to recover slowly. After a week or so, he was well enough to talk to me and discuss his share in 'The Spirit Murder Mystery', as the Press have called it. I must admit that his story bears out the accuracy of your deductions in the case to a marvellous degree, Mr. Vereker. I take off my hat to you!"

"You found you were wrong in ascribing Thurlow's murder to him?" asked Vereker eagerly.

"One minute, let me tell you his story. He admitted he was the writer of the notes to Clarry Martin and Ephraim Noy. As you surmised, those stills were in the underground chamber under Church Farm, when Orton took over the place. They must have been there for ages, because the entrance to the vaults had been bricked up many years ago. Orton, out of sheer curiosity, demolished the wall sealing the entrance and discovered the ancient distillery. He started working it for the mere fun of the thing, and finding that the results were good, decided later on to run it for profit. This was as you had figured it out. Eventually he roped in Miss Garford as an agent for collecting orders. This she did very discreetly and eminently well and received a thumping big commission. Things were going on quietly and successfully, when something went wrong with one of the stills. Orton was no hand at repairing such a contraption, and Miss Garford introduced Clarry Martin into the business as a stand-by copper-smith. He carried out his duties secretly and well. The sky was again clear. Then that arch crook Ephraim Noy appeared on the scene. Somehow he'd got wind of the business in London, and promptly came to Yarham to inquire into it. It was directly in his line. He interviewed Orton and, as you've already described it, he muscled in. By this time, Orton was getting rather tired of the whole business. At first he had found it exciting and interesting, but the novelty gradually wore off and Noy took matters in his hands more and more. Orton became, so to speak, almost a sleeping partner. His love of music stole him away from his interest in whisky. By this time he would have liked to quit, but Noy had him in a vice and wasn't going to stop the racket just because Orton had got sick of it. There was nothing for it but to carry on and hope that the cat wouldn't get out of the bag. The cat, however, was going to give trouble long before they expected her to. Clarry Martin, crossed in love, took to drink, got into debt, and found himself faced with bankruptcy. He tried to beat off his creditors by extorting money from Orton. In this he was at first successful, but there came a time when Orton would give him no more. He thought he'd try the game on with Noy, but he didn't know what a tough guy he was pitting himself against. On the night that he went up to mend the soap box and spirit taps, he was rather drunk and decidedly aggressive. He approached Noy for money, and on Noy's refusal, threatened to twist his tail. Noy soon showed him that he had made a big mistake, and before Martin knew where he was he took a beauty on the point that knocked him senseless. When he recovered, he found himself bound hand and foot to a heavy post in the underground brewing chamber. He struggled, the post broke, and he fell with it. A stiff dose of carbonic acid gas had evidently collected along the floor of the chamber, which is not ventilated, and soon Martin was beyond recall. When Orton heard what had happened, he was beside himself, but after a couple of days of thinking over it, he foolishly agreed to keep his mouth shut about the business and carry on. He was also now thoroughly afraid of Noy, who put it to him that it was better to take a chance of being hanged than a certainty of being shot. The next step was to dispose of the body. It was decided to bury Martin in one of the tunnels. If this had been done, and Thurlow hadn't been interested in spirit music, possibly nothing more would ever have been heard of Martin. But the very best laid plans go wrong. Now, Joe Battrum had been the first to discover that Martin had died at his post, so to speak. He was in the know, much to his own bewilderment. So he and Noy were just going to form up for a burial party, when to their horror and astonishment Thurlow blundered into the brewing chamber. As you've described it, Mr. Vereker, he fell, his revolver was discharged, and the bullet passed through Martin's shoulder. Battrum, thinking that a ghost had appeared on the scene, bolted for all he was worth and never quite recovered his mental balance. Noy, realizing the deadly importance of what had happened, picked up a fold-drift and knocked Thurlow on the head, smashing his skull. The fat was now thoroughly in the fire, and the disposal of two dead bodies became the burning question. At first it was decided to bury them together in the tunnel, but after some discussion, Orton correctly pointed out that this would be a fatal mistake. Thurlow's unexpected arrival at the secret distillery declared that there must be an entrance to the tunnels from Old Hall Farm. A search party would eventually come along and the whole ghastly secret would be out. The argument seemed irrefutable. So Noy and Orton racked their brains for a plan of disposal and finally thought of planting the bodies at Cobbler's Corner. This, Joe Battrum and Ephraim Noy did next night. It was hoped that the story of the rivalry of the two men for the hand of Miss Dawn Garford would make it appear as if they had fought and killed one another. This was weak, especially when they had to reckon with detectives of our calibre, Mr. Vereker, but neither was in a state to think clearly. The rest of the yarn you both know."

"But what about Orton? Has he recovered, Heather?" asked Ricardo.

"No, the poor chap died after all. He was mortally injured, and though he seemed to make a bit of a recovery at first, he couldn't maintain it. There came a bad relapse, and he snuffed out quite peacefully. As a matter of fact, I don't think he wanted to live. He was, I found, very fond of Miss Thurlow and would never have been able to face things, had he recovered. The illicit distillation was bad enough, but to be accessory to a murder was beyond the limit."

"Thinking back over the case, Heather," said Vereker, "we can now see why Orton called at Old Hall Farm, the morning after Thurlow's disappearance. He must have been eager to find out about the entrance to the tunnel and whether anyone in the house knew of it. He evidently learned little, but fearing that they would possibly discover that entrance in their search, decided that the bodies must be removed quickly from the distillery chambers. In a way he was right, because once we had discovered the tunnels, the finding of the bodies would only have been a matter of time. There's another point I'd like to know more about and that's the struggle that took place in Noy's bungalow before he vanished."

"That's the one point on which you were a bit off the mark, Mr. Vereker. You thought Battrum had beat him up. I, too, was wrong, for I blamed Orton. The man who made a mess of Noy and his bungalow that midday was Barney Deeks. He had been employed by Noy to do some digging at his well. At the end of the week, when Deeks called for his wages, he found Noy about to depart. Noy tried to get out of what he had agreed to pay him, and a bit of spirited boxing took place. Deeks owned up to this to me, and seeing that he'd had his nose broken in the scrap, I gave him half a dollar to go to the pub and forget he had a nose."

"What are you going to do about the ladies, Miss Garford and Miss Shimpling, Heather? Were they accessories?" asked Ricardo.

"Only to the distillation racket. Orton swore that neither of them had the faintest inkling as to how Thurlow and Martin met their deaths. We shall get hold of Miss Garford very soon. We've got a man on her spoor already. She'll be fined heavily for her share in the game, but seeing that she's in for a legacy of ten thousand pounds, that won't break her back. Miss Shimpling admitted frankly that she knew all about the secret liquor traffic but had no hand in the business whatever. She had always tried to get Orton to chuck it up before he was discovered."

"And what has happened to Ephraim Noy, Heather?" asked Vereker.

"You'll be delighted to hear we caught him hiding in London, Brixton way, yesterday," replied Heather triumphantly.

"Got a hanging case at last, Heather! You ought to be thoroughly satisfied now," remarked Vereker.

"I don't know so much about that, Mr. Vereker. Noy may escape the gallows by the skin of his teeth. He has admitted knocking Thurlow on the head with that iron bar, but he'll put up the defence that he did it in self-defence. Thurlow was armed with a revolver and had already fired one shot. Noy was indirectly the cause of Martin's death, but can truthfully say he didn't kill him. We must wait and see and I hope the prosecuting counsel's a brilliant man. I'm not too happy about it all. Besides, I've had to buy you a box of fifty cigarettes."

Heather tossed the box of cigarettes to Vereker and buried his grief under an upturned tankard.

THE END

Lightning Source UK Ltd.
Milton Keynes UK
UKOW06f1801150616

276381UK00017B/272/P